A UNIVERSE GONE AWRY

AWRY

ELENA DELGADO

Paperback: 979-8-9953077-1-6

Hardcover: 979-8-9953077-0-9

eBook: 979-8-9953077-2-3

Audiobook: 979-8-9953077-3-0

Library of Congress Control Number: 2026907992

Edited by Melissa Ousley.

First Edition.

Cover design and interior illustrations by Elena Delgado.

All parts of this publication were made without the use of AI.

Book 1 of the *A Universe Gone Awry* trilogy.

TABLE OF CONTENTS

The sun shines brightest in its latest hours.

PROLOGUE

Marathene looked at a floating map of Earth, pondering what to do. Her eyes focused intently on the map, but her mind couldn't help but go back to the attacks on her city the day before. She could remember the report handed to her, describing a fire on the city's northeast side. Her eyes widened slightly, recalling the smoke that had covered the city all weekend, which only slowed reconstruction because of other attacks. She returned her focus to the situation, tapping her fingers swiftly on the hologram keyboard as she searched for an Earther to take to her world. Mother Everealm sat in distress in a nearby chair. She bit her lips and picked at her fingernails.

"Anything?" she demanded quietly.

Marathene, her closest daughter, grimaced and huffed sharply, stepping back to gaze at the hologram. "Come see for yourself." Marathene moved aside. Lined up vertically were profiles of people—each a life that would be uprooted and changed forever at her mother's whims. "Mother… why must we always select Earthers as imports?" Marathene asked, her voice apprehensive. "To fight a battle that isn't theirs… it feels sort of wrong."

Mother Everealm sighed deeply, her weathered turquoise eyes glinting in the light from the hologram.

"Because," her expression lay fixed on the hologram. "The imports don't know what we did. They have no magic. They lead simple lives and are easily rewritten." She turned to Marathene, her expression reflecting decades of exasperation, desperation, and fear.

Marathene gave a blank nod in response and went back to the profiles. She knew it was better to oblige than bring up the past.

They went through a number of profiles, weighing things like social connections, abilities, and age. They generally got people who were young teenagers, since those were easiest to train. *Easier to brainwash*, Marathene thought bitterly. Once they grew a little older, they sent them on more important missions.

"Who is she, Isavna Belanis?" Mother Everealm asked, pointing her pale, slightly wrinkled hand to the softly glowing profile. "An awfully strange name for an Earther."

"American, potential magic reading 1200, which is about the upper limit for imports. But the potential hasn't always translated into performance," Marathene said. After a long pause, she sighed, her guilt evident. "We don't have a choice, do we?"

Marathene watched her mother adjust her crown, rubbing her neck and grimacing, as if the crown was heavy. Millenia of decision-making for the world had taken a toll on her, both physically and mentally.

"Isavna Belanis then," Mother Everealm said. "We have no time to hesitate."

"Will you be her tether?" Marathene asked. Her mother nodded tensely. Imports had to tether to a strong magical source. Their biology wouldn't be able to sustain life in Avukena.

"Yes, I will."

"Do you have the energy left for it, though?"

"Yes," Mother Everealm said hesitantly. "But it will have to be my last."

June 4th, 1:12 AM Avukena City Time, Lakondra Star System

Asleep and unaware, Isavna lay curled up in the far corner of the space pod, hugging a pile of clothes splayed over the cold metal floor. The pod quietly whirred as it traveled through the emptiness of space. An internal radar showed a cosmic tear, which was their route back to their home universe.

"Another successful retrieval. Have you selected a proxy?" Marathene asked quietly.

"Sirani Maligari will mentor her," Mother Everealm said. "She will help her adapt quickly. They're the same age, and she has excelled in magical and academic disciplines." Marathene nodded, vaguely recognizing the name.

"So what will we do when we get back?" Marathene asked.

"There's an old sitting room on the twentieth floor of the palace that I had the servants furnish with a bed and a kitchenette. That is where Isavna will live, and where we will leave her tonight. I will send Sirani there tomorrow to introduce herself." Mother Everealm said, watching the stars pass by outside. "Then we will enroll her in military training and the Academy. I don't believe she has finished high school on Earth yet. We will let them figure things out while we do periodical check-ins with her." Marathene felt uneasy by her mother's vague plan, but didn't say anything.

"What about her Earth life?" Marathene asked, tapping her knee restlessly in a nervous rhythm. She felt more anxious than her mother did.

"That's taken care of, Marathene. No one will know she's gone, for now." Mother Everealm said, growing irritated by Marathene's constant questions. Isavna, snoring quietly, began to stir. Marathene looked down at her, hoping for someone else to talk to.

"Where am I?" Isavna croaked, sitting up. She fixed her round, black glasses, which fit a little crooked on her face.

"In transit," Mother Everealm replied tersely.

"We're in a system of galaxies that lie at the border between our two universes," Marathene added.

"Two… universes?" Isavna said. Marathene saw Isavna shift her position and look outside as they were nearing the edge of one universe and entering the next through a large tear. Isavna trembled and sat as far from Marathene and Mother Everealm as she could.

She looked at the tear, squinting from the lurid light beaming from the distorted stars just beyond the opening. She glanced fearfully at Marathene and Mother Everealm a few times.

"We have to go in there?" she whispered fearfully. The pod sped up, and time seemed to slow slightly as they passed through. Isavna braced and didn't look up until she felt the pod slow down dramatically.

They approached the orbit of a planet with numerous floating vessels. She looked at Mother Everealm, and her eyes widened in terror and amazement as her breath quickened. Marathene felt a bit of pain and pity watching her. She thought about how Isavna must have felt so small, compared to the eight-foot-tall Mother Everealm and Marathene. An hour passed as they neared their destination, Isavna's gaze never leaving the window.

"Who… are you two?" Isavna finally asked.

"I am Mother Everealm. This is Marathene. We're taking you to our home planet, Avukena, because there is something we need you to do," Mother Everealm said. The pod slowed down further. "You were chosen, Isavna, and we need your help to fix… a problem." Marathene looked down. What Isavna didn't know was how many times Mother Everealm had told the same thing to the previous Earthers, which made Marathene uncomfortable.

"And here we are," Mother Everealm affirmed as she pulled a lever to land on the planet. "This is your new home." Isavna's breath reached a frightening intensity and speed, and Marathene worried that she might pass out.

Two Years Later

June 4th, Thursday, Year 2041 New Era, 8:42 PM, Avukena Palace

Mother Everealm stared out of the stained-glass window into the early summer sunset as the colored light poured over her body and the floor before her. Her silky, snow-white hair fell to her shoulders and down her back. Her shiny blue crown sparkled in the evening sunlight. She looked out at the ocean, rippling gently as if it were breathing in and out. Seabirds flew and squawked while their forms cast tiny black shadows on the sand and glassy water. She squinted slightly as she watched the fluffy clouds, painted with the sun's blushing tones, drift gently across the sky.

She smiled wryly with the tenderness of a mother upon the world she had created, at the same time feeling anxious about its potential demise.

She tightened her hands and let out a shaky breath, trying to distract herself by looking at her rings.

"Do you remember when you gave me this ring, Marathene?" Mother Everealm asked, looking down at her slightly wrinkled fingers, staring at a glittering crystal. Her voice reverberated in the hall of her throne room. Marathene, who had just walked in, came close to her mother.

"I do. Didn't you say it was your favorite ring?" Marathene asked. Mother Everealm nodded, then gazed at the other rings, colorful and sparkling in the evening sun. "Was there any reason you needed me here?" Marathene ventured.

Mother Everealm stayed quiet and focused on her rings as she held her arms up to the light. She observed another one, a small blue diamond with white edges.

"How is Isavna's mission going?" Mother Everealm asked, not turning to look at Marathene. A bird squawked outside.

"I don't know. They've made some progress."

"The past imports have greatly advanced her mission, and I was hoping this would be the last one we'd have to bring—"

—"You said that last time we brought one." Marathene interjected. She saw her mother's shoulders raise slightly. She realized her mistake and spoke quietly. "Continue."

"Progress seems to be slowing down. I anticipated her to do well—and she is—she seemed really promising. She and the others have gone on many successful reconnaissance missions. But it simply isn't enough." Mother Everealm let out a troubled sigh and looked outside, though she could not bring herself to enjoy the view. She knew that beyond the respite of the palace walls lay the world she couldn't protect.

"Well, at the end of the day she is still an Earther, and she is young, too. How can we expect so much of her? Of any Earther?" Marathene asked hesitantly. Mother Everealm was silent, then said something else.

"I feel very unwell, Marathene. The military is becoming resistant to advancing our mission, and I do not know if I need to put out more public messaging on the importance of the mission, or what must be done. Isavna at least has her head on straight, since she's not contaminated by the open-minded agenda like the others are. I need Cavaris and Jovnelle dead as soon as possible." Mother Everealm bit her lips, omitting the rest.

Because I can't kill Jovnelle myself. Because I failed her once and I will not live peacefully if she survives her tether with Cavaris.

"It'll be very difficult to convince her that Jovnelle *must* die," Marathene added, hiding her unease under feigned agreement. "Same with the others in the military and the public."

"Don't question my doing. We'll use magic if we must," Mother Everealm retorted sternly. The harsh edge came more from fear than certainty. "Cavaris is becoming quite strong. I can sense it; it's eating into my own vitality. We *have* to do this. If I die, her tether will be transported to the next strongest source of energy, which will be Cavaris himself. And she *needs* this tether, otherwise she won't be able to use her magic or live on Avukena." The admission left her feeling exposed. She gripped her own hands, the sharp edges of the rings digging into her skin. She hoped Marathene wouldn't notice the shaking.

"Have you told her how you feel?" Marathene asked. "About your anxiety."

"Not yet, I cannot find an opportunity to tell her," Mother Everealm said. It was difficult for her admitting she was afraid. "Though I don't want her to wait much longer."

"Is it really that soon?" Marathene asked, a little appalled. "It seems only a little while ago we brought her from Earth."

"If we cannot lessen Cavaris's power, it will drain my vitality and I shall die. Isavna's tether will be rerouted to him. She will be a slave, like Jovnelle, or worse. Imports have no magic, so they are easier to control." By now, Mother Everealm was circling the room, looking around nervously. "Her potential magic reading means *nothing* as long as she's tethered to me; her magic fades as mine does. Oh, how I wish magic in this world was infinite. Every tether since four hundred years ago has aged me a millenium or more. The reason why I called you here is because I need you to give something to Isavna in case I die." Mother Everealm said, removing her crown. Her fingers glowed as a small, white, irregular gem came out of the crown. She cupped the small gem in her hands, and when she opened them, it had duplicated.

"This jewel is a decoy; it is the one I shall keep," she said, placing it back in her crown. "This one is a shard of my essence. It is inert while I am alive, but will serve as a tether when I am dead." The real gem levitated above her open palm and glowed purple as it was set into a pendant with a silver chain. It was pretty, but unremarkable. She passed it to Marathene. "Rough it up a bit more so it seems less conspicuous." Marathene accepted it, looking stern. "The most important part is that no soul can know of its strength. If it is lost, we will be able to locate it; your foresight is strong enough. But if it is destroyed or she is too far away, within a minute her tether will go to Cavaris. The burden will be too heavy for her, so she cannot know. And if she knows that activating it would fix her fading magic…."

"She may target you," Marathene said. "I understand. If she starts to feel weary, she may allow the mission to fail and let you die."

"She cannot know." Mother Everealm asserted. Marathene cast her gaze out the main window to the ocean. She watched the shadows stretch and engulf the throne room as the sun set.

I

After years knee deep in this world, I couldn't quite figure out if I belonged in Avukena, Earth, or neither.

I looked down at my cellphone. I still had an Earth phone, even though everyone here used more advanced magic and technology. Even after all these years, I liked the tangibility.

I was a twelfth-year student at the Everealm Preparatory Academy, and it was my last day. Everyone around me moved through the city with ease, and while I haven't accepted Avukena City as my home yet, the buildings and routines have become familiar.

I joined up with two of my friends from school, Sirani and Sakuraci. Though, I had only ever heard teachers call her that. Most of us just called her Saku.

"Hello, Isavna! Good morning!" Sirani said. Her vanilla blond hair bounced to the rhythm of her step. Even running, she seemed graceful. Her uniform draped over her body in a boxy way; she had the tall, androgynous type of body you'd see in European fashion magazines. She knew a lot of people, too. It was a social circle I was able to enter easily.

"Do any of you guys wanna hang out later?" Saku asked.

"We have scouting today as AHL work. It's in Nojuni, remember? We're just checking on the old palace again," I said, watching her expression remain indifferent as she stared ahead. I thought about Nojuni. It was where Cavaris and Jovnelle lived, north of Avukena. There wasn't much these days but the old run-down palace and ruins of the village. The AHL often sent younger sophomore operatives like us on reconnaissance missions, since they were easy, low-risk, but necessary.

The AHL was the Avukena Homeland Legion, the nation's military. I was introduced to it on only my second day on Avukena, and I've been in it ever since. They also had the same mission as I did: destroying Cavaris and Jovnelle. It functioned as the global military. While I never really liked their morally absolute way of thinking, I made many friends and respected the people there. But that was *despite* the AHL, not because of it. It's not like I could leave, anyway.

"Oh yeah, you're right. Hmm… maybe I should go buy groceries," she said, still facing the school.

"If we even have time for that, who knows when we'll get back," I replied. We continued walking until she nervously started digging in her bag.

"Did you lose your check-out sheet?" I asked.

"I lost my gym shoes. I must've left them in my dorm. I'll see you at school!" she said hurriedly. As she ran, her brown hair with blue ends flew. Sirani and I continued idle conversation about Earth movies, school, and work. As we approached the building, the school colors of black, white, and cyan could be seen on posters decorating the interior, made by the leadership club.

Saku had been recently appointed to our scouting shift with Sirani and me. Our jobs mainly revolved around reconnaissance missions and various paperwork tasks at the AHL office.

Cavaris was a being with the power of Mother Everealm, but was her complete opposite in every way. Where she was obsessively ordered, he craved ultimate chaos, which wasn't necessarily *bad*, per se, because for millions of years, both beings coexisted peacefully, as two sides of the same scale. The stories conflict, but he came to possess Jovnelle, one of the original six daughters of Mother Everealm. No one really knew why—or how—it happened. Mother Everealm had always been far stronger than Cavaris, but with his and Jovnelle's combined magic power, it tilted the scales of balance further away from Mother Everealm.

In my time here, despite what Mother Everealm declared as truth, I had seen that many people did not believe killing Jovnelle to be justified, though I had not made my mind up myself on who was right. Jovnelle was possessed under unknown circumstances, and she is not someone who has any mental or bodily autonomy under Cavaris' control, making people feel strange about the need to kill her. Mother Everealm argued otherwise, saying that the destruction spreading is objectively bad. Who were we to argue with her? Mother Everealm was the one who created everything, so she was never wrong, supposedly.

A storm swirled around the mountain range beyond the eastern side of the city. To the west was the ocean. As we walked, the landscape changed from tall, looming buildings to flatter land, right as we arrived at the school campus. A teacher walked by me, wearing a heavy perfume that reminded me of the smell of a department store. My heart hurt a little as I tried to recall the foggy memories of Christmas shopping with my family back on Earth. I thought about how my sister and I would smell so many perfumes in the fragrance section that my nose would be stuffy for the rest of the day. I looked up at the sky, sighing. I had come to terms with the fact that my life was just different now.

There were trees that released blue flower petals to the breeze that found their way on the ground and sometimes in people's hair. The foot traffic bottlenecked at the school's two sets of double doors.

"So my cousin in Sjasa told me that he was almost killed in the Mahifer attacks," I heard someone say to their friend as they walked by me. "Those attacks are pretty bad there."

"Oh, really? That's pretty crazy. Last I heard, the attacks are still mostly in the northeast part of town. Hopefully they don't close in on the city center."

"I heard from someone in Spellcasting say that his dad got possessed. He said his voice sounded funny, and his shadow disappeared— it was bad. But they were able to get him to the hospital in time."

I thought about the Mahifers as I rushed into the school. They were black ghosts, shards of Cavaris, sent out to feed on magic, also known as "Mahis." They fed on magic by possessing people and sapping them dry of magic, with the ultimate goal of returning to Nojuni and using any leftover magic to feed Cavaris.

I proceeded with my day as usual, heading to my locker and getting my things. I observed the drab, black metal interior of my locker. I had already emptied out most of the contents over the course of the week.

My mind was preoccupied with the recon mission, despite it being my last day of school, which was arguably more significant than a routine mission. I felt little attachment to this school; I had only been there for four years, the whole time being somewhat alienated by most of the students. It didn't affect me too much; the other things I did in my life took up more of my time and energy anyway.

I entered my first class and sat with Sirani, the girl who was assigned to be my mentor from day one. She was native to Esco, a city about a hundred miles south of Avukena City, just down the coast. She, like many in the Academy, was of noble blood—her parents being the king and queen of Esco. Though, she spent more of her time in Avukena. I didn't like to ask much about her parents, since talking about her family always seemed to strain her emotionally.

"Are you ready to be done with studying magic?" I asked her. Today was a catch-up day for homework. I had turned everything in already, I was just chatting with Sirani.

"Oh, absolutely. Some of these skills are useful, but many of them are just useless. I never had much of a liking for the very specialized skills. That was more my brother's thing. He tried to learn weird and difficult stuff like combat delay," Sirani explained. "He had been trying to learn it for years."

"You think he ever actually got it?" I asked.

"No, well, not since he left, I don't know," she said. I dropped an eraser on the ground, and I tried to levitate it back up to my desk. It wouldn't float.

"Are you okay?" Sirani asked, noticing my straining.

"I'm fine," I replied. "This is… weird, I don't know why it isn't working."

"Maybe it's because you're an Earther, or something?" suggested Sirani.

"No, my magic was strong when I first got it," I said, slightly offended. "It seems almost as if it's starting to fade or something."

"Well, be careful. You don't want to hurt yourself," she replied.

I kept the thought in the back of my head to ask about later. Something felt different today, good or bad.

I glanced over to Saku and Sirani as we stood atop a building. I saw the burning, fiery sunset, then turned around to find the rest of the city covered in darkness. I sometimes likened the looming towers and density of the place to Earth cities, which was consoling. Something so beautiful and strong could surely last forever. I raised and pushed back my shoulders, causing giant brown wings to unfurl from my back, about ten feet on either side. Here, anyone could invoke wings at will. It was a part of being—or becoming—Avukenan.

"So when do we plan to leave?" Saku asked, putting on her flight helmet. They were not only practical but also required by Avukenan law. Not wearing one would be like trying to stick your head out of a moving vehicle.

"Right before the sun is completely gone," Sirani replied. "By the time we get to Nojuni, it will be fully dark. The long shadows make it hard to hide. Darkness is the safest way to go, even though I prefer the visibility of sunlight." We were in Sjasa, a city north of Avukena and on the way to Nojuni. We took the portal systems to save time.

We watched until only about half of the sun was showing.

I took off, hearing the loud flapping of my wings. Saku and Sirani followed, though they quickly got ahead of me.

"Palace," a voice said to me. The voice shot a throbbing pain through my skull. It was scary and unusual. I lost my balance and panicked as I looked down to see cars passing by on the street, about eighty feet below me.

"Did you guys get that?" I asked the others telepathically, and I steadied again.

"Get what?" Sirani asked.

"Never mind." I squinted, almost expecting it to happen again, though it wouldn't for the rest of our flight.

When we arrived at our destination about an hour and a half later, I took a deep breath, having thought about the strange message the entire time. But I also knew that to perform effectively right now, I needed to disregard it. I saw the small glowing plants of Nojuni, which in any other situation would be beautiful. There were some flowers that had glowing stems and blooms. Something so tiny and persistent in a really harsh environment. I turned to Saku, who was standing with her lips tightened nervously.

"Remember to take note of what you see, but try to use telepathy sparingly so we don't attract Mahifers—oh, and watch out for guards. Wing invocation is fine, the magic is too weak to attract anything. Did you bring everything?" Sirani asked her quietly. She opened her belt packs, and Sirani inspected them. Then, we dispersed.

I was doing the palace court that evening, the riskiest of the protocols. I flew, briefly inspected the palace from above, and landed on a sketchy-looking roof gable that groaned under my weight. I gripped some of the gray slate tiles. The palace was mostly stone; we believed there may have been timber at some point, but it has since rotted away.

"Palace. Go to... palace. Inside... enter." It was the voice again. *"We need you to go to the palace... east wing."* A stinging, pulsating pain came into my head that knocked me off balance again and made me slip down the gable. Rocks tumbled down as I gripped the slate roof tiles.

The feeling left as quickly as it came. I took out my wand, realized what I was doing, and quickly put it away. *Dammit! I can't use magic here. It would attract the Mahis.*

I reached for my knife instead. Magic would be useless—dangerous even—at least for me. No matter how much progress I made in understanding magic and Avukena, it still wouldn't be enough to catch up with my friends. I dug my boot into a crevice between tiles, trying to stabilize myself in case another strange message came. Looking around tentatively, I decided there wouldn't be anything new around the palace.

"Hey, Saku, Sirani, let's leave. I don't feel good about tonight," I told the two telepathically, hoping they wouldn't be annoyed about having only been here for thirty minutes.

"Okay, I'll see you guys out by the woods, near that big yellow pine," Saku said. Sirani complied without protest.

I found Saku and Sirani waiting for me anxiously, next to the tree, as a gust of wind swirled away some fallen pine needles.

"What's wrong, Isavna?" Sirani asked.

"So, uh… there's been… a voice I've been hearing?" I said, realizing how ridiculous it sounded. I popped open my water canteen as they both looked at me intently. "I heard it earlier during our flight. I thought someone had sent us a telepathic message, but I guess it was only me that heard it. It's been hurting my head, too." They looked at each other, as baffled as I was. A slight breeze crescendoed into a gust.

"Does it mean anything? Do you know? Which palace?" Saku inquired, brushing away hair from her face.

"It would have to be Nojuni if Isavna said she felt the signal strongest there. Was the voice discernable to be anyone in particular?" Sirani deduced. "And furthermore, you can't just message someone telepathically unless the receiver consciously consents to first contact… how did this person bypass that? And cause the pain?”

“I don’t know. All I can really infer was that it was definitely male and probably not that old,” I said. “He spoke really weirdly though. I don’t think he speaks English very well, whoever he is. Or *whatever* he is.”

Saku put her hand to her chin and bit her lips. “Hm. It would have to be someone in the palace who isn’t a servant or a ward since they don’t have access to telepathy, if I remember right. It’d have to be some other kinda person with power there and it can’t be Cavaris or Jovnelle. But besides them, I dunno who’s powerful enough to cause a *headache* though.”

“Maybe you’ll have better luck checking whoever we have on file for Nojuni Palace? I don’t know how restricted that data is, but you surely will be able to get it if you ask,” Sirani added.

“Oh well. I suppose we can figure out who it is tomorrow,” Saku explained as I let out a big sigh. We took off to go home. *I can’t wait until tomorrow. Who knows what’ll happen?*

Saturday, 1:09 AM, Avukena Palace, East Wing Lobby

I quickly thanked Saku and Sirani for coming with me and bringing closure to our scouting. I turned to take an elevator, but instead sat on the scarlet red sofas in the lobby to rest for a moment. The room looked a lot like the lobbies for hotels on Earth. There were pale tan walls and bland, abstract art that a child could make. I caught a glance of my reflection in a shiny metal pitcher that was being wheeled past me. I looked like a mess. The person pushing the cart went down the halls towards Mother Everealm’s throne room.

I still couldn't wrap my brain around what she expected me to do here. I closed my eyes, and for a moment I felt like I was back on Earth. The air smelled like a clean hotel, crisp early summer air, and flowers from the gardens.

I didn't know why *I* was chosen to do this. Not because I thought poorly of myself, but because it didn't seem logical for a deity to recruit someone from another planet to fulfill a gargantuan task. I stirred in my seat. The sofa wasn't very comfortable.

I decided to take the elevator upstairs. Most tall buildings had balconies on many of their floors where flying people could land, but not the palace, because of apparent criminal concerns in such an important building.

I saw my unit at the end of the long, drab hallway, as familiar as ever. I walked towards it, hearing my feet padding on the carpeted ground. The hall smelled of incense; perhaps one of my neighbors was using some. My door creaked open after unlocking, and my lamp illuminated the room in a bath of warm light. I quickly opened my wrist-projected hologram to file a mission request because the software wasn't cellphone compatible. I talked on the phone with my supervisor, Renee Rotura, explaining the situation, and tried to convince her why I needed to do it tomorrow and not some other day. I didn't tell her about the telepathic messages. Instead, I told her it was simply scouting in an area where there was "non-possessed human activity." I also added a request to view the files we had on hand for Nojuni Palace's known residents. She reluctantly approved it, requiring that I take the same team.

As I waited for my leftovers to heat up on the stove, I looked over the AHL's files of known non-possessed Nojuni inhabitants. *Cavaris.* *Jovnelle. The palace chamberlain. Resident 0401. Resident 0412.* I went through more of the files displayed on my wrist projection's hologram as I ate, squinting, but I didn't feel anything. *This is pointless.* I walked around my sunken floor to my bed and immediately fell asleep.

2

Cold. That was the only way to describe the atmosphere, the people, and the weather. *Cold.* We had landed far enough from the palace to not be noticed. As we approached the grounds, I felt the voice rattle in my head again.

"Enter the palace. Go to the… east wing," the voice pleaded, sounding more urgent and painful than ever. Once Sirani and Saku arrived, we hid behind the ruins of a fallen building, waiting for the right moment to enter the palace.

"Sorry you guys had to come. Renee wouldn't let me go alone, she required the same team," I said.

"It's fine," Sirani said, yawning. "It wouldn't be wise to go alone."

"What do you want us to do?" Saku asked, her voice rumbly and tired from the short night's rest. She zipped her jacket a little tighter.

"Come with me. It'll be easier if we're together," I answered. We were several paces ahead of the front gates, hiding behind a dilapidated stone wall. I watched the pallid, possessed guards pacing across the front way. They must have been human at some point, but now remain in an eternal state of limbo and possession. Their metal spears dragged across the cobblestone ground, letting out an eerie, piercing screech. I had to use as little strong magic as possible, or else I would attract the Mahis. Anything stronger than wing invocation was a no-go. Mahis fed off of magic, absorbing any use of it and following the source for more. They were more of an annoyance than anything, since they were easy to kill. But they multiplied like weeds. Trying to contain them was useless unless we stopped the source.

I threw a rock to lure in the guards, drawing their attention away from where we planned to go. Sirani and Saku were behind the other stone fence, and they had their weapons drawn. They were perfectly still, like our training had taught us. We couldn't afford to make a sound.

The guards were getting dangerously close. I checked my hips for any other weapons I had. I had a regular Earth-style pistol, a .22, that I would use in regular combat. They've been common in the military for years since Mother Everealm copied the design from Earth. They were pretty effective at hurting and slowing down possessed people, though not super effective on Mahis themselves.

Together with Sirani, we struck a guard. I shot him in the head twice, and Sirani sank her short sword into his chest. He collapsed and died quickly, not having much life force to begin with. Saku took on the other guard with her pistol. I heard her retching.

"Relax, Saku, it's not like his brains are falling out or anything. He's not even alive! You're lucky he's wearing a cloak that covers up most of the damage," Sirani said.

Sirani passed her a full canteen of water. Saku looked back at the bloody body and retched again.

"Alright, let's head in," I said as we passed the outermost gate. There were still the court and the palace doors themselves to breach. Under the cover of darkness, we didn't worry about being seen. Being heard or smelled was a bigger problem.

The palace was structured strangely. The left wing looked large, like it was supposed to be a keep, though it was filled with empty, dilapidated ballrooms. The other wing looked more residential, with lit torches.

There were two balconies at the end of each wing. The one on the right had a live millin bush in a pot. Millin was a flower, somewhat like a large, unfurled rose. It had grown wildly, spreading in many directions. *Someone must live there.* Otherwise, that plant wouldn't be alive. *Maybe I should go there first.*

The balcony to the left of me was so overgrown with dead vines that I couldn't imagine anyone was there. Not to mention it looked like it would cave in if anyone set foot on it. *Why am I even here? This is too dangerous,* I thought, second-guessing my decision. I grabbed the sheath on my left hip, which was where I kept my combination knife, a type of knife issued by the AHL that turned into a short sword, no longer than two feet, when flicked.

We quietly ran around the court, keeping to the walls, as the possessed zombie-like people were doing simple things like sitting and hobbling around aimlessly. They were few; military efforts had largely removed Nojuni of humans strong enough to transform into the final evolution—large, frog-like creatures, covered in boils filled with acidic, black ooze. The rest were beyond saving. I squinted my eyes, trying to find the main door in the darkness. Shuddering, I creaked open the massive wooden door. I was sure the guards wouldn't notice.

The first thing I noticed was the smell. The air felt thick in a way that made me yearn for a clean shower. The style of the interior of the building was late-medieval, as far as I could glean. There were dusty statues, peeling wallpaper, and broken objects everywhere, along with the occasional servant limping slowly around the palace. We ran to a secluded corner and quickly threw on servant cloaks we carried with us as disguises, smearing ourselves with dust from the ground to mask our scent.

Our stealth boots made our steps silent, but didn't stop the wooden floorboards creaking under us. We walked around as I felt the headache to intensify. I whispered my plan to explore the east wing, which the map on our wrist projections showed was on our right. We continued down a corridor.

I saw something covered in fabric on the side of the corridor as I passed by. It appeared to be the same mauve cloak everyone was wearing, likely with someone inside. As we got closer to it, a horrible, rotting stench filled my nose and stung my head. *Is that... dead?* I asked myself, feeling cold spread on my back as I passed. *I feel like how Saku must've felt out there.* I heard her suppress a retch behind me.

The end of the corridor led to two smaller hallways on the left and right. I winced at my ever-ringing headache, but I knew it was the right place.

At the end of the left corridor was where I felt the pain intensify. I also smelled the sweet millin bush. *This had to be it.* Saku and Sirani kept watch in the corridor as I surveyed the area.

It was hard to tell the colors of the chamber we were in with the darkness masking the room's far side. The ochre paint on the wall—the only thing that wasn't faded—was chipped, and bits were scattered on the dark wood floor, looking like stars in the sky. I kept scanning the room. The bookcases were covered in dust; the varnish felt rough against my fingers.

To my right was a door leading to the balcony I'd spotted before. I looked outside, seeing the possessed guards we'd killed below it. *We should clean that up before they're seen.* I had made it to the end of the wing, meaning that I could escape to the outside of the palace if I needed to. I saw a canopy bed pressed against the wall with faded, red curtains. This room in particular smelled like someone had been living there. The smell was just too fresh. It smelled like herbs and clean bed linens.

One of the bookshelves covered in dust had a new shadow there. I jumped slightly, and my first instinct was to draw my weapon. I ran forward with my combination knife as I flicked it and slashed at the figure.

I knew I must have missed it because I was facing the opposite wall, feeling disoriented. I turned to look, and the person was still there with a different guy next to him, although they were hard to see since it was still barely dawn. I rapidly put on my helmet while the two began muttering things to each other. The taller one had red eyes, which I had never seen, not even in Avukena. The slightly shorter one had scruffy vanilla blond hair.

They started speaking slightly louder in a strange pidgin. It sounded like a mix between the local language, English, and Hakon, Avukena's lingua franca, which I understood most of.

They must have thought I didn't understand, because they were talking about the blond one's use of combat delay, a magic technique. Most people don't bother with that skill because of its difficulty.

The taller one was looking at my disguise and helmet. He had a sword in his other hand. He took another step towards me, still gripping it. I prepared my stance to guard myself.

"You're not from here..." he said quietly, in thickly-accented Hakon. We stared at each other for a long time, waiting for the other to strike.

"Here in palace." The voice said again, louder and clearer than ever. The sensation burned, causing me to fall to the ground in pain.

This must be him. I barely managed to look up, seeing him nod thoughtfully. I saw his eyes widen, and all the pain suddenly left. I stood up, panting and sweating.

"You… one I try to talk to." He stumbled through the words. He must have heard me speak, or he wouldn't have known I spoke English.

I didn't let my guard down, but I lowered my short sword to hip level. He dropped his sword entirely, backing away from it. "The reason why I message you is because our need you help." He said, several feet away from me. His words were jumbled. It was difficult to understand what he was saying. He continued. "We trying to get—"

The blond one, close to a wall, partially fell through an old floorboard, the rotten wood splintering around his leg. I saw a faint purple glow. *What is that?* He blinked vigorously as the hole released a faint cloud of white dust. He lifted his leg out and looked at Zandos in fear. They muttered things to each other in their strange language. I could vaguely understand some words like "alright," and "leg."

I observed the shorter guy as they spoke. His resemblance to Sirani was uncanny. The hair color, the faint freckles, and the protruding ears, all of it was really similar. The only difference was his slight underbite. They hadn't yet seen each other; she was still outside the room in the corridor.

The black-haired one looked really eager to talk to me after concluding with the blond one, so I set down my short sword and lifted my visor to show I wasn't hostile. He smiled earnestly, but it could very well have been a trap. Even a crocodile could look like it's smiling. Our training taught us that until cleared by the senior officials, anyone we encounter in Nojuni should be treated as volatile and a high-risk threat. Saku and Sirani still had their weapons on them, and I had my gun too, if it came to that.

I gestured for Sirani to enter, and she retracted her visor too, though she and the blond one locked eyes for a moment. She lurched back behind Saku and me, activating her visor.

"I can't believe he's alive…" she whispered quietly, sounding shaky. The blond guy approached us, trying to chase Sirani out from behind us, only managing to hit her helmet and deactivate her visor. Even the black-haired one looked like he thought it was strange.

"Is this some kind of trick?" The blond one asked Sirani, looking angry, approaching her further. "What's the joke here? Did dad send you all? I'm never going back, and you just made me sure of it!"

"No, he didn't, leave me alone!" Sirani demanded, shoving him away, pulling out her short sword.

"Jace," The black-haired one cautioned.

"Then what the hell are you doing here? You don't just stumble here by accident!" Jace sneered, continuing to stomp around, chasing Sirani around the room. "How's your palace life going? Live with them still? Do they even want you anymore?" Jace asked, jeeringly.

"Jace, is enough," The black-haired one urged, trying to intercept him. Sirani ran behind me and Saku, holding her sword in a short stance. He must have been important, otherwise she would've just attacked him like any other guy.

"I don't care, Zandos," Jace spattered as he was held back by the black-haired guy, who I supposed was Zandos. "I bet you don't even live with mom and dad still, I bet they kicked you out already!"

Sirani stammered. "I don't—"

—"You knew we'd never be enough!"

"Please, this isn't what you think it is," Sirani pleaded. "I'm not here because of you, I promise."

"Jace, stop it," Zandos said firmly, tightening his grip on Jace, who only became angrier. He clawed at the Zandos's arms. Moments passed while he and Jace wrestled on the ground, and Sirani took deep breaths to compose herself. Saku looked at me, perplexed and scared.

"You're pathetic." Sirani stood, arms akimbo.

"I don't care," Jace barked. "I don't care about you or what you have to say." Zandos loosened his grip.

"Do you realize what happened? I barely know you, yet you caused us so much pain by running away like you did."

"You're not going to make me feel guilty. I'm over it. I don't care about that stuff anymore, and neither should you." He said. I connected the dots. *Yesterday... Sirani's brother... the combat delay... this has to be him.* Jace contorted furiously and swatted away Zandos's grip. The sun had risen and made us cast long shadows. All but Jace, though it was hard to tell as he slinked away to the hall.

I turned to see Zandos in the corner staring intensely at my group. Saku looked uncomfortable, wringing her hands and pursing her lips.

"Zandos, tell us who you are," I said. "And why were you giving me those headaches?"

"I Zandos. Jovnelle my mother, I'm she child," he said. "That are why I live here."

Fear came to my mind. *Would he tell Jovnelle that we were here? Why didn't I expect him to be related to her?* It would explain the painful telepathic messages and his red eyes, being from someone so powerful.

"Alright, but that doesn't explain *why* you were sending me those messages," I said cautiously, aware of how horrible this could be. He didn't answer me immediately.

"First, tell... why I see you and... Sirani, who were here much times while fly and search?" he asked, sounding annoyed. He paced closer to me, and I rested my hand on the pommel of my short sword, alert to his approach. I knew I shouldn't tell him about the AHL right away, so I pressed.

"No, answer me first. Why did you send me those telepathic messages if you're part of the Nojuni Empire? Aren't you allied with them?"

"I… are believing that what Cavaris do is not right," he said, his eyes saddening. "With thing how it are, I do not want to die, with world and mother in possess… and… destroy."

"So do you want us… to help you?" I said, slowing down my words for him.

"I assume you working to stop the destroy… and Cavaris, so I talk at you."

That's a courageous thing to do. He didn't even know that we were against Nojuni at all. I felt a small bit of relief, but also wariness—I couldn't divulge too much information. "Yeah. We do something like that."

"We can finally go see the rest of the world… " Jace said, his voice low and almost robotic, as he stood at the doorway.

That can't be right. His appearance almost seemed tainted by something. I couldn't tell whether or not he had a shadow, but I was immediately suspicious. Losing a shadow was the first sign of possession. His fingers trembled. Saku was pleading with her eyes, begging me to leave. I felt bad for her, as it was only her second recon mission.

"We should probably leave soon, then," I suggested. Both Zandos and Saku nodded vigorously.

"I… am sorry," Jace grumbled, his eyes growing wide, and a bit of drool dripping from his mouth like a rabid dog. He stepped forward, and I lurched back. His shadow was fully gone.

I drew my weapon.

"It's the sign," Saku said quietly. "Losing your shadow."

"Zandos, I am le-eaving and telli-ing Jovnelle," Jace spattered. He gripped onto the doorframe as he shook violently and slipped. He hit his head desperately with the heel of his palm, in a flash of consciousness, trying to regain control. He looked in horror at all of us, before suddenly falling motionless, his eyes glassy. "I am t-telling Cavaris you… are leav—leaving."

Zandos looked appalled, blinking and stammering. Saku stared fearfully at me. Sirani was the first to speak.

"Jace. What are you doing?"

"Sirani, don't you… do not… see? They are going to a war, which is—is obvious. We will be rewarded for telling Jovn-n-nelle. It would be an honor to help her," Jace said with an unnatural tone and cadence. Even the words were weird. Zandos stood by the doorway, preventing his escape.

Sirani stepped forward. "Jace, stop, you don't know what you're saying." Jace's expression looked unchanged.

"You can come with me, Sirani. And you too, Zandos. All of you. We can all be praised," Jace said. The color had left Sirani's face.

"Sirani, he's possessed," I said, trying to rope her away from emotions.

"Please, we must go," Jace grumbled. He suddenly shot out of the door but hit the wall. Zandos lunged towards him, tackling him to the ground and drawing his knife. Sirani's pale brows furrowed as she restrained herself. She held her arms close to her body and wrung her hands. All we could do was watch. Struggling, Zandos kept Jace in a headlock while his legs were flailing and kicking. I looked at Sirani, torn between what was right and her own love for her brother, whom she barely knew.

Suddenly, Jace stopped struggling from exhaustion. Zandos put away his knife and dragged Jace over to the next room.

I heard Zandos say something angrily to him in their Frankenstein language. Sirani held her arms tight to her body. I put my hand on her arm. We had to get out of here, and fast, but this new problem needed to be resolved. He had to be restrained before we left.

Zandos came back and started looking around the ground, trying to find what triggered his possession. Meanwhile, I walked into the adjacent room to see how severe Jace's condition was. As soon as I entered, he locked eyes with me, the way a cat does before pouncing.

"No," I whispered, shaking, horrified by the look in his eyes. His head spasmed, and what should have been white in his eyes darkened to an inky black. The Mahi had taken complete control, and he was about to transform. After possessing someone, Mahis try to transform into a monster if there's enough life force or magic available.

Jace gurgled, his mouth foaming. I saw his hand become enveloped in a deep purple, scaly skin covered in little red tendrils that writhed like an octopus' arms. He morphed into a frog-like monster, almost twice his height, as his clothes ripped. If it weren't for the high roof, he would have certainly broken it. I backed away, turning towards the door.

The creature screamed in a distorted voice and lurched an ugly alien hand towards me. I didn't have time to check if it alerted any guards or servants. Shaking, I lunged toward the beast. I stabbed his shoulder with my shortsword. I wasn't able to evade his black, piercing claws, for they tore the cloak I was still wearing and left a small, raw, bloody gash on my thigh. I felt a wave of pain and nausea as I glanced at my wound. The creature looked at me loathingly, growling in pain. It snapped its jaws at me. I stumbled on the ground and ran away, slipping and yelping through the small hallway.

"Zandos, your friend just transformed into a Mahi monster," I yelled, panting.

"What is?" he said, looking confused. I felt a rush of panic and exasperation.

"Monster," I mimed desperately. "Your friend is a monster now. He is too big to fit through the door, but still dangerous." He blinked as he tried to understand. Then his eyebrows raised as he suddenly understood.

"What... how, how fix... him?" Zandos said, stumbling over the words. I looked at him gravely. He bit his lips. "No fix. Yes?"

"We have to neutralize him here for now," I said. He blinked in confusion. "I mean... we hurt him and he stays here. Then, we go away." He nodded and left for the adjacent room.

I grabbed my emergency first aid kit on my hip to quickly dress my wound with Sirani's help. It wasn't too deep, but the claws did scrape off a good chunk of my skin. Meanwhile, Saku called a van to take us back, since we didn't think Zandos could fly. His being seen in Sjasa was risky, too.

I dashed out of the room to the next one, the adrenaline overpowering my pain. Zandos was already there and had the creature backed into a corner. The creature didn't seem to want to fight Zandos. The wound had slowed it down somewhat.

I knew my .22 wouldn't be enough to dent its thick skin, but Sirani's 9 millimeter could at least distract it. I ran back into the other room while Zandos fought the monster with his dagger.

"Sirani, I need your pistol," I said as quickly as I could. Worry crossed her eyes.

"Are you going to... hurt him?" Sirani asked.

"Sirani, please, we have to do this," I said, being intentionally vague. "It's nothing that won't heal if he transforms back into a human. We just need to knock him out so he doesn't follow us back—"

—"*If* he transforms back? Knock him out with a *gun*, too?" Sirani said. "I'm sorry Isavna. I can't let you do this."

"He could follow us back!" I said as I started to get frustrated. "I don't even know what could happen—"

—"Sirani, please just give Isavna the gun," Saku said, terrified.

"No, I will not do that," Sirani said. I heard a crash in the room where Zandos and the Mahi monster were. It made us all flinch, but Sirani was firm.

As soon as we heard another crash, we ran over to investigate.

Zandos was holding onto the horns of the monster, his shoes on its nose and one of its eyes, as the monster threw its head around. It spun once forcefully, and Zandos lost his footing. Sirani didn't blink. Saku drew her Mahi blaster.

"Don't shoot," I told her. "Those only work when they're still in Mahi form. The skin is too thick now." I drew my shortsword and walked into the combat, and for a second, I thought I saw Sirani put her hand on the grip of her gun.

I slid under the neck of the beast as Zandos wrestled with its head and stabbed its shoulder again, opening the wound further. I heard Saku retch as the muscle was exposed and blood squirted from an opened artery. The monster screamed, causing Zandos to fall off and hit the ground.

The monster grunted in pain and fell on the other shoulder. The blood loss caused it to weaken temporarily. After checking that Zandos was fine, we barricaded the room with a bookshelf and a few other pieces of furniture.

"That'll hold him for a moment," I said, walking back to the bedroom. "Until he regains strength. But hopefully we'll be gone by then." If we lingered too long, it might follow our scent. "Saku, what's the ETA on that van?"

"Any moment now." She said. We waited for a moment, drinking from our water canteens and listening to the helpless cries of the Mahi monster from the other room. We all knew that leaving him here would mean dooming him to death, since monsters eventually ran out of life force and died, if they didn't sacrifice themselves to Cavaris first.

"Isavna," Sirani said meekly. "Do you think we could take Jace back to the AHL and find a way to extract the Mahi?"

"Not safely." Her eyes pleaded hopelessly. I sighed. "I'm sorry Sirani. There's nothing we can do." She cast her gaze downward.

"I know we have to leave him. It's just... hard for me." I nodded and hugged her.

We heard another crash. As I walked over to the doorframe to see if any of the furniture had budged, I noticed a strange mechanism under the broken floorboard. It looked like a magic bear trap, but without teeth.

"Zandos, what's this?" I asked, taking a picture of it with my wrist projection, an object that confused him for a second. He knelt down.

"I not believe," he gasped. "Is a magic trap. Is why Jace get Mahifer. I thinked I destroy all of them...."

He explained to us how it was inert now that it was already activated. Apparently, those traps were pretty common in the palace, but he tried to remove as many as he could. He told us how Cavaris had placed them there to try to kill him and others who wandered in places they weren't supposed to go.

"Van's about a minute away, I can see it from here," Saku said. I took the deactivated trap and turned to Zandos.

"Do you know how to fly?" I asked him.

"Everything... I know come from books," he said, pointing at the many bookshelves in the room. "Like... this language. I have no book on magic anymore. I never learn."

"Do you know any other way to get down besides going through the palace?" I asked.

"Yes, I have," he said, standing up to go to the balcony. He gestured for us to follow him. He pointed to a ledge right next to the balcony. The stone bricks were large and close enough together that they seemed like a usable way to descend. In fact, there appeared to be a worn-down pattern in the bricks that was probably his usual route. I looked up and saw the van in the distance.

"What is?!" Zandos exclaimed. "Oh… Is vehicle?"

"Yeah, it's our hover van from the AHL. Your books look old, so maybe the ones you saw had these circles, wheels, on the sides." Saku explained, miming a circle with her hands. "We don't use those kinds anymore. These types of vans can fly both low and moderately high off the ground. Flying low to the ground is safer." She spoke so quickly, I was sure Zandos had trouble following along.

"Slow down, Saku," Sirani said.

"Right," she replied. "Sorry."

Zandos climbed down the stones with practiced ease, while Sirani, Saku, and I flew down.

"Ready?" The driver asked as we piled in and departed. I looked back at the palace as we left. Something rustled within the forest, running parallel to us at a scarily fast speed. It disappeared into the thick brush.

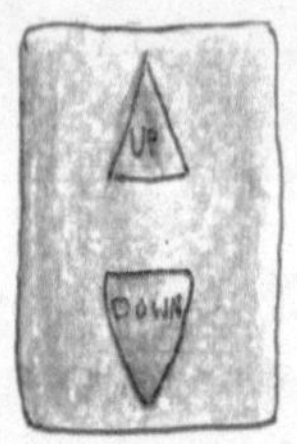

3

While we drove, we filled in Zandos on the history of Avukena that he missed, and about the AHL. We also explained about our city, the council, and whatever he needed to know. I told him Avukena's creation story, which he knew only vaguely.

"The first person in space was Mother Everealm, and she was created at the same time as Cavaris."

"Who is?" Zandos asked.

"She's, like, the closest thing we have to a god. She raised the six sisters, patron goddesses of the elements," I said. He nodded slowly, as though he was pretending to understand. "Your mother is one of those sisters, the one representing darkness There's five others. Marathene, the light sister, lives in the palace, she's closest to Mother Everealm. The other four live elsewhere," I finished explaining slowly. I glanced out the window, wondering if the thing I saw running was still following us. The forest was too dense to see.

When we exited Nojuni country, we flew to a slightly higher elevation to clear the trees. Zandos was startled as his body was pulled back, having never been in a vehicle before. While we flew, I messaged my supervisor telepathically about my suspicion of being followed by the Jace monster so we could tighten security. After another while, we arrived at a small above-ground concrete building, the AHL Central Base's main entrance. Most of the building was underground. We went down a ramp into the garage. As I got out, I saw more security personnel than normal. An operative and mutual friend, Keya, was sitting at the desk. She smiled, but her expression flickered as she took notice of Zandos.

"Morning," I said. "I didn't know you were on so early."

She nodded and stood up. "Morning. Yeah, I was sent here to cover someone's guard shift. They should be on in five. We moved the sign in sheet there," she added, gesturing vaguely to the other side of the office. I typed in our names in the hologram, giving Zandos a guest tag to wear.

"Real early shift," Saku commented as she waited. Portals made commute time virtually nonexistent, but six fifteen was early, even considering that. I walked over to her.

"So Keya, the new guy is Zandos. Correspondent for Nojuni," I said as she looked him over.

"Correspondent? Wouldn't he be *from* Nojuni then, or at least live there? I thought only senior and exec officials could assign correspondents, and you're only a sophomore official...."

"It's sort of hard to explain," I said hurriedly. "Renee approved this mission. He claims to be able to help us. There was also, a, uh, Mahi incident over there." I unwrapped the inert trap from my cloak, just enough for her to see.

"Jeez, you'll have a lot to tell our supervisors,"

"Yeah, I'll do it after getting Zandos situated here. Again, Renee knows. I don't intend for him to leave the AHL until the supervisors look him over."

Keya looked concerned. A different guard arrived to take her spot.

"Hi there, Zandos. Ready to go?" Keya asked him. We all agreed, even though Zandos looked somewhat nervous, as if he knew himself that he stood out.

The AHL elevator had a bulletin button. One could press it, and a hologram would reveal updates and notices. A small propaganda poster caught my eye. *DEFEND. DEFEAT. SUCCEED. Made possible through your efforts!*

As we approached the next subfloor, Keya explained each division. She detailed the first and second divisions. Division One dealt with administration and logistics, while the second was our task operatives and actual manpower. The AHL was essentially our national military, though at the moment, we were mostly preoccupied with fighting Mahis and possessions and protecting cities from Cavaris.

I looked up at Zandos. He seemed to be trying to pay attention, but was overwhelmed with the new information. I wasn't paying much attention, either, and neither was Sirani. Her eyes were reddened, and she cradled her arms close to her body. The action from the morning led us to be more tired than usual.

"Division Three is composed of our science and magic team," Keya explained. *Those are the people I'll have to give my artifact to.* I thought.

"This is our watering hole," Keya said as we hit the second subfloor. "The lounge is right there." I stepped across the blue and white tiles, and I felt the gentle whirring of the appliances. I quickly poured a cup of black coffee and dumped in a packet of sugar as I ran back to the elevator. *It'll at least keep me up for a little while.*

We proceeded to the weapons floor, where we could see an instructor teaching combat to some recruits. It smelled sort of like a locker room back on Earth. Different universe, same sweat. All the earthlike things here were taken from Earth by Mother Everealm, including humans, in her pursuits to customize Avukena to her liking. She was very selective with what she decided to introduce and keep, almost to an obsessive point. All the little details that weren't quite Earthlike enough gave me a weird, uncanny valley feeling sometimes, which really messed with me in my earlier years being here.

The weapons floor was divided into three: the training mats to the left and aisles of practice weapons to the right. There was a room with a lock on the end that had the real weapons, ammo, and other things.

A guy came out of the training sword aisle and talked to Keya for a moment.

"Who's he?" I heard him speak rapidly and quietly. He was Levi, a young operative, a few years older than I. He was dating Keya; they had been since before I got here. He mostly did Division Two work. I hoped he would overlook Zandos, but I supposed he stuck out too much.

"He's Zandos. I'm doing a quick tour since he's important, apparently." Keya said, pointing at the back of Zandos's head; he was focused on the mesmerizing collection of weapons. I glanced to see Sirani next to me. Her eyes looked glassy.

"So where you from?" Levi quickly asked Zandos, as he hefted a bag over his shoulder that held broken training swords. We were back in the elevator, going farther down. I always saw him around running errands; sometimes it looked like he was in multiple places at once. Even just by hearing him speak or looking at him, we could tell he was restless and full of energy like a small child. Levi asked again, "Zandos, uh, you from, like, Sjasa or somewhere close by?"

Zandos looked at me like he needed me to answer for him. Not to mention that Levi spoke so quickly, it made it hard for him to understand.

"Yeah, he's not from too far away. He's a new correspondent." Correspondents were what we called spies.

"Oh, cool," Levi replied. "I like your felmine leather knife sheath, by the way, my brothers would kill for one of those." Felmines were large, wolf-like creatures with wings and antlers that were commonly eaten and used for leather.

Zandos, still bewildered, blinked at him. We stood awkwardly until a rumbling made me clutch the wall.

The lights suddenly flickered and shut down.

I turned on my wrist projection's flashlight, and Sirani invoked a light orb. The elevator slowed midway while we fell and suddenly jolted to a stop. I heard thuds, jumps, and heavy breathing that sounded like it belonged to the Jace monster. Sirani extinguished the light orb upon realizing that it might be a Mahifer, and they're attracted to magic. I listened to a few booms of what sounded like gunshots, and the instructor and others yelling at the other people.

I couldn't see anyone in the darkness, only the barely illuminated ground from Sirani's wrist projection. I didn't need light to sense the electric panic around me.

"We'll be fine," Keya said, trying to maintain composure. I worried about Zandos. Standing next to them, I could smell Keya's hippie citrus and patchouli perfume, and Zandos's raw, unwashed body odor—two very contrasting smells. I had to imagine that Zandos didn't have access to proper hygiene or running water while in Nojuni. Being around so much decay probably doesn't help, either.

The roof kept shaking so much that I nearly fell down. I could even hear magic weapons firing, the distinctive *schwoop* of a Mahi blaster shooting something.

A piece of metal fell from above, down through the roof of our elevator with a resonating clang, Keya barely dodging as it fell to the floor. I stared at the metal I-beam now on the ground. Half of it was melted by some kind of acid. I looked up through the tear in the roof of the metal elevator. I could see a silhouette of a black creature bouncing around the metal framework, with the same scary, purple, shiny scales as the Mahi-possessed Jace monster, though it was hard to tell in the low light. Even so, we knew it was him.

The creature descended from the cables of the elevator, and so did the instructor. The monster screamed and slashed at the gaping hole in the roof with sharp claws, widening it as we all ducked and tightened into balls on the floor. I caught a glimpse of the purple scales as they passed by the light. Zandos was the only one who seemed undeterred. Levi grabbed one of the swords he had and hurled it at the monster. It roared again, saliva dripping from its sharp fangs.

"Throw another!" Zandos shouted at Levi. Levi obliged and threw one, which missed just to the side of the monster. The monster looked for it, trying to investigate.

"Dammit! Sorry," Levi said, seething in frustration.

"No, is perfect. Do again," Zandos said. He knew we were running out of time. People on the other floor managed to open up the door by now and started shooting at the monster. The fluorescent lights illuminated the creature's fangs.

"Hold on!" Keya shouted at them, and the shooting ceased. Zandos gestured to Levi to throw another sword, which again missed the monster. Zandos climbed up the hole, stepping on the half-molten I-beam. The monster followed the source of the thrown sword, buying Zandos just enough time to leap onto the creature's back.

We all watched as Zandos dodged most of the spikes on its back as it threw him around. Zandos, unsure whether to kill it or not, grabbed the horns on its head like a horse's reins. The creature was so focused on getting rid of him that it didn't focus on defending itself from anyone else. Mahis weren't particularly smart, which is why they weren't worth taming. Someone on the second subfloor, a few doors up, shouted, getting the attention of the monster. And in that moment, we watched as a blast of golden-white magic hit the creature, knocking the wind out of him. Zandos dismounted and leaped to the side to catch his breath.

"Hey, you good?" Levi asked Zandos, who was slumped on top of the elevator, almost out of view.

Brev, a lab worker, invoked her wings and somehow flew down the super cramped elevator from the second subfloor to where Jace was, still in monster form. Jace was squirming helplessly. His spikes could easily impale us if we weren't careful. She gently clipped the claw and put it in a jar for further investigation, among other samples. Jace kept squirming and roaring in confusion and pain until he relented, heaving on the ground. I looked at Zandos. Levi was already up there, helping him up. When the lights came back on, we could hear hydraulics whirring and felt the elevator move up. When it went as high as it could go safely, Brev, Sirani, Zandos, and Levi dragged Jace out of the elevator. The Jace-monster was put in a room with a glass wall, where Brev and the whole lab and medic team tried to extract the Mahi out of him with specialized, bulky machinery as he sat there appearing nearly lifeless. People stared as the body was transported—curious, but not daring enough to get within a dozen feet of it. The machine, which looked like a small vacuum cleaner, was strapped to his head. It looked primitive and experimental. Sirani turned around, not strong enough to look.

Sirani and I stepped into the sterilization chamber, holding our arms up as the machines around us hissed disinfectants.

"Isavna, I think you were right," Sirani said. "I should've given you the pistol. Maybe… maybe he wouldn't have followed us here." By now, she was no longer unsettled by what had happened. Or at least, she didn't show it. "He wasn't who I remembered him being."

"Don't worry about him now, Sirani. What matters is that we're all safe." We turned around to the people scrutinizing the monster's nail clippings and scribbling things in notebooks or holograms. The lab had colors of white and silver, with the sterile, concrete floor under our feet. I saw Sirani take a deep breath. The lab smelled like bleach and cleaning agents that stung my nose a little. People were carting around buckets with biohazard signs on them. The scientists here were trained in the three disciplines of magic, science, and technology. Such things were what allowed my phone to be tweaked to connect to Avukena's universal wireless network, since they didn't have cellphone towers here.

"Ms. Belanis," I heard. I whipped my head around to see who was speaking. It was a lab worker, waving a clipboard. Sirani and I walked over to him.

"We confirmed that it was indeed the friend of Zandos who triggered the trap. He is doing fine now."

"What's the deal with that trap?" I asked. "And how was he able to keep up with the hover van?"

"Zandos told us they were ancient traps that the palace chamberlain had implemented to control people from wandering in places they weren't supposed to go. Most of them are apparently deactivated. The monster's speed—and the ability to transform at all—is based on the magical aptitude or physical strength of the possessed individual; whichever is stronger. That is why he transformed into such a large creature capable of extreme speed. In fact, most people sustain the injuries they take in monster form once they transform back, but he only has scrapes on the surface of his skin."

"That's why the regular servants can't transform monsters, because they're too weak physically and magically," Sirani deduced.

"Precisely. We ran some tests, and it looked like this individual had very strong magic." *Maybe because he mastered skills like combat delay.*

Sirani and I went back into the elevator to find Zandos and decide what to do with Jace. Keya was there, so Sirani explained what we were told.

"Really?" Keya asked, eating a sandwich. I could smell the capers and a distinct Avukenan spice. "So are we gonna keep these guys around or what?"

"That's the hope," I said. "They know Nojuni in and out. I suppose you can imagine why they'd be especially useful for recon missions, as a guide or an alibi." I walked into the mess hall with Sirani and Keya. who levitated four drinks.

"Oh, I told Renee about them. There's gonna be a hearing with some senior officials soon." Keya said as she looked at the clock. "Gotta split, see ya. I have a meeting with Div One AHL south to talk business," she said playfully, as she left.

I saw Zandos and Levi talking by a vending machine. *How did Levi beat us to the mess hall? He was still there when we left.* I sat for a proper breakfast with Brev and Sirani.

Sirani and I both pressed buttons on the glowing interface of the table, and before long, two plates rose from a compartment.

"Zandos, why don't you join us?" Brev asked, blinking her sleep-deprived eyes. She had a messy brown bun that sat on top of her head like a cinnamon roll, and an anxious wrinkle line between her eyebrows. I waved from our table. Zandos sat down at our table and looked at us awkwardly. There was a lot of information he needed to know, but I had to go easy on him.

"So, Zandos," I began slowly, trying not to sound patronizing. "Just letting you know, there's going to be a meeting later today to talk about your place here." He looked perplexed and cast his eyes aside. "Well, I suppose we can cross that bridge when we get there."

"How are you finding your first day here?" Sirani asked, wearing a reassuring smile.

"Is much. Is much world I do not know. Levi just tell me about much of wild thing like vending machines, which he say are bad, terrible, not useful invention, and also the teleport." He seemed curious, but apprehensive. He pursed his lips and looked between Sirani, Brev, and me. "Jace doing... how?"

"Jace is in recovery right now," said Brev, sipping hot coffee. "Tell me something, Zandos, how did you first meet him?"

"Maybe sort of remember," He said. "I was maybe... fourteen when Jace first come to me. He in woods, and I feel... for first time, that someone else need me like my mom need me. I have no... brother or sister. He feel like one. I taught all I knew for combat. He liked combat more than I, which was not a surprise. After combat, he practice he magic skills." *Gosh. This guy has more of a maternal instinct than I do.*

"He would've probably liked the weapons room then," Sirani said, smiling wryly. "Such a shame that we didn't get to tour all the subfloors."

"Well, we got to the important ones, I suppose," I said.

"The elevator incident cut it short," said Brev.

I finished my salad as quickly as I could. The slight, warm draft from the air conditioner made my hair flap around. Zandos just looked around, perplexed, but also amused at all the new sights.

I spotted somebody who looked like Jace being followed around by a guard. I stopped eating and watched as he was escorted into a special elevator, the one that went to the fifth subfloor, the detention cells. It needed a keycard access level that mine couldn't access normally. It was specially armored for criminals and blocked telepathic messaging. I could see Zandos wanting to follow, but Sirani gestured otherwise.

"His memories will take time to come back," Brev said. "But soon he'll remember what happened." Brev pushed up her glasses. "Well, best I get back to the lab." She upturned her wrist and flicked her hand for the wrist projection to appear, this world's version of a phone. She pinched the bottom of it, and it detached from her wrist, viewing images of the samples she took from Jace. She walked away, leaving just Sirani, Zandos, and me. A guard approached us, taking Sirani.

"Jace?" I asked telepathically. She looked in my direction and nodded. They disappeared into the elevator.

After a little while, Zandos and I went up to my office. I explained what we knew about Jace, other basic things about Avukena, and some things that interested him. I withheld a lot of information, not trusting him enough. After all, he could've been a spy. I heard a knock on my office door.

"Come in," I said, realizing it was Reid, a friend.

He looked at Zandos in the same distrusting way Zandos looked at him. A long pause made the situation even more awkward.

Making a quick decision, I decided to introduce the two.

"Hi, Reid, this is Zandos. We found him during recon. He'll be our new correspondent for Nojuni. He helped in the disaster in elevator three, if you heard about it." I winced internally at how bad I knew this looked, but tried to keep a smile on my face. Had I been told this, I would also be suspicious, as Reid was at that moment.

"Oh, really? Zandos, huh. I've heard some stuff about him this morning. Crazy good at combat, apparently." Reid said, with ill-suppressed worry and anger. He stood in the doorway.

Zandos pointed at Reid. "So… Reid?" Zandos said to Reid. "Friend? Work here?"

"Yes, anyone who wears this works here," Reid said tensely, gesturing to his tan blazer. He sighed, relaxing his shoulders. *I wonder why he's so agitated.*

"Look, I just met him today, on a scouting mission. I would've told you but it was like, four in the morning."

"Can we talk for a sec, Isavna?" Reid asked. I felt a tingle of fear. I followed him out while Zandos waited inside.

"So?" I asked him, as if I didn't know. Reid looked at the door and back at me.

"Isavna, what were you thinking? He's from *Nojuni.* What on Mother Everealm's planet compelled you to bring him here?"

"I couldn't have just left him there," I retorted, trying to keep my voice down. "He's not some regular citizen. He was sending these powerful telepathic messages to me to try and get me in the palace so we could talk."

"And you *listened* to them? What if it was a trap—"

—"I know how ridiculous it sounds. But these messages hurt like hell, I don't know why. I had to do something about it."

"SO what's the deal with the Mahi monster everyone's talking about?" he interrogated, still agitated. He didn't seem mad at me, more... anxious. I explained how we found Zandos and Jace in the palace.

"Things went south, and, well, Zandos proved to be really useful. He also seems to have gotten acquainted with Levi so I think he can watch Zandos for now."

Reid looked concerned and incredulous. "Did Renee or anyone even know about this guy yet? You're really asking a lot. We've never had someone from Nojuni, much less the *palace grounds* come here without proper inspection." Reid propped his chin with his hand, looking concerned. He knew there was no going back now. Zandos had definitely seen too much. I sighed, understanding the gravity of Reid's unease. "Well, dammit, we can't exactly send him back now. I don't think this was a good idea, Isavna."

"I get it," I said, sounding firm. "But Counterintel didn't have anything on him yet, I've already checked. But for now, I need you to humor me on this. He has valuable information about Nojuni. He knows the palace, everyone in it, and how to speak to them," I said. I refrained from telling him that he was Jovnelle's kid. "So can you just... bear with me, and keep an eye out?"

Reid hesitated, his dark eyebrows furrowed with worry. "Okay, but I still don't trust him. He's not someone we know. Don't let him out of your guys' sight." He looked at me with sincere worry. "Please, be careful with that guy, especially in public."

I nodded in understanding and proceeded into my office.

"I go see rest of building," Zandos said awkwardly, noticing my unease.

"Yeah, but just one more thing," I said. "You, uh... you should bear in mind that not everyone's gonna like you."

He blinked and furrowed his brows, appearing puzzled; an expression I had seen on him very often by this point. "Why? Because I not wear… jacket… uniform?"

"No, just because you're you," I said. His expression remained unchanged. "Yeah, I know, it's kind of strange. That's just how this world is. Even if you saved a bunch of people like you did in the elevator, they're still not gonna like you."

His face hardened. "I… understanding," he said without conviction. His eyes looked past me.

"You don't have to lie," I said, smiling wryly. "I know what it's like."

I silently escorted him down to the second subfloor, leaving him in Levi's supervision. I went back up and slumped in my chair. *I hope he doesn't hate it here.* I suppose that, unlike me, he actually wanted to come here. I thought about my interaction with Reid, too. And about Sirani and Jace. *Ugh, why does it all have to be so complicated?* I turned to my desk and began to fill out some paperwork I had pending. I turned on my wrist projection and detached the display, then accessed the AHL's camera system to keep an eye on Zandos as I worked. *He's looking at the vending machines now.* I was not very high ranking, so I mostly filed meeting minutes for all the Division One committees. *Safety committee papers here,* I thought. *Contingency Planners is here, and, uh, oh—here's the PR committee.* I saw Renee's name on that paper as I put it in a folder. *Maybe I should take that as a sign.* I closed the filing cabinet and started writing an incident report for the mission.

Suddenly, I heard footsteps. They were commanding and confident, which told me they were my supervisor, Renee. I heard her open the office next to me, Sirani and Saku's. They talked a bit, and then she moved to my office.

"Come in," I said. Renee opened the door and walked in, sitting down on the chair on the opposite side of the desk. Her face was lean and somewhat masculine, with orange eyes that glinted with concern and resolve. Even during slow days in the AHL, she always seemed to have something she was hung up on.

"Good morning, Belanis. We will be holding a meeting in thirty minutes," Renee said. "Please let the others in the event from this morning know. Jace will be released into the Safety Committee's meeting room, and Sakuraci will go down to collect Zandos. Some other sophomore officials will be at the meeting, so we don't have to repeat ourselves; we will leave Zandos and Jace to be among you. Fill these out during the meeting." She handed me a packet: *Zandos and Jace Review Meeting Minutes*. "But really quickly, we need you to sign this." She opened her wrist projection and pulled up a file. "Sirani and Sakuraci have informed us of the situation. They wrote an incident report, and due to your involvement, we just need you to confirm this is what happened." She flipped the hologram, and I reviewed it quickly before signing. *I guess I won't need to write one then.* She nodded curtly and left.

I thought about Zandos and Jace. I honestly didn't know what could happen if the officials didn't buy their story. Nojuni refugees with this amount of insight into the AHL and with that kind of power were very unusual. It's not like these guys were ordinary, either. The higher-ups obviously knew something was strange about them. Whatever the case, their screening had to go well.

4

Sunday, 7:47 AM, AHL Central, Subfloor 3 - Armory and Training Facility

"What weapons is… you favorite?" Zandos asked Levi. They were both going around aisles of training weapons in the armory, returning repaired swords to their places.

"Broadsword," he replied, pointing to the sword sheathed on his back. "I keep it here cause it's annoying on my hip."

"I see earlier Isavna and other people use wings, board-sword not get in way?" Zandos asked.

"Nope, I'm not great at flying, so I use the vans, portals, or just run, y'know?" Levi said.

Zandos widened his eyes and nodded. "Yes! Yes, I not can… fly, I not know how, never… learn. I not like… like use magic, difficult, hard to work with." Zandos explained passionately, as fast as his words could go.

"Exactly! Man, it's like everyone likes using magic these days. The most magic I use is, like, the portals." They heard footsteps coming from the elevator, which poured out to the main combat training area. The door buzzed as someone tapped a keycard to the armory entrance in the small hallway. Saku rounded the corner first, followed by someone significantly taller than her. Same features, but his blue eyes held a steadiness that hers didn't. He was also far taller than she was. He was quieter and calmer than his sister, and often found himself watching out for her. He stood in place, squinting at Zandos, while Saku drifted away towards a rack of suppressors.

"Are you Zandos?" he bellowed. Zandos blinked, looking to Levi.

"Yeah, he is." Levi said. "New guy. Correspondent. And Zandos, that's Kairo. He's Saku's twin. If you have any questions about our organization or magic, you should ask him. He's way smarter than I am. Or if you need to reach for something on the top shelf of the supermarket. He's in the SO8 like the rest of us."

"SO8?" Zandos asked, not having understood most of what Levi said.

"That's what they call our group of sophomore operatives, hence, *Sophomore Operatives 8,* or SO8. When they need us to do something they're like, 'Hey SO8, mission briefing next week' and stuff."

Saku emerged from the aisle. "Hey Zandos, they exterminated the Mahi that was possessing Jace."

"Jace Mahifer…" Zandos said, lost in thought.

"Right. We're here to get you." Kairo said.

Levi shifted around. "I'll go with him. I don't know a ton about this Jace guy but we should make sure he doesn't try to punch a hole into a wall or something."

"Or into he self," said Zandos, nodding thoughtfully.

Sunday, 7:54 AM, AHL Central, Subfloor 1 – Command Center & Office Wing, Meeting Room 203

I led Zandos to the meeting room where Jace was, who had a small entourage of guards, looking uncomfortable.

Zandos entered after me. "Jace." He studied his friend with concern etched on his face. Levi, Kairo, and Saku were with him, standing at the doorway. Jace looked up from his trance, as if he didn't even notice the squeaky door as we entered.

"Hello," I said, which he ignored. I couldn't help it if he didn't like me. Zandos came close to Jace and spoke with him in their Frankenstein language. Despite Zandos's attempts, Jace still looked very resistant to the idea of staying here. Or, well, that's what I assumed they were talking about. I couldn't really parse their language anyway.

I heard footsteps and voices as Sirani and someone else came to the conference room.

She passed Levi on the way in and stood beside me. She turned to Zandos and Jace. He was sitting in place, his arms crossed and his expression sour.

"You got me here. Are you happy yet?" he asked bitterly in Hakon.

"Well," Sirani said, smiling apprehensively. "I am." All but one of the guards left the room. "At least more than before." Everyone was quiet for a little while.

"Did you saw the Mahi?" Zandos asked Jace awkwardly in English, trying to include Sirani and me in the conversation. Levi started idly spinning one of the metal award pins on his coat, one of many. He was unusually decorated for a sophomore official, bearing the awards and honors for risky missions and distinguished service.

"They exterminated it." Sirani said. "Or so I've heard."

Jace leaned back in his chair, with his arms crossed over a plain black crewneck. It was standard issue from the AHL to any refugees we processed. He had a pair of the AHL's boots, too. All of his clothes must've ripped when he turned into a monster.

"What do you even want to do with us?" Jace asked bitterly. "Are we going to stay here forever?"

"We'll keep you here until we decide to leave later today. We'll get you situated in the city, where you will stay indefinitely," I said.

"And what if we leave?" he asked, testing me. The guard in the room shifted around.

"We will catch you," I said. "I don't know how long you've been gone, but whatever you can do won't be enough." The door opened, and Renee was there, her expression stern.

"We will be having your meeting. Come with me," she gestured. Jace grumbled, though Zandos quickly shut him up.

We continued down the hallway. Sirani and Zandos were exchanging telepathic messages; I could barely detect their communication. It was like people talking across the room—you could tell when others were doing it even if you didn't know what they were saying.

The guard at the door trailed Jace, who was in the back of the group. I sensed how on edge everyone was, especially Renee. Her shoulders tensed. She had been running around all morning, dealing with incidents like the Mahis, Zandos, Jace, and the elevator. All of us knew better than to argue with her—all of us, excluding Jace.

"What do you want from us now?" Jace demanded. I heard Saku inhale through her teeth in fear.

"We need to discuss with executives your role and place in the AHL—"

—"Can you just let me leave? I don't even want to be here, so there's no point in discussing my place here," Jace retorted.

Renee whipped around. "There is no room for argument. Resisting will have consequences." Her boots clunked on the ground as she approached him. "The more problems you cause, the worse those consequences will be."

Jace's neck stiffened. I could see his jaw tense behind his stout, red cheeks. Zandos straightened out, alert, if not sort of freaked out.

Renee turned back around and continued leading us down the hall as she began to speak. "Now, if you all could please—"

Jace grunted and let out a spinning kick to Renee that barely missed her head. Had it hit, she would surely have been knocked unconscious. He used his combat delay, freezing Renee momentarily as she glowed purple. He ran behind her and grunted as he forcefully swept his leg low to the ground, aiming for her knees.

In that moment, the guard tackled Jace, with Zandos grabbing Renee out of the way before anything happened. Jace began contorting furiously, managing to freeze the guard and escape. He stood up, faced Renee, and whipped his head forward, casting a glowing ball of combat magic towards her.

"He cast that spell with his *head?*" Kairo asked. I had never seen that either. Zandos lunged at him and socked his liver. Jace grunted and lay on the ground, unable to move.

"What did you do?!" Sirani cried, bleary-eyed.

"He fine," said Zandos, his expression neutral. "Only temporary. He want to hurt, he get hurt. See how it feel."

The guard used a small crystal wand to levitate Jace along with us into the conference hall. We then went into an elevator, making it more awkward, especially since Reid was there, taking a ride to the same meeting. He looked sort of bewildered as he saw Jace floating unconsciously.

"*Isavna, what's his deal?*" Reid asked telepathically as he and I observed his floating body.

"*Zandos's friend. He lived in the palace and was there when we went there. Also, Sirani's brother, apparently. He, like, really hates her though.*" I watched as Reid turned to Sirani, standing next to me. She looked entranced watching Jace float. I wanted to help her somehow, but I felt like telling her the wrong thing could make things worse. "*I don't know how long he's been stuck in Nojuni, but he'd probably rather be there right now.*"

"*Really? He would rather be in Nojuni of all places?*" Reid asked. "*He seems like a stoic or silent type from everything I've seen.*"

"*You think so? He tried to hurt Renee just now. That's why he's in suspended consciousness, if that's what you were asking about initially. He honestly gives me the impression of someone who's unstable and violent.*" He squinted and turned his head. Renee was finger-combing her short cobalt blue hair, made messy from the fight.

"*Wow. That's not like Sirani at all. I guess I severely misjudged him.*" We exited the elevator, and after some turns in the halls of the fifth subfloor, we reached the right door.

"*I agree. I don't know how Sirani's dealing with all this; she hasn't seen him in so long. Since eight years ago, at least. She said that he's not who she remembered him being.*"

The subfloor we were in had our detention centers, questioning rooms, conference halls, and shadier things that I wasn't allowed to know about. Out of the whole drab, gray, and lifeless AHL, this room was the eeriest I had been in.

Renee used her fingerprint to unlock the door. *I hope they don't get too suspicious of Jace and Zandos…* I thought. *If the senior and executive officials decide they're too much of a problem, who's telling which punishment they'll get?*

We walked into a room with folding chairs everywhere and a big table in the center. Various people were sitting in the folding chairs, some new and some familiar. Zandos was with the rest of the group, but Jace and his guard were in a holding cell for everyone's safety. The cell was one of a few that flanked the main room.

An officer opened a panel near the door and turned on some switches. Suddenly, all telepathic messages were interrupted and suspended. Many schools, prisons, and government buildings had this technology—anywhere where you wouldn't want secret communication.

"We would like to have a meeting with supervisors and sophomore officials present regarding this morning's situation," a middle-aged executive official bellowed from the end of the table.

He blathered on some more preamble, then asked me to explain what happened. Reid took meeting minutes on a hologram as I explained the headaches, the messaging, and the mission, noting that Renee approved it before I went. We had to switch to Hakon halfway through to accommodate Zandos's language struggles. Apparently, he assumed everyone in Avukena City spoke English because he only heard me and other operatives speak English during missions. They interrogated him, and Zandos explained why he wanted to come here. He changed the minds of some, but not all.

"We can offer you this, which will be further negotiated during your individual screening," Renee said in Hakon as we were about to close. "You may stay with us if you are helpful, but you must agree to go on missions and conduct yourself properly. In exchange, we will offer housing, education, and whatever else you may need for the time being. If you prove yourself, we may consider giving you a position."

"And Jace?" Zandos replied. "Will he get that too?"

Renee sighed. "If he's helpful. And complies with orders. We'll see."

The executive official called for the adjournment of the meeting. I looked at my group, trying to read their expressions. Reid wasn't convinced. Levi and Keya looked optimistic. Both Sirani and Kairo were warily hopeful.

I returned to my office and went back to work. I could hear Sirani and Saku talking about something on the other side of the thin walls.

"Hey," Kairo said, opening my door, trying not to hit his head on the doorframe. He was the tallest out of all of us, enough that he almost always had a small bruise on his forehead from bumping into things. "We were thinking of going out for lunch today, and Zandos wants to go see the city. Wanna come with?" he asked. I nodded, getting up from my desk.

"Is Jace going to be coming?" I asked quietly. He tightened his lip and shook his head.

"No. I think they decided he's too much of a risk to do any of that."

I was walking between Zandos and Sirani as we left the portal terminal and entered the city. I couldn't quite figure out much about Zandos yet. I glanced over at him. He had black hair in a very ordinary side part, but it looked slightly disheveled because of the events this morning. He wasn't particularly attractive either, or at least not to me. He had very thick eyebrows that made his emotions easy to read. Sirani tried talking to him, but was not able to get along further than small talk.

"Where are we eating? How about Mohaba on Sorbruck and eighteenth?"

"What them make? What... food?" asked Zandos in English.

"Mohaba has all kinds of stuff, I'm pretty sure they specialize in steak and soup. They serve unicorn meat with salt sauce," explained Kairo.

"Salt sauce?" I asked.

"Oh, it's not just straight salt and water, obviously," Kairo said. "It's a fermented fish sauce. That's just what they call it."

The sounds and smells of the city wrapped around us as we entered the main dining district. Smells of fresh-baked bread, heavily spiced broth, and grilled meat wafted through the air and lingered in the streets. We passed the cloying colors and smells of a candy shop as a mother tried to pull her crying child away from going inside. There were also people on the perimeters of restaurants eating fancy meals in outdoor seating, and the cultural aromas clashed with interesting combinations of flavors. A hoverbus whirred by, carrying more tourists.

We entered the place. It was a homely sort of mom-and-pop restaurant. Physical photographs and antiques lined the walls, looking decades old. I saw some other AHL officers there eating lunch.

Reid, Sirani, and I picked a booth on the far end, with a view of the street outside. I observed him while we looked at the menu. He was stealing glances at Zandos at the table across from us, who was oblivious, looking at the city around him. Much like a child. *How could Reid be so suspicious?*

Jeez, I thought, staring into my glass of water. *Why does everyone here have to be so wary of people from different places? I mean, I've gotten plenty of weird stares and pity after people learn I'm an Earther. Gosh. Avukenans are so full of themselves. And they didn't even thank us for all the stuff Mother Everealm took from Earth.*

A lady came out with a small notepad.

"Ready to order?" she asked. We all nodded.

"Yeah, uh, I'll have the steak with cinnamon rice." I said after the others had ordered. When I first came here, I was surprised they had so many Earth foods, but by now I was used to it, and have even come to like the strange uses like black pepper in sweet food. I handed back the menu and looked at the others.

"I heard the individual screening for Zandos and Jace is happening tomorrow." Saku said.

"There sure are a lot of strange things about those guys…" Reid said, lost in thought. His eyes were intently focused on a stain on the table, as if it would move if he weren't looking.

"What are you thinking about?" I prodded.

"Well there's just so much we don't know yet. Why would Zandos ask you, if so many people go scouting over in Nojuni every week?"

"We're not the only group?" Saku asked.

"Our group is one of five that cycle for scouting. We usually get the slots where they don't expect much to happen since we're still sophomore officials," Sirani explained. "You're right, Reid, it's strange. Maybe we look the least threatening?" she shrugged. "Why don't you just ask him, if there's so much you want to know about him?" Reid stared again at Zandos, who was smiling with Kairo, Levi, and Keya at the table across from us.

"I'm good." Reid replied quietly, staring at his cup.

"Sirani's right, you should at least try sometime. Couldn't hurt," I suggested.

"Don't be so quick to assume, you only just met him today," he replied.

"Well, you're jumping to assumptions too," Saku said. Reid remained silent. Our food began to arrive.

"Hey, Sirani," I asked her telepathically, as quietly as I could, since the others would still be able to sense we were communicating. *"What do you make of… Reid's attitude about Zandos and stuff?"* I glanced over to her, though her blond curtain bangs covered her expression. Maybe I asked the wrong

thing. It was kind of a loaded question, and a territory that our friendship between us three hadn't really brought us to explore. I looked over at Reid, who seemed to be staring past me, out the window.

"Can we talk about this later?"

"Do we have a plan for the rest of the day? It's barely noon," Saku asked, putting her utensils on her empty plate.

"Not really, just get Zandos and Jace situated and go back to the AHL," I said. "Renee told me that we'd be rooming Zandos and Jace together in the room next to mine and tracking both of them. Unless something crazy happens between now and then." We finished eating and left, not worrying too much about trying to conceal Zandos. Avukena City was a large enough melting pot of cultures that they wouldn't look too unusual.

"What's that over there?" Levi asked as he pointed at something that flew low to the ground and disappeared into another street. It was a black spirit. It could really only be one thing.

"Let's go," I told our group firmly, trying not to draw a scene. We all opened our wings and took flight a few at a time, except for Levi and Zandos, who kept to the ground. I put on my flight helmet, as did everyone else flying, as we chased after the Mahi.

5

Sunday, 12:06 PM, Avukena City, N Pryne Street

We surveyed the area from above until I caught another glimpse of it—a *Mahi*.

"*There!*" I shouted both out loud and telepathically, tightening my wings to descend, getting closer.

"*Did you guys leave your Mahi blasters at the office?*" Keya asked. "*I think I forgot mine.*"

"*I got mine,*" Reid messaged the group, taking aim and trying to shoot it. We were in a quieter part of the city, and the Mahi had slipped into an alley, making it hard to fly.

"*Keya and I will watch the other side,*" Saku said as we landed. They flew a little higher to clear the building.

The group that stuck to the ground had caught up with us, their faces gleaming with sweat. I turned my attention back to the Mahi. It whipped its tail into the side of a dumpster, causing a mess. Reid kept shooting with the blaster, which made *schwoop* sounds that reverberated in the alley. The Mahi hissed and contorted furiously. Someone came out of a door on the side of the alley.

"What in the hell is going on out here?!" he shouted. "Are you the police?" He had an apron on with a few stains and a bandana around his shiny bald head.

"AHL members, sir, and there is a Mahifer we're trying to eliminate," Sirani said frantically. "Sorry for the commotion!"

Reid kept shooting at it with the blaster, and Levi ran to the back of the Mahi. He leaped back as the Mahi's tail threw a rusty pan from the dumpster at him. The Mahi went for Reid, but Levi got behind it and sank a killing slash with his broadsword at the right moment. Levi gasped and darted away as the Mahi burst into black goo, coating the area in the sticky, acidic sludge. *That's weird. Usually, they just turn into a pile of goo, not explode.* The goo let out a hiss as it burned into the asphalt and bricks. Kairo took a picture with his wrist projection to file a report with the AHL and the city.

"You got a whole damn sword? Isn't that thing illegal?" The man bellowed as he narrowly missed the goo himself. I could smell steak from inside his shop.

"Not unless it's an emergency," Levi said, panting. He fumbled with his wallet, pulling out a license. The man grunted and looked at the destruction.

"Sorry, sir, we'll find a way to clean this up," I apologized.

"Eh, it's fine," the shopkeeper said, sizing up the mess. "I'll call up my insurance and see if they even *cover* Mahi attacks." He went back inside the building without saying another word.

"That was weird," Saku said. "I hope that guy isn't mad at us."

"This is more than weird, and I don't mean that guy," Reid said, approaching the remains of the Mahi. He grabbed a piece of rebar and poked at the black goo. "It's bad. This is actually *really* bad. I don't think we've ever had Mahifers come this close to the palace before."

"Yeah, this is the first one, I believe. The next closest one is almost on the mountain border with Sjasa," Kairo said, as he focused on plotting in the Mahi in his wrist projection. "This isn't a regular Mahi either. Notice how it exploded with goo? Regular ones just turn into a puddle."

"Zandos, don't touch that," I said, running over to him. He was touching the goo that was on the wall. It was known for burning flesh and concrete, though it didn't seem to damage him at all.

"Yes, is Mahifer from Nojuni. Strong Mahifer, not… normal type, like… Kairo say. Is why hard for you… to make Mahifer die," Zandos said, pointing at Reid with his goo-covered finger.

"I wasted like half my ammo on that thing," Reid said. "How do you know all that?"

I was more surprised about why it didn't hurt him. *Maybe it had to do with him being Jovnelle's kid?*

"I can… tell," he replied, wiping the Mahi goo on the wall, which began to sizzle. "I live with many Mahifer. They never hurt me or my mother."

"Wait, you still live with your mom? How old are you, even?" Levi asked, confused.

"I do not know." Zandos said obliviously. He continued observing the sizzling goo. "I not see my mother… much, she… live on other side of castle."

"Wait, but you're like, from Nojuni, right? There's only one castle there, which must mean that your mother…" Levi said, the realization dawning on him.

"Jovnelle," Zandos answered plainly. I could almost sense my group lurching back, except for Saku, Sirani, and me. "My mother Jovnelle."

"What? You didn't say anything about that!" Reid exploded, looking at me. He seemed to be more fearful than genuinely mad.

"I told Renee already, the senior officials know," I insisted. "It's not… it's, uh, something we're trying to keep secret."

"Are you crazy? She *let him in?!* And the senior officials are in on this too?!" Reid said, holding up the Mahi blaster to Zandos. He stared down the barrel of the blaster, more confused than scared.

"I… not enemy, I not like her," Zandos urged.

"Then how come you touched that stuff like it's nothing?" Reid barked, the goo still sizzling.

"I leave Nojuni because I *hate* Nojuni, I not spy, I not want to make pain, you think I like what she do?" Zandos said, trying to stay quiet. Reid lowered the blaster and didn't rebuke Zandos's statement.

"Um… we should probably go, guys," Saku said. "We don't wanna look suspicious."

"I'm gonna tell Renee about that Mahi thing when we get back," Kairo said, trying to change the subject. We turned a corner in the city.

"Isavna, about that thing you said earlier," Sirani messaged.

"About Reid?" I asked, looking at her. She was gnawing on her lower lip and squinting.

"He's definitely got something against Zandos, I don't really know why though. I think we ought to keep an eye on him until whatever's going on fully blows over."

"I do not… understand. Mahifer usually slow. How it go all way here… with no person notice?" Zandos asked.

"I dunno, I've seen 'em get pretty quick," Levi said. Everyone was silent, except for Saku singing softly to herself, something in her native language. Her singing was drowned out as we entered the loud and busy portal terminal. It felt like an airport back on Earth.

"Do you think Renee will know what to do about the Mahis?" I asked Kairo. We scanned our AHL IDs to get into the portal terminal. Jace's guard used provisional IDs for Zandos and Jace.

"She's seen plenty worse. I'm sure she will. I bet she's already seen the report I filed," Kairo replied. We heard our wrists buzz just as we entered the line full of other officials to enter the portal.

"Oh, what's this?" Sirani asked, opening her notifications. "Looks like Renee and the higher ups want to take us on a little field trip to Nojuni. The whole SO8." "Wow, that's sudden. I wonder why," Reid said, reading the notice. "Looks like they want to meet to discuss logistics."

"Oh, in that conference room with the squeaky door again," I said as I read my wrist projection. I checked the clock. It was about one, so we had half an hour.

I heard Saku groan as we dispersed. "I was hoping I'd never have to go back to Nojuni ever again."

I sat in my office, dressed and ready for the mission. Sirani was in a chair across from the table. We were waiting on Reid.

"I wonder if the people at Nojuni have noticed Zandos and Jace have left," Sirani said, picking at her fingernail.

"I hope not. I mean, we didn't change much besides—" I suddenly remembered something. My mouth went dry.

"What?" asked Sirani, alarmed by my physical jolt. "Are you okay?"

"The bodies. The guards. The room Jace smashed up. We forgot to hide it all."

Sunday, 1:03 PM, Nojuni Palace, Main Gates

71

The chamberlain of Nojuni Palace walked the corridors, inspecting the servants' work. He was one of the few people in the palace with free will, which he used to control others who did not.

He walked into the east wing. He spotted a Mahifer dash in front of him. It stopped briefly to hiss at him.

There was a dead body of a servant that had not yet been cleaned. He raised his ghostly, bony arm over it and squeezed his palm, causing it to disappear. He kept walking to the end of the hall. There were bedrooms there, occupied by Jovnelle's son and his friend. He didn't usually interact with them after Cavaris commanded him to "let them rot and fester."

He glanced out the smashed window at the end of the hall, surveying the land outside. From his angle, he could not see the mountains. Some trees flanked the side of the building. He looked at the main gates, and he saw more dead bodies, which were not unusual.

He flew out the massive window, invoking black, leathered dragon wings and landing outside the main gate. It wasn't strange for people to be dead around Nojuni. Mahifers would often possess bodies, drain their magic, then stay stuck inside, unable to transform into a monster, as they continue to eat away at the body's vitality until it has nothing left to give. The Mahifers could only take from the living; the dead were removed. As he landed, he inspected the scene. There were footsteps imprinted on the mud. They had to be from after the morning's rain, otherwise they would've been washed away. They looked like boots. He felt a sting of agitation.

He continued to study the two dead guards. They had apparent bullet wounds, with caked blood staining the fabric. *It's fresh.* He knew someone had been there, someone from the outside. He looked around the area for more bodies, realizing there were none. *Who did this?* He frantically scratched at his bald scalp. He decided that some measure had to be taken, so he returned to the palace.

He made his way towards a ballroom and focused on a seemingly blank wall. He approached it and thought a spell, and the door opened.

Cavaris spoke without words but with feelings and sensations. The chamberlain could barely make out his form from inside the labyrinth. Inside were swirling colors, shapes, and sounds that shifted ceaselessly, though the chamberlain had become accustomed to it.

"I am here to warn you of intrusion. I saw evidence of outsiders who murdered our guards. We need to be wary," the chamberlain said.

He crumpled in pain at the sudden feeling of his gut being twisted. The labyrinth swirled violently, leading to a black void in the center. Hundreds of Mahifers flew out of the hole, hissing at the chamberlain as they passed.

Sunday, 1:22 PM, AHL, Subfloor 1 - Command Center & Office Wing, Isavna's Office

"Really?" Sirani asked, slightly surprised. "I thought that the wand crafter's shop got shut down because the owner had gone bankrupt." She was busy tying up her long blond hair for our task. We were talking about city news we had heard while we waited for the meeting, to distract ourselves from what we both knew. We didn't want to tell Reid just yet; he didn't need one more thing to worry about.

"No," Reid answered, gently rotating back and forth on the spinning chair. "Or at least, that's not what I heard. I mean, the owner and her wife were already pretty old. I think they retired, but their kids didn't want to take over the business so they decided to shut down." The air conditioner above us whirred quietly as our conversation lulled. As soon as I was going to bring up something else, we heard knocking on my door.

"Come in," I called.

Renee opened the door. I remembered the rumors among recruits from a few years ago of people saying Renee must be an alien because she never smiled or cried. At least, not in front of anybody.

"The meeting is about to begin," she said. *Had we really been talking for that long?* We followed her into the conference room, the door squeaking as it opened. Renee and the other executive official sat down at the head of the table. It was the whole SO8, so essentially, my group of friends.

We discussed the logistics of heading back to Nojuni. Everyone was dressed to go, except for Zandos and Jace, though it was better if they didn't change. Zandos told them everything they needed to know about the mission, and Jace mostly remained silent. His guard wasn't there.

"Excuse me, Mr. Makorod," I asked. He was a man in his mid thirties, who managed the finance interns and sent us on mission along with Renee. He turned and gestured for me to ask my question. "What is the purpose for this mission?"

"Counterintel told us there's a high-pressure area of Mahifer activity somewhere in Nojuni Palace, about 300 percent higher than normal. We have until about tomorrow at noon until the pressure of their magic causes an explosion. We believe it will likely consume most of the immediate area, and will release additional Mahifers to spread out to nearby cities. A few scouting Mahifers were sent from there, that is the one you encountered. Normal Mahifers don't explode like that," he said gravely.

I thought about the numerous hours of study we all had to do to learn about Mahis. They're constantly seeking magic to feed off of, ultimately with the goal of bringing it back to Cavaris to make him stronger —sort of like how bees bring nectar back to the hive. However, Mahis aren't intelligent creatures—they often forget where to go or get caught up in their own gluttony. When they're killed, they normally melt into a puddle of acid. Some especially fat Mahis, however, like the ones for scouting that can go long distances without food, are prone to exploding.

But here, an explosion would happen because of the pressure of malevolent magic in such a compact area, and it would force them all out of any openings in the labyrinth. It was the simple principle of matter moving from a high-pressure area to a low-pressure area.

Mr. Makorod continued. "It confirmed our suspicions of a node full of Mahifers which could send out thousands of them. This is not unseen, but it is uncommon, and would make good practice for you all. This mission will go into your record, and will be considered during promotions for higher paying positions." I thought more about Nojuni, and wiped my nervous, sweaty hands on my pants. *I really, really have to do something about those guard bodies.*

"We will go on a scouting mission only, locate the high-pressure area, and find the fastest route in and out. A hybrid unit will visit the location tonight. They'll seal any openings, so that when the explosion happens, it doesn't breach containment. Hopefully Cavaris will choose to reabsorb the Mahis before then, but we are prepared for the worst-case scenario."

"They can just do that?" Saku asked.

"Yeah, those Mahis are a part of Cavaris. But they need to be feeding on magic to survive," Keya explained.

"If they don't consume magic for twelve hours then they die or get reabsorbed," Kairo said. "That is, if the pressure doesn't force them all out of the labyrinth by then."

"And that is all the time that we need," Renee said.

"Well, I suppose there's nothing we can discuss here that we cannot discuss on the way," Mr. Makorod added, standing up. "I suggest we gather weaponry and leave as soon as possible, Officer Rotura," he said, addressing Renee.

"Please, it's just Renee," she corrected.

We all made our way down the elevator to the garage, not before picking up weapons on subfloor three.

"So what's the inside of Nojuni Palace like?" Reid asked me as we collected boxes of ammo and spare wands.

"It's pretty gnarly," I replied. "Everything is broken, super shabby, smells like crap, and there's dead bodies." I only saw one, but I wouldn't have been surprised if there were more.

"Wow. That sounds pretty bad."

"I mean, the land around it really is quite beautiful, if you can ignore the eyesore of a castle that is Nojuni Palace." I saw Zandos behind me. "Sorry, Zandos."

"No, no, is true. Palace very bad. I… do not like. My mother… want better, but no time," he explained.

"Sounds like a big ol' violation of zoning laws," Levi commented as we walked back into the elevator.

The elevator slowed to a stop as we landed at the sixth subfloor, the garage. A door opposite to the one used for the fifth subfloor opened, which led to the garage. We all walked out, into the din of power tools and motors. Mr. Makorod counted us and the weapons, though we were packing light. It was only a scouting mission. We worked quickly, piling the small items under the seats, which opened like boxes, and the oversized items under the van or wherever else. We got into the hover vans and swiftly set off, my worry gnawing at me.

6

Sunday, 1:49 PM, 2.1 km N of AHL Base Central

Renee had put the car into autopilot, headed towards Nojuni Palace. She was busy trying to establish a connection with the other hover van.

"Hello? Can you hear me?" We heard Mr. Makorod say over the hologram. I peeked over Saku's head and saw his image on the hologram. He and Renee both discussed things for a little while. The weather was warm, so we talked about things of that nature, like cold drinks and sunburns.

"My arms are getting tired," Saku complained, as she tried to tie up her hair.

"Do you need help?" Sirani offered.

"No, I got it."

"Let Sirani help you," said Kairo. "Your grunting is driving me crazy." Saku tried a few more times and failed, finally relenting. Sirani quickly grabbed her thick, wavy hair and put it into a perfect ponytail.

"There," Sirani said. I could hear Keya sending telepathic messages, possibly to Levi in the other hover van. I could listen to the faint static of their conversation in my head, like a conversation in the next room over, but much quieter, though I could hear her slight laughs. *They must've been dating for as long as I've been here. Gosh, like four years?*

"Hey, look at that," I told Reid, pointing out the window. It was a herd of unicorns in the distance, though they were hard to see in the dense grass of the meadow. The hover van was moving extremely fast, so they were only visible for about six seconds.

"All the unicorns in Dekerei got hunted to extinction," Reid said, reminiscing about his homeland, an icy northern region. Almost inhospitable. "It's refreshing to see some out in the wild."

I saw a herd of felmines, too. They were horse-sized wolves with wings. They were often eaten or used as beasts of burden, though large wild and feral populations existed in the plains. I tried to enjoy the scenery, but the thought of the dead guards poked at the back of my mind.

We were passing through an area with trees. I looked out, watching the hover van rise. It got a little shakier. We were about twenty feet above the ground now, just enough to clear the most hazardous of trees. Two metal plane wings folded out from under the van, reducing the shakiness.

The climate around us was slowly becoming colder. Most of the trees here were evergreens. Flecks of white snow dotted the ground, melting into the strong rivers of snow runoff.

"How much longer?" Saku asked Renee.

"About twenty more minutes," She replied. I heard Saku groan.

"You'll be fine," Kairo said quietly. "You've survived the nine-hour flight back home multiple times."

"Barely," she said. "Oh, I wish we could just get there quicker, this feels like pulling teeth. Maybe you should be more interesting, Kairo, so I won't get bored."

"Maybe you should learn how to relax for once," Kairo retorted. Their bickering continued quietly.

"How's your sister doing?" Reid asked me. I had a sister who mostly stayed on Earth, but occasionally visited Avukena. Three years ago, my sister and parents learned about my whereabouts, after a spell Mother Everealm cast on them had worn off. I had come from Christmas that year, and tried explaining everything that had happened. They were worried, yes. Terrified, even. But they accepted it, saying that it "made sense somehow." I still didn't know why they said that. It certainly didn't help with trying to adjust here in Avukena.

"She's fine," I replied. "She's on her way here, actually. She really missed Levi's little sister."

"Yeah, they're the same age, right?" Reid said. "Levi has like, a million siblings or something."

"I know, right?" I said. I waited a little, then got curious myself and asked Keya.

"Two, I think? Taren and Salia. That's not counting his older half-sister. Actually, he has six older half-siblings on his dad's side."

"So nine of them?" Reid glanced at me wide-eyed. "Might as well be a million," he said quietly. My sister was friends with Salia, both being tenth years.

"How far are we now?" Saku asked after a small while had passed.

"Ten minutes," Renee replied.

"Has it only been ten minutes?" Saku said. "Fine. I guess I can wait ten more."

"Also," Reid said, looking at me. "Are you doing anything tomorrow?"

"No," I replied. "Toniska might want to do something, but I doubt it. She'll probably barge into my unit at some point in the evening."

"Well, Mr. Makorod asked me to review a map that a Div One general prepared. It has locations where he intends to deploy some task ops and vehicles, but I don't have access to the files that show me how many personnel and vehicles we *can* deploy in the first place. Since you mostly do files I assumed that you had access to the database that I need to look at." He said quietly. "Honestly, I think he meant this task for someone else with file access, but I'll do it if it gets on my record."

"Sure," I replied. We waited a bit longer. I looked outside in the snowy woods. I felt my hands go cold as I saw what I thought were Mahis.

"We're five minutes away," Renee said. "Make sure you have everything." We straightened ourselves and checked our satchels and pockets. I prayed that what I saw was just a really dark-colored felmine or deer.

We watched the other hover van pull up next to ours. We parked at the foot of a forest. The vans changed color to match the area perfectly. We piled extra gear into the pockets of anyone who had space. We chattered a bit in anticipation of the mission.

"Gotta be ready," Levi said, checking each of his pockets with practiced ease. "Never know who's gonna make it back home."

"Remember: we are here to find the high-pressure spot. We aren't here to go inside it or defeat whatever is in it. We're just here to record information and find possible weaknesses." We all acknowledged Mr. Makorod's statement as we made sure everyone was there. Renee, Zandos, Mr. Makorod, and Jace got together to begin planning our entry.

There were three main areas. The same as before. Outside of the court, a village lay in ruin. There was an area east of the AHL that was modeled after this to train us for urban warfare. There were main gates that led to the court, and then the palace doors. We gazed at the dilapidated palace, visible over the gray, forgotten rubble of the court walls. There were noticeably more Mahis, and despite being able to kill them rapidly, Renee looked anxious.

Zandos had told us bits and pieces about what life was like in Nojuni and what Jovnelle was like. There had always been conflicting stories about her, some saying that it was her choice to let Cavaris possess her, and others saying that she was abused and became possessed under duress. The story I believed was that Mother Everealm raised the six sisters, favoring some and neglecting Jovnelle because she represented shadows, causing her to leave when she grew up and make a deal with Cavaris, unaware of his power. I also believed that light cannot exist without shadow. For that reason, I pitied Jovnelle and wanted to help her.

Zandos stopped us a little bit before the main gates.

"I and Jace are walk in, no problem is. You all, not know palace… need different clothes. The clothes you wear early today." He explained, pointing to Sirani, Saku, and me. All of us made sure to bring servants' clothes beforehand; it was standard practice for any Nojuni mission. We also had to intentionally wear them down so they wouldn't stick out. As we walked in, I felt a sudden rush of nervousness and fear. I couldn't tell who was who because we all looked the same. The only way I could differentiate everyone was by height, build, and gait. We passed through a hall with mirrors, some of which were cracked. Not even some, most of them had some sort of imperfection, and a thick layer of gray dust on the ridges, like the way snow falls on a mountain.

"Watch out!" I whispered to Sirani, pulling her from a broken floorboard. I looked at Saku, who was walking between her brother and me. This was only her third total mission in Nojuni, but she seemed significantly calmer than this morning. I saw Zandos talking to Renee and Mr. Makorod as we searched for the high-pressure spot.

"What are you doing with the servants?" A Nojunian guard asked in Hakon. *Strange. I wonder why not the local language.*

"We need them for the south side of the palace for Sir Horuo," Zandos replied, also in Hakon.

"Who's Sir Horuo?" I heard many of us whisper.

"The chamberlain for this palace, as we understand it. He is one of the few people with free will, and controls and cleans the palace," whispered Mr. Makorod. *He must be bad at his job.* As we reached the end of the corridor, we saw a strange man in a long, impractical robe. He was bald and had ashen, almost blue skin. He wore nothing on his head. He had a long, cruel face. The light behind him gave him a godly aura.

He descended the stairs, approaching a servant. He had not yet noticed us; we were in a hallway perpendicular to the stairs. His robe was musty maroon and black, with long, fine, brocade sleeves that nearly brushed the ground. He looked like a vampire or something of that nature.

"Is that him?" I shuddered, whispering to Jace.

"Dammit. We gotta get out of here," Jace told the group. He tensed his lips, looked around, and started directing us down a hall. But we had already been noticed.

Zandos walked over to make conversation to distract Sir Horuo while Jace led us away. I heard his accent, which was identical to Zandos's; guttural and rhotic, like a weird mixture between Arabic, Spanish, and American English. Jace took us behind another corner.

"You guys have to be careful here. They kill people onsite if you're suspicious or seem to be against Cavaris in any way," Jace told us quietly. "These halls also echo like crazy, so none of you better scream or anything."

"I still have my map," Renee showed Jace the picture projected on her wrist.

He nodded. "I know where that is."

"So would it be okay if you went to tell Zandos and meet us there?"

He nodded. "Keep some distance, too. Servants don't usually travel in groups unless they're led by someone."

I suppose Jace can be sensible in high-stress situations. We all followed Renee, keeping about a yard between each person in a loose group. Three or four armed guards noticed Reid and me. They barreled at us clumsily, but they were easy to kill with our short swords. We covered their wounds with dust to hide our tracks.

We pushed onward to the stairs, which looked like they might break with the weight of all of us climbing them. I was scared we would fall. They creaked terribly, and it reminded me of the first time I was here. As we walked, I thought about the guard's bodies. I hadn't seen them on my way in, meaning someone must've dealt with them already. *Maybe the increased Mahi activity has something to do with it.*

We approached the end of the staircase with all the grace of a three-legged elephant in our robes. I was too short for mine; they made them in one size to blend in with the servants. The room was gigantic, and the bits of light that poured in through the broken stained glass illuminated dust particles in the air. I observed the stained glass, artwork, and motif of the ballroom, trying to imagine what it might've looked like in its prime.

The glass had images of Jovnelle and the surrounding nature of the palace, but it was hard to tell because most of it was cracked or smashed. The ballroom we were in was pretty empty. The chandelier was shattered on the ground, in the middle of the carpeted floor, with a thick layer of grey dust on it. Statues lay broken beside their pedestals, and artwork hung crooked or infested by moths. The smell reminded me of a basement, repulsive and stuffy.

I felt a slight buzz in my body that was hard to describe. It was as if my phone was buzzing in my chest. It felt invasive and uncomfortable. Renee stopped. *This has to be it.* I looked at my group. They felt the same thing.

"You all feel that?" she whispered. "It's what happens when you're in range of malevolent magic. We're here."

We saw a small crack in the wallpaper. Renee put her ear to it, and I saw her eyes widen. She pulled away and whispered to Mr. Makorod. She gestured for us to form a tighter group.

"You all have to be extremely careful, Cavaris doesn't use regular magic."

"Cavaris?" Levi asked, alarmed. "You're telling me *Cavaris* is in there?"

Mr. Makorod nodded gravely.

"He uses extrasensory magic. He can seriously mess with your memories, I think. That's what they told us in basic malevolent magic training," said Reid.

"Yes, he is known to cause that. He may try to give you false visions of the future or past and show you the worst extent of humankind. Do *not* trust them." Renee explained the next part of the plan, which was to try to send in drones to investigate the aperture, but we quickly had to disperse, hearing footsteps. Jace came up, panting.

"And Zandos?" Mr. Makorod asked.

"He's still caught up talking with Sir Horuo." He gasped for air. "He'll be back in a moment."

We heard more footsteps followed by some conversation in the local language, which seemed to come from the staircase. These sounded sharp and resonant.

The two speakers bid each other farewell. The one coming up sounded like an alto female voice, low and graceful. I saw a tall gold and red crown rise from the staircase. My hands got cold. I saw a head with pale skin and long snow-colored hair, and what should've been white in the eyes was black, with red irises. *Just like Zandos's eyes.* She had a long, red, and black dress with several designs that made it confusing and mesmerizing to look at. She also had a black cape with a red collar. Her figure looked emaciated. She looked the most terrifyingly beautiful I had ever seen.

"Hello, your reverence," Jace said cautiously as his body trembled with fear. Her height overshadowed us, though she was undoubtedly shorter than Marathene and Mother Everealm. The crown probably helped.

Suddenly, the black in her eyes turned white. I saw her gasp a bit. She blinked intensely and looked at us. *Cavaris must not be paying enough attention to keep her possessed every hour of the day.*

"Hello, Jace, who do you have with you?" she asked in Hakon, slowly enough that I could understand. Her voice sounded fragile, as if someone moved wrong, she might crumble. This was not the Jovnelle that Mother Everealm and the media talked about. I looked beside me, and Reid had his weapon drawn. He looked even more afraid than Jace.

"Conceal it," Kairo huffed. Jace waved his hand, as if trying to tell us to be quiet.

"Outsiders," Jace said, barely loud enough for me to hear. He got closer and whispered in her ear. Jovnelle looked happy and smiled.

"I cannot believe you did it." She had a grateful expression on her face that seemed to illuminate the depressing ballroom. I heard Reid stumble back.

I looked at her. She was observing us with such warmth and hope. I compared that to Avukena, where death and despair were all anyone could think about when Nojuni and Mahis were mentioned. Most people's exposure to Nojuni was through the news and destruction. But behind all of that, tucked behind where no news station dared to go, was someone who had never been loved.

For as long as I had been here, I had been only driven to move forward by fear, of what could happen to me and the world if I didn't try hard enough. When Zandos contacted me—the enemy—it didn't seem logical. Now I understood. He was driven by sort of purpose that love gives you, and the will to preserve the little he had left. It was the kind of love that compelled him to risk everything.

In that moment, I finally felt purpose. Jovnelle truly needed us. Except, if I wanted to save her, I would have to go against Mother Everealm's command.

I observed Jace, who had the same resolve I saw in Zandos. He had been cold to us all day, but I thought I saw his eyes redden. *Who even is this guy?* I thought, wondering what he was truly after.

"I… I will become possessed again soon, please…" she wiped her eyes with her long, graceful fingers. "Please be careful. I will try to leave before it happens." She backed away down the stairs. She looked at us with such hope, happiness, and love, but there was nothing we could do. Her eyes turned black as she fell to the ground. We all looked at her lifeless body splayed on the staircase for a few moments.

She began to shuffle on the ground and float. She levitated away, by some force other than her own. A servant passed by from a corridor, picked up Jovnelle's glittering crown, and descended the stairs. *I guess that's what they're for.* I began to worry more and more about Zandos's whereabouts. He hadn't come back yet.

We tried to go back to our work. We looked at the crack in the wallpaper, which had begun to glow more intensely. Suddenly, there was a noise that began, and I felt a low rumbling. I ducked a bit to brace for anything worse. I heard footsteps and panicked, just to see it was Zandos. *Finally.* Jace filled him in on what happened.

Some of the wallpaper was missing. The wall under it was stone, with strange insignias and runes on it. Mr. Makorod took pictures with his wrist projection. I squinted, trying to dig in my memory for anything similar I had either seen before or learned about in my training or at school. *Hm. Nothing.* It was obviously some kind of magic *thing.*

"This is indeed a high-pressure area," Mr. Makorod said, looking at his detectors. "It appears the possible concentration of Mahifers has risen to 340 percent higher than normal levels." The rumbling got to be too much to ignore, and the large stone wall began to crack further.

A large piece fell into it, large enough for a person to fit. Even from afar, I could see it was a bright world, dancing with vibrant, lurid, hideous colors. I shielded my eyes. Renee and Mr. Makorod took pictures of the void and documented it.

"So this is Cavaris's labyrinth?" Kairo asked.

"This doesn't seem like the sort of place it would be," Sirani said. "I would have expected somewhere better hidden, perhaps even not connected to the main palace."

"That's strange," Mr. Makorod said as he tried doing a scan with his hologram. "It appears the use of magic is not possible inside of the labyrinth." With furrowed brows, he kept working the hologram in front of him. *Maybe this magic is a whole other kind, opposite to the one we know. Like how shadows and light are mutually exclusive, yet related.*

He took out a small hologram-operated drone, and we watched as it slowly went in. Even as it barely entered, we saw the red dot on the display of the GPS start to convulse and appear to be everywhere. I looked back into the labyrinth. We could plainly see the drone, right there.

A massive black figure flew right beside the entrance, looking like a freight train passing by. It swept away the drone and caused a strong gust of wind to hit us, toppling Saku.

"You okay?" Keya yelled, louder than she should have.

"Yeah, I'm fine, I can take a little fall," she said, wiping off dust from her cloak and putting up her hood.

"I suggest we leave soon, Officer," Mr. Makorod told Renee. "Our presence will surely be suspicious, and I believe we have gathered sufficient evidence. Our path is mapped out, too." She nodded. "I already contacted the hybrid unit, they might want to come sooner because of how big the aperture has grown." They went over exit plans. I was starting to panic. *Why couldn't the AHL just let us deal with Cavaris right now? He's right there.* I knew it was impractical and probably impossible with the tools and knowledge we had on hand, but a large part of me just wanted to be done with it all.

I looked back into the labyrinth. I saw Cavaris swirling around inside, with a mass of Mahis staying behind, already beginning to fade into wisps of purple steam, little by little. Cavaris appeared and reappeared at different distances. *Maybe he's a fourth-dimensional creature or something.* Sirani was visibly anxious to leave. Beads of sweat formed under my servant's cloak.

"We have gathered enough information for today. We will now be leaving," Mr. Makorod said, addressing the group.

From the staircase, we saw three Mahis rise, and then, Sir Horuo's ghastly figure.

"Let's go!" Reid yelled as Sirani pulled me along.

7

Sunday, 4:47 PM, Nojuni Palace, Upper Ballroom

I scurried like a mouse as I tried to get my footing. Once I got a steady run, I followed everyone down the stairs, barely able to move without tripping because of the cloak. Sirani tripped, taking me with her as she fell, and we scrambled in a panic to get up. We reached the end of the ballroom, and the spiral staircase convulsed violently under the weight of all our feet slamming against it. Zandos and Jace took us to a smaller passageway that led to a broken window, where we all climbed out. I fell onto the dirty, wet ground. The snow had melted and created cold and musty-smelling mud. We jogged to a broken part of the stone fence surrounding the perimeter of the palace that Zandos knew about. It was short enough to climb over.

"Could've gone cleaner," Levi said quickly, his tone tense as we walked to the vans. "Can't exactly tell them I almost got taken out."

"Who's 'them?'" Kairo asked.

"People back home," he said quickly, trying to move on.

We threw off our cloaks and tucked them into our hip satchels.

"Come on, we have no time to lose." Renee barked at us as we sprinted to the forest where we left the vans. After a fast but necessary system inspection, we were back on the road.

We spent about ten minutes in silence, trying to get over the initial shock of seeing Sir Horuo and being chased. I closed my eyes as I felt the light shaking of the van, the hushed conversation between Renee and Mr. Makorod on the holocom, and Levi restlessly tapping his fingernails against his belt. No one spoke until we were in the plains north of Sjasa.

"Consider this a mission well done," Renee said to us and the holocom to the other van. It didn't sound like she fully meant it, but the fact that she didn't seem panicked comforted me enough. I was glad to have the mission under my belt because I knew I needed all the experience I could get, being a sophomore official. As scary as it was, having gone to Nojuni and meeting Jovnelle for the first time helped me understand her more, and understand Mother Everealm a little less.

I stared outside. I vaguely recognized some structures and mountains from this morning.

The landscape changed from the unicorn plains to old fences and defunct sawmills, also watching as long-ago abandoned villages passed by. Nature had fully reclaimed them.

"So what do you want to do when we get back?" Sirani asked me as she drank from a water bottle. By then, we had been driving for a while.

"Hey, where'd you get that?" Reid, who was next to me, asked Sirani. She produced one from under the seat in front of her. I kept staring out the window.

I thought about where my loyalties were bound. I was obligated to serve Mother Everealm, but I felt loyal to Earth. But now, I felt some loyalty to Zandos and Jovnelle, too. It wasn't quite in me to rebel, but I could sense the complexities I was inviting into my life.

As we walked into the AHL, I approached Brev on the second subfloor and talked to her about what had happened. Most of the people on the mission had filtered out through the building. Levi was talking to Zandos and Jace, who looked very frustrated. Reid was watching them while Sirani and I talked to Brev.

"Ah, I see. Hm… well, we know where Cavaris is now," Brev said. "Good work."

I saw Zandos heaving, his neck tense and his lips thin as taut wire. He marched up to the main table where many of us were sitting.

"So we knowing where Cavaris is at," Zandos grunted, suppressing his anger. "What of my mother?"

"What… um, what does your mother have to do—" Brev stammered.

—"Jovnelle!" his voice cracked. I saw desperation in his eyes. "You say you try to save my mother!"

I tensed. I had told him we were saving his mother, but that wasn't exactly the AHL's official goal.

"Right now HQ's mission is to neutralize Cavaris and stop the damage," Sirani said, omitting a key detail. "Believe me, we all *want* to save your mom…."

"You mean what?" Zandos asked, nervous.

"Well, we want to, but we're under Mother Everealm's command," I said, trying to placate him.

"Mean what?" he insisted. "What she say?"

"She instructed us to eliminate the tether, so… your mother…."

His eyes widened, and he gasped, seeming to freeze.

"You… try to kill my mother?" he asked quietly, his voice flowing with grief and rage. Tears fell. "But I risk much to help, I was think you…

try to help save my mother, she all I have." Jace stood beside him, silent except for low, ragged breathing.

"She chose Cavaris," Reid said.

Zandos spun, his eyes a sunset of pain and emotion.

"What?" Zandos simply said, quietly and shocked.

Reid didn't flinch. "She chose Cavaris and the life she has. We're not obligated to save her."

Zandos blinked. "But you never see… my life, what is, and she is, and… and… she want me to have good life."

"But I've seen enough to know that we've been too quick to trust you. You're dragging your family drama into this hoping that your emotions will make the AHL and Mother Everealm bend the rules," Reid said.

"I want to save my mother because she matter," Zandos said, wiping his eyes and facing Reid head-on. "I make choice to save her because she all I have."

I tried to back away. I didn't know if they were going to fight, or what. Zandos's eyes began to glow. They flashed black as Reid collapsed, his eyes glassy. He began to shake on the ground, as if having a seizure.

"What are…?!" Sirani cried out. Levi, Kairo, and Brev recoiled back. I stumbled forward in horror. Zandos voice suddenly appeared in my head. It was *the* voice from before.

"You think I just savage. You hate me." I felt. Everyone in the immediate area winced. *"He right. He not trust me. No one trust or believe me."*

I couldn't even begin to parse what he was doing. Mind control? Some other form of magic? Reid went limp. I ran towards him, thinking that maybe he was dead.

"He's still breathing," I announced. I turned to Kairo, the only one who could probably carry Reid with ease. "Can you take him to the medbay?"

He nodded, picking up Reid's limp body and carrying him over his shoulder. Everyone stared at Zandos.

His face was ashen. Even more tears than before began to fall. His mouth quivered, and he fell to his knees, hunched over.

"I… not mean to…" he said, covering his face with his hands. "I not know…how I do that…." The people around him began to inch back. "I promise I not monster, I just want…." He lay on the ground with silent sobs.

"What just happened with that guy?" someone asked.

"Some kind of episode," another said. "Whatever this is, it looks dangerous."

I would have been lying if I said I wasn't scared, but I also knew this couldn't be intentional. *I hope you're not a monster.*

Jace stood in front of Zandos, his fists clenched. I saw him with a short sword in Nojuni, but he must've left it there, or the AHL confiscated it. "If any of you guys touch him I'll kill you! I'll kill you!" he cried out, his eyes wild. Some bystanders filtered out.

Brev tried to get closer. "I don't want to hurt him," she said, at a good distance.

"What are you thinking?" I asked her, running to her side.

"This… what he just did, it has been highly speculated upon among the magic and science team. I've peer reviewed some papers on this." She observed Zandos. *"I believe that Zandos may have a weak form of tether magic. I'll need to do more research on it."* She told me telepathically. I gasped.

"What?" Jace demanded, standing in front of us. "Will you stop staring at him like some kind of freak?"

"We don't want to be enemies," I said.

"Shut up already, Isavna. You lied to him." He turned to Brev. *Do they really not trust me anymore? Did I mess up that badly?*

"May we take him to the medbay? He'll be safer there," Brev asked.

Jace thought, tensing his lips. "Fine," he conceded. He helped Zandos up.

The medbay was on the seventh subfloor, near the lab. The hallway was wide. Our footsteps resonated clearly and loudly on the clean tile floor. There was a direct portal to the main hospital in Avukena City.

I stopped in Reid's cubicle. He was sitting on the bed, pale and shaking. Kairo was standing next to him.

"Isavna?" he asked, his voice shaky and quiet.

"Where's Zandos?" Kairo asked.

"He's also in the medbay. Jace, Sirani and Brev are with him. He's fine, but super shaken up."

"He snapped and entered my mind… I heard… I saw things, I saw his memories, I thought I was getting possessed."

"Brev thinks it's some kind of tether magic."

"Is that all you know right now?"

"Yeah. She's on the case, though. I honestly don't know much about tether magic myself. All I know is that it's like a magic Ethernet cable that's keeping me alive, and in this kind of situation, I know even less."

He managed a weak nod, probably not knowing what Ethernet was. He sounded congested. *Is he sick?* I went to the other side of the room, to Zandos's cubicle.

Jace was standing at the front, arms crossed. He had a staunch expression that made him look sort of like a bulldog. Sirani and Brev were hovering over Zandos. He was sitting on the bed, fine, but clearly shaken. Brev held a vial of blood in her hand. I saw the bandage on Zandos's arm, having rolled up his sleeve.

"This may be the first confirmed case of a human using tether magic," Brev said. "It's stronger than a Mahifer but not quite as strong as any of the six sisters."

"How are you?" I asked Zandos, feeling more anxious about having lied to him than whatever crazy magic was going on.

"Am I… danger to all? I not mean to hurt Reid, I not mean to, believe! I… please, I not want… to go back!"

"We won't," Brev said gently, staring at the vial. *They would sooner imprison him or simply execute him before they'd consider letting him walk free.* "I need to test this." She pulled a hologram from her pocket. It was more powerful than the average wrist projection. She tapped in credentials and placed the vial in a floating disc. Results began appearing, and she adjusted her glasses. "Give me a moment. I have to go over to the lab to interpret these results." She left without another word. Sirani went to stare at Jace from afar.

That left me with Zandos. He was pale, shaking, and anguished. I sat on a stool in his cubicle, but I didn't say anything. I didn't want Reid to be right, that I was blindly trusting him. But I also couldn't know for sure who was good or bad in the world.

"Wow. You're lucky you didn't kill Reid." Brev said when she came back.

"He could've killed him?" Sirani asked, eyes wide.

"Your blood has traces of compounds commonly found in Mahifer secretions, similar to malevolent magic. There's also foreign DNA here." She took a moment while she cross-examined the DNA. I looked between Sirani and Zandos. "As I thought. It's Reid's."

"Is that bad?" Sirani asked.

"Zandos's white blood cells will eliminate the foreign particles, so it's not permanent. It may cause mild congestion and drowsiness, like any normal respiratory disease. From your vitals, I couldn't detect enough magic energy to trigger the reaction again, so you're probably safe until tomorrow morning." She opened her wrist projection and took a picture of the results. She turned to him. "Zandos, I know you didn't mean for this to happen. But we do need to learn how to control your ability before something worse can occur." She gave him further instructions, and Zandos consented to help them with their research.

I reconvened with Reid right after a different doctor had left. Kairo was still there.

"How are you?" I asked.

"I... don't really know." He mumbled. "I don't know what happened and I don't know what to think of that... Zandos," he said. "Whatever it was that happened out there was terrifying and hurt like hell. I couldn't move, and for a few seconds I couldn't breathe. I thought I was going to die, and at the hands of Zandos, no less!" He was irate.

"Reid—" Kairo began.

—"If this happens again, whoever Zandos ends up possessing could die. I know I got lucky, but the next person might not be as fortunate."

"Reid, you said you saw his memories," Kairo said. Reid's hands tensed.

"Yes. I did, and that's the weirdest part." He stared past us, at the white and blue tile ground. "When I try to remember them though, they're all at once. I still can't... see them individually." He held his head in his hands. "It hurts when I try. And that's not something any of us signed up for, Isavna. I don't want someone else's life in my head."

"I know you don't," I said.

"Do you?! Do you really?!" he said sharply. "Because *you* brought him here." Kairo shifted uncomfortably.

"I couldn't just *leave him there*, he knew way too much. And he helped us in the elevator, and as an alibi and guide in Nojuni Palace. I won't lie, I took him because he's useful, and I trust the AHL will contain him or do whatever they need to do to keep the rest of us safe."

"And now we've got this weird and dangerous scientific anomaly on our hands," he said. "What if he kills someone next time?" Kairo glanced at me. I felt uncomfortable. Reid was staring at me bleary-eyed, asking me to pick a side.

"I don't know. But I know it won't be a good outcome for him. He'll probably be sequestered in subfloor five, or worse." I said. "But whatever happens is leadership's decision. Brev says it's malevolent magic, and I know they won't take it lightly." He smiled wryly. He anxiously tore a small hole through the paper lining of the medbay bed.

"Malevolent magic… wow. I… I don't have words. I hope that leadership knows damn well what they're dealing with." He said. "We can't risk someone actually dying next time." He stood up, the color returning to his face. I took it as my cue to leave.

I took the portals back home and put away my AHL uniform in my closet. Sirani and I decided to have a sleepover and debrief. I stayed in my unit and took a shower while she got her things from the dorms. The hot water burned on my leg wound from the morning. My hair wasn't very long right now, so washing it was quick. As I put on my clothes, I heard some people in the hallway arriving in the unit next to me. It had been empty for a while.

"Yeah, just send me a message if you have a question," I heard someone say. It sounded suspiciously like Levi. "Isavna's in the next room over." *Has to be him.*

"Okay." I heard the other respond plainly. I couldn't tell if it was Jace or Zandos, but it was one of the two.

Sirani came back, looking like she had showered. I didn't tell her about the new neighbors. We tried to talk about everything *but* the things that happened that day. We gawked at photos that people we knew posted on their social media accounts. She lay down on my chaise lounge. It wasn't even nighttime yet, but I could tell she was tired. I went to my kitchenette to make dinner.

"Did you talk to Reid?" she asked, after we ran out of topics.

"Yeah. He said something about seeing Zandos's memories. I can't tell who he's mad at, exactly."

"That's crazy," she said, swiping and closing her wrist projection. "I'm fully speculating here, but perhaps in the same way that Mahifers possess someone, and they become one entity, something similar happened there. Maybe they didn't fully turn into one entity like with normal possession, but just enough that they started to exchange some DNA and memories. If that makes any sense."

I sat down at the table nearby and gave her a bowl of fettuccine from a box my sister gave me last time she visited. "Yeah, I see what you mean. I guess we'd have to see if Zandos experienced the same memory thing."

There was vigorous knocking on my door that scared me for a moment.

"Yes?" I asked, getting up. I saw Saku, beaming. Behind her was basically… everyone. Even Keya. "What's going on?" I asked. They were all out of uniform, so I guessed it had to be for fun. *There goes my cozy evening.*

"We're going downtown," she said. "We'll stick to the west side. But we wanted you and Sirani to come." Sirani came behind me and groaned.

"Oh, fine," she relented. I saw Levi and Kairo go next door to get Zandos and Jace. We had to take him since he couldn't be left alone. Renee deemed it too risky. They both came out, looking like they'd also showered. I heard Sirani in my bathroom wrestling with her makeup bag. "Gosh, I'm such a mess right now."

Levi came out, followed by the two. Zandos looked like he wasn't actively panicking, but he was clearly still somewhat agitated. Jace was right behind him, scanning the hallway like there was an invisible threat. Sirani emerged from the bathroom with a small perfume bottle in one hand and a bracelet in the other.

We were going downtown as a group of young people, not as scouts or operatives. It was nice, for once, to have a little piece of the teenage years that were taken from me.

8

The city's evening lights were beginning to flicker on. Daytime flowers closed, and night flowers opened fluorescent blue and purple. Birds with warbling calls echoed through the street.

"How about we go back to Beris Street? They've got some interesting stores that open late," Kairo said. Our group agreed. I glanced behind me, where the palace was. I couldn't tell if it was because there were no clouds, but the palace looked especially pretty tonight. I found myself lagging.

"Isavna, hurry up," Reid told me at a crosswalk. *Have I been going that slow?* He seemed to be in better shape after the incident. I ran past him and to Saku, who was closing her wrist projection.

"Do you want to come over for a sleepover tonight with me and Sirani?" I asked, expecting Sirani to be okay with it since it wasn't uncommon for us. "Except, no staying up late."

"Lame, but okay. I'll go," Saku said, yawning. She was obviously tired herself. I looked up to see several people flying, with a white light on the front and backs of their flight helmets. Avukenan law required that we use those when flying at night.

"Zandos, is it hard to find food in Nojuni?" Sirani asked.

"I bet it's as hard as Spellcasting Five," Levi said jokingly. "I barely passed the final. Don't take Spellcasting Five, you'll regret it. God, that class is so useless. Just take, like, metaphysical philosophy instead. There's less speculation than in Spellcasting Five."

"What... what is?" Zandos questioned, clearly lost. I understood, seeing myself in parts of him. I recognized the shame of not knowing things. Sirani began to explain the way schools worked. He seemed to be aware of them, but more so... grammar school, not the modern education system.

We ran into Marathene coming out of a bakery in town. She came up to us excitedly. From what I could gather, she had envelopes in hand and seemed to be handing them out to the businesses.

"Isavna! How are you?" she asked.

"I'm doing fine. We're taking the new correspondents on a walk here to get to know the city. The ones Renee registered as wards, maybe you've heard."

"Yes, I did get notified about that. I suspected you were involved." She walked up to us and explained an upcoming event I had heard whispers about. A flower festival, something held every four years. This would be my first one. She also told us her other sisters were coming.

"Really? All your sisters from all their kingdoms were able to make it?" I asked.

"Yes," Marathene said, with an edge of sadness in her voice. "Excluding of course, Jovnelle."

Zandos looked at her with shock, stopping in his tracks. "What... you sister, with Jovnelle? She my mother."

Marathene tilted her head and grimaced in confusion.

Kairo intervened to explain. "Marathene, this is Zandos and Jace. They are the new correspondents for Nojuni. He—well, Zandos, is Jovnelle's son." Marathene nodded slowly. "And Zandos, Marathene is Jovnelle's sister. I'm sure you know about the other four sisters of the elements, they have their own palaces around the world. Anyway, your banquet ball sounds cool. When will it be?" Kairo finished, trying to distract her.

"A week from next Third day," Marathene replied, furrowing her brows but conceding. The Third day was essentially Wednesday. "We have been planning this for some time now. We decided that it would be best to have it soon, because of what's been going on with the city." Marathene said. *I see. It's strategic.* "Obviously, we contacted vendors and such in advance. We would also like to have AHL members present for respective regions and looking at your records we decided that you guys could do some speeches for your crown regions."

"Why not the senior or executive officials?" Sirani questioned. "It seems they would have more to say. I mean, Renee is eloquent. She would be perfect for this."

Marathene tilted her head, wincing a little. "We've asked the Division Three panel, and they've declined. Nearly all of you have enough public speaking experience that we decided you would be articulate enough for the job." She looked around as we continued walking down the street, leaning in a little closer. She leaned quite a bit, she was probably close to eight feet tall. "Frankly, the public thinks of anyone higher than a senior official as being either biased or corrupt. So strategically speaking, it would be best if we have you do it. Furthermore, you are the future of our organization and it will look good on your record." We all nodded silently. We trusted her far more than Mother Everealm, since Marathene was more involved in the AHL and public affairs. "Aside from that, how is your mission going? I heard you went on a reconnaissance mission today."

"The mission led us to discover a lot about the palace and its people. We succeeded in our scouting and found a route for the hybrid unit tonight," Sirani said.

"Well, when do you expect the mission to be completed?" Marathene asked, sounding nervous. She asked for my prediction every few months, like clockwork. I knew Mother Everealm must be sending her to ask.

"That's hard to quantify," I said. "I mean, to kill an evil that's been terrorizing the world for centuries won't be easy. I intend for no more than a year or two. This is just my prediction." Everyone there knew I was lying. It was just impossible to tell.

She smiled hopefully but looked aside. I could tell that I hardly made her feel any better. We kept walking, inching closer to the palace. I heard the squawks of evening birds. Zandos looked around at the buildings around us, beaming with pure curiosity. His eyes lingered on the glowing facade of Enva and Reion Legal Services. A somewhat drab blue building, but the letters were floating a few inches away from the building like a hologram. Marathene was watching him.

"He has her eyes," she murmured. I felt sympathy for her. Who knows how long it had been since she last saw Jovnelle?

As our conversation drew to a close, we slipped into the *Dewdrop Tea Shop*. Marathene was still with us and took the opportunity to speak to someone at the counter about the event while Kairo put in our orders. I walked to a small table with four chairs and sat down. Reid, Sirani, and Saku came over with me. Saku was playing with her drink; she had levitated the liquid out, which had become an oscillating ball of cherry tea that hovered above her cup.

I looked over two tables down, where Zandos, Levi, and Jace were sitting. Sirani was watching him from afar, too, but never spoke to him. Marathene was interacting with Zandos, but I could tell it was somewhat awkward. Jace was still vigilant. I could see that the others at my table were also observing them.

"I guess we figured out what happened," Sirani said. "But… why did you act the way you did in the first place?" she said to Reid.

"What do you mean?" he asked, somewhat defensively.

"You said that Jovnelle chose Cavaris," I whispered. Reid leaned away and stared at the roof.

"Sirani, do you remember three years ago, about what happened with Renee's husband on the Division Three board? Reban?" he asked. I had heard mentions of him before. I knew it was a double agent incident that occurred before I got here.

"Yes," she said firmly. "And I know exactly where you're going with this."

"Can you remind me?" I asked. "I wasn't there for that." Sirani began to explain quietly.

"Reban was Renee's husband. He served on the Division Two board for a few years." She looked to make sure the other table wasn't listening. "He got exposed as a double agent for Nojuni. Now he's either being held captive in the fifth subfloor, or he's dead."

"And he was able to marry *Renee* of all people?" I asked, appalled.

"This was back when she was a bit more reckless," Sirani added. "She had only served in the AHL in her position for a year or two. The incident broke her so much, because she couldn't tell whether or not she should love him anymore. Anyone would be changed by something like that. She turned into the Renee we know now. But now *Reid* thinks that somehow, Zandos is the same." I inhaled deeply, preparing myself for his justification. Reid nodded at Sirani's explanation, staring at the tea.

"When he tethered to me, I saw some of his memories." He gripped his cup. "It's like trying to think of a movie I saw as a kid. I saw them all at once, but since then they've started to split. They were blurry, but I felt... this intense emotion. Like, I saw this woman with white hair smiling and holding her arms out to me, and then another flash of her again, and me screaming, but it wasn't my voice. It was Zandos's. Then the lady fell. I think it was Jovnelle." He squinted, boring his eyes into the table. "It felt... wrong, like I was just showing up uninvited into his memories. It didn't feel like a hallucination. I think it was real." Sirani folded her arms and tilted her head as if listening thoughtfully, but she remained apprehensive. "I mean, it wasn't all bad, I don't think," Reid added quickly. "A lot of it was really... human. Like memories of the forest and Jace. It wasn't exactly evil, but I saw and felt like twelve or thirteen memories at the same time and felt like I was drowning." He didn't sound defensive anymore. There was a slight quaver to his voice that I could only liken to the warbling birds outside. "I still can't tell if it makes him more trustworthy or less."

"He and Jace are risking their lives being here. Today, we made it nearly impossible for them to return to their normal lives in their palace without being questioned. He's stuck here," I said.

"You *saw* his memories and you still think he's a threat?" Saku questioned.

"He nearly killed me with magic he doesn't know he has. Maybe he even has *Cavaris's* blood, and that could mean he has even worse magic we haven't seen yet," he said. "The reason why I brought up Reban at all is because he was just a regular guy. He turned Renee into a different person, caused investigation hell, and unleashed a PR disaster in the AHL. And he was just a regular guy. Zandos is not."

"I get that you're stressed. All of us are. But we can't let our fear and worry dictate how we move forward, because that's what we've been doing long before I got here, and we never got anything done," I said.

Saku nodded vigorously. "Levi trusts him, he doesn't even trust the mess hall vending machine," she said earnestly.

"Levi does have a good sense of judgement," Sirani added.

"I'm not saying we should kill him or anything, but I'd be an idiot if I didn't say we should be careful around him. Don't let hope blind you," Reid said. "Renee probably knows what it's like better than anyone to want someone to be a good person so badly that she'd ignore the signs." Sirani bit her cheek and turned her head away. I didn't have a retort. He was right, at some level, but not completely.

After spending some time in the tea shop, we went on over to explore the rest of the city. *I think we got somewhere. If nothing else, we got a coupon for our bulk tea order.* Once we decided the tour of the city was done, Marathene brought us all back to Avukena Palace, and everyone else returned home for the night. I stood for a moment in the lobby, checking my phone.

"Isavna, please come here," Marathene said after most of the group had left. Her tone was serious. I closed my phone and faced her.

"Yes?" I responded. She opened her palm and showed me a pendant. It was a small white diamond in a thin platinum chain, but it was a little scuffed.

"Please take this," Marathene said, presenting me with the object. "The stone is quite valuable, so I suggest you do not take it off. It could mean life or death." I tilted my head in confusion. *This is sudden.*

"Okay, I… understand," I lied. I paused, wondering if she would explain. "Uh, could you elaborate?" she looked behind her at the palace and then slowly drew her eyes to me, shaking her head morosely. She looked immeasurably guilty. I nodded sympathetically.

As I walked into the palace, I thought about it a bit. Strange request, but I trusted Marathene. I rushed to the elevator and ran down the hallway, approaching my unit. My friends then arrived soon after.

Sirani was the first to come, so I decided to talk with her. In sleepovers like these, we always began with gossip. We talked about a breakup of people neither of us cared for, and Sirani went on about some other couple I didn't know about.

"Alright, enough gossip," I said after a while. "What're we actually gonna do? Movie?"

"Not sure," Sirani replied. I leaned back in my sunken floor, covered in a blanket from the waist down. Peering outside, the darkened sky was beautiful. My floor-to-ceiling window next to my kitchen showed me the city. The clouds, like cotton, settled onto the mountains like a blanket, behind the purple evening haze.

"Y'know," I said to Sirani, who was also gazing out the window. "Sometimes I forget how beautiful Avukena is."

"It's really nice, especially with this view you have," she replied, twirling her hair. "All I see from my dorm is Avukenan State Bank."

Saku entered without a need for an introduction, with arms full of snacks and an overnight bag. "I come with gifts for the village," she declared.

"You didn't think to put them in the bag?" Sirani said, furrowing her brows. "Never mind. Do you need help with that?" Both of us got up and grabbed some snacks to put on the table, packaging rustling as they went.

"What did you bring?" I asked, inspecting her bounty.

"Whatever I raided from Kairo and Reid's dorm. They left the door unlocked, and Kairo always has some," Saku replied, smiling.

"Oh, so it's plunder we're looking at here," Sirani said. "I see." I saw her bounty had local snacks with labels in Hakon and other languages from nearby regions. They were just as flashy and bright as the snacks on Earth. There were chocolates, chips, cookies, and what appeared to be candy geodes.

"I got all the essentials, and then some. Kairo's in his dark chocolate phase right now, so he had a lot. I'm sure he wouldn't mind if I took just a little box," Saku explained. As we sat back down in the sunken floor, surrounded by snacks, we continued to talk about everything and nothing.

"Were they even there when you went to pillage their snacks?" I asked Saku, biting down on a crispy, salty, and somewhat spicy red potato cube. The speckled brownish powder got on my fingers and probably around my mouth.

"No. Kairo was shopping for food at Bahana's using my employee card again and Reid was… well, I don't know. The light in his room wasn't on, maybe he was on a walk or something."

"Maybe," I said. "Hey, Sirani, how's it going with Jace?"

She reached for a candy geode. "I don't really know. I think it'll take at least a few days before I can get through to him," Sirani said.

"At least it's not like this morning. Maybe he even likes Avukena now. I mean, he seemed pretty happy in Dewdrop," Saku said.

"Oh, I wouldn't say that just yet. It's only been a day," Sirani said. "He's never been one for socializing. That's probably why he left."

"But why Nojuni of all places?" I asked. "Seems like the last place anyone would want to go. There are some hermit villages past Sjasa I've seen that seem way more viable and less hostile."

"Well, I don't really know," she said, fiddling with a wrapper.

"What happened in your family for him to leave?" Saku asked.

"My grandparents had passed the year prior. Our parents were really bad to Jace and I and… I suppose he couldn't take it anymore, so he left. Then they sent me here for a semester and never asked for me to return." She sniffled. "I just couldn't believe I couldn't depend on anyone, not even my parents."

"We're here," Saku said, handing her another chocolate pyramid and smiling earnestly.

"And we're not going to leave you in the dust, okay?" I told her.

"I suppose you're right," she said, taking the candy. "Thank you."

"So do we have a plan for tomorrow?" Saku asked us.

"Besides our normal work at the AHL, I don't think much else. Actually, I do have that thing with Reid, but I think that'll be in the evening," I said. "Sirani has a date. I guess everything else will just kind of… happen."

"Yeah," Saku replied simply. She pointed to my neck. "Is that new?" I unhooked the necklace, which didn't go down farther than my collarbone, handing it to her to inspect.

"Marathene gave it to me during our walk. It's not in perfect condition, but it's nice. She was pretty adamant that I should keep it on all the time, so I'm guessing the stone has some kind of value." She handed the necklace back to me.

Sirani looked it over. "It might be a magical item," she said. "Probably more of a reason to keep it safe."

We watched about half of an awful romance movie until it got to be too much to handle, and then went to bed.

I switched off the light and lay awake for a few minutes, thinking about my pendant and other events of my day. I thought about the mission, Sir Horuo's face, and the tethering incident.

I remembered what I had told Reid. *I wish I knew more about tethers.* I knew it had to be what was keeping me alive here, and something to do with my magic, but Mother Everealm was sort of resistant to talking about it. I decided to put a pin in that thought for the next time I saw her and Marathene.

Sunday, 10:01 PM, Avukena Palace, Floor 20

Sirani quietly stepped out of Isavna's room. She had forgotten her retainers and other toiletries in the dormitory, and Saku and Isavna were already in their beds. *It's just a quick portal trip.* She glanced at the door right beside Isavna's, which belonged to Zandos and Jace, sighing quietly. She only made it a few paces when the door suddenly opened.

She stopped, looking back at the door. She could hear some conversation between the two. Jace stepped out with a cardboard box turned laundry basket, likely headed for the nearby laundry room. She tightened her hands, held close to her body.

Jace averted his eyes. "Didn't think anyone would be out this late," he remarked quietly as he went into the laundry room.

"Well, I didn't either," Sirani replied in their native tongue. "Are you adjusting well?"

"No." He replied in Hakon. Escan was the primary language in southern Avukena State, which included Esco, but having spent so much time away from there, he had forgotten most of it. "I lost most of my Escan. And I hate it here."

Sirani tightened her lips. "Yeah, don't you ever. You always have a problem with something."

"Like you don't either," Jace said, throwing the laundry into the machine. "Unless you never do, which wouldn't be a surprise."

"My life isn't perfect," she said, closing her eyes and sighing. "But I'm always trying to make it better, if I can. Even if I fail… my conscience is clear."

"What are you talking about? And why the hell do you care so much? I barely know you."

"Because you're my brother," Sirani said. "Forget our parents, and Esco."

"And that's supposed to mean literally anything?" Jace said firmly.

Sirani leaned against the doorframe. "Well, all I'm saying is… just —I don't know. We—we don't have to be, um, strangers."

"And then what? You suddenly expect everything to be fine? For me to suddenly be okay with it?"

"I just wanted to *try*, and maybe I'm asking too much. To… to tell you the truth, I just can't live like this weighing on my conscience. That I didn't try. So you can just go ahead and tell me no and all of this can be over with." She stood still. A few moments passed.

"Jeez, you're really dramatic, y'know?"

"I've been told." She focused on the blinking cycle button on the washing machine.

"You tried, I guess. What do you expect me to do?"

"I just told you," she said. "I gave up on a happy reunion already. I don't want to fix you."

Jace exhaled sharply and leaned on the washing machine. "You used to be annoying as hell. You'd steal my socks all the time."

"Only the ones that fit," Sirani said quietly. Jace diverted his gaze. "Was that why you left?"

Jace scoffed. "Course not."

"Then why?"

"Is it so hard to understand?" Jace asked. "For the freedom we never got. I was the happiest I ever was for like a week. The further I got, the harder it was to turn back."

"Jace, this is the last thing I'll ask if you'll be honest with me," Sirani said, so quietly it was almost a whisper. "Were you trying to die?"

Jace's brows furrowed as he tapped his nails on the washing machine. "I expected to be caught, so I didn't care what happened. But then, a week went by, and nothing. No one noticed. If no one else cared, why the hell should I—I thought. I went farther away and didn't care what happened."

Sirani didn't flinch, but spoke slowly. "Jace, you're still *missing*, as far as Esco's concerned. You're lucky that you were in that holding cell during debriefing, so the AHL doesn't know your last name yet. But I promise you that they will know soon."

"It must've been the same awful luck that took me to Avukena. I thought I would finally be left alone in Nojuni." Sirani thought about her choice not to give Isavna her pistol back when they were fighting him.

"Would you rather have died there?" Sirani asked.

"Yeah," Jace said, as if it were obvious. She felt a little selfish for having made the choice to keep him alive. She didn't tell Jace, though."

"The AHL is going to find out who you are eventually. In fact, they already might. What happens to your plan then?"

"I don't know. Maybe I'll get what I earned and be thrown back into our parents' claws."

"You think that's what you earned?"

"If I get what I deserve, that would be it. I definitely haven't earned the right to stay."

Sirani crossed her arms, her expression hard to read. "So be it, then."

"That's it?"

"Yes," she said. "I've done all I can. That's all I wanted."

Jace stood still, waiting for a catch. His nostrils flared as he exhaled, partially annoyed, partially relieved.

"And for what it's worth, um, Zandos's leather coat is going to get damaged if you use hot water. You should probably hang dry it too." She left, smiling weakly, closing the door quietly behind her.

Monday, 7:49 AM, Avukena Palace, Isavna's Unit

I looked towards Sirani as we did our makeup.

"You look tired," I said, noting the puffy dark circles that she covered with concealer and powder.

"Yes, I had trouble sleeping." There was a knock on the door.

"Yeah?" I shouted, walking over to unlock the door. It was Kairo and Levi.

"Morning, guys," Kairo's voice rumbled as he walked in. "Am I too early?"

"Yes," Saku croaked, finally stirring in the pullout bed.

"We checked your mail on the way up. You got a couple of letters from Angeten Palace." Levi said. His voice sounded kind of squeaky compared to Kairo's.

"Thanks guys," I said. They had both sat down at the table.

"Have we told you about Saku's and my crown city anniversary?" Kairo asked.

"No?" Sirani said, joining us at the table.

"Oh, New Klethorog is having their tricentennial in about a month and a half. Nothing like the gravity of the festival, but it's an important event for us, so I thought I'd deliver an invitation personally," Kairo explained. "I already told Marathene about it."

"Oh, that sounds good. Well, I should be able to make it," I replied. Just for fun, I tried to levitate the letters into a stack to move them over to the kitchen counter, just to have them fall. Kairo finished the job for me.

"I still don't get it," I said. "I haven't been using much magic but when I do, it doesn't work. I just hope it doesn't affect flying and stuff."

"Has it always been like this?" Levi asked.

"No," I replied. "This is very recent. Like, less than six months ago. I wake up tired, and even after the thing with Zandos I'm still getting these headaches."

"Weird," he replied. "You should probably ask Marathene or someone."

I tilted my head up to look at my ceiling. There was a small cobweb in a corner I had neglected to clean.

"So should we get going to the AHL? Get those hours in?" I asked my group. Saku looked like she was barely alive.

"Saku, you can't be serious," Kairo said.

"I'm just kinda tired," she complained quietly. I looked towards Sirani.

"Yes, Isavna. I'd like to find out if Zandos and Jace have gone through questioning yet."

"He's doing that right now," Levi replied. "He messaged me a little earlier saying they were taking him to subfloor five and he'd be there for a while."

We continued out into the hall. I spotted Zandos's coat hanging to dry on a rack in the laundry room as we passed by.

Thinking about magic made my pendant feel a bit warm. I tucked it under my shirt in case it was some kind of magic artifact.

"I hope they have beef rolls today," Saku said as the elevator chimed. "Those always run out first." As we descended, no one said anything. I adjusted the strap of my work bag, intending to fill it with food containers I had left at my office. They had begun to accumulate. I tried not to think about Zandos and Jace. Or Reid. Or Jovnelle. Or my magic and the weird pendant. Even though it was sort of impossible.

9

Monday, 8:09 AM, AHL Central, Subfloor 5 - Questioning Room

Zandos shifted uncomfortably in his seat and blinked repeatedly. He was given brown contact lenses to disguise the true nature of his eyes. The guard had just cut off telepathy. He and Jace were seated directly across from each other in the gray, drab room. A guard stood in the doorway by the one-way glass. A well-known officer, Mr. Novet, sat between the two.

"What language would you prefer?" The man asked in Hakon. His voice was loud and intense.

"Do you speak Nojunian?" Zandos replied in Hakon. The man shook his head. "Good. I am better at Hakon than English. I am terrible at English."

"We will now proceed with our questioning. Please state your full name and region of origin."

"Zandos... I do not know my last name. Sorry. Whatever Jovnelle's last name is, that is mine."

"Everealm?" Mr. Novet said, raising his feathery eyebrows.

"Yes. My region of origin is Nojuni."

Mr. Novet turned his attention to Jace.

"I'm Jace," he said simply.

"Last name? Region of origin?"

Jace felt his palms get sweaty, but conceded reluctantly. "…Maligari. I'm originally from southern Avukena State."

"Esco?" Mr. Novet interjected, looking surprised. His lips curled into a toothy, wry smile. "You're that missing kid, huh?"

"I… I, uh, yeah. Somewhere around there. I got possessed by a Mahi yesterday and somehow came here. I didn't want to come," He replied, looking aside anxiously. "Maybe you've heard."

Mr. Novet tilted his chin up and narrowed his eyes pensively. "We will deal with that in a moment. But for now, we must continue. Now, how did you two meet?"

"It was in Nojuni," Zandos said. "I lived there my entire life. Some time ago Jace came, and he was… lost, so I helped him." Jace tensed a bit more, looking down at the white tile ground. He could hear the guards shifting.

"What was your role in Nojuni?" Mr. Novet asked.

Zandos prepared for a long explanation. "I am Jovnelle's son. She was possessed almost all the time, so apart from my early childhood I never got to speak with her much." He said, trying to remember. He had nearly forgotten what it was like to have a full conversation with her. "I was not happy. Cavaris is cruel to her. She is kind when she is not possessed. I want to help stop him, and free my mother."

"And you, Jace?"

"I—I didn't do much. I didn't grow up speaking Nojunian, so the only people I could understand were Zandos and some guards. They know Hakon to understand outsiders. Zandos had to convince them I wasn't a threat so they wouldn't try to kill me."

Mr. Novet nodded, his fingers moving swiftly on the hologram. "And you, Zandos? Did you have a routine? What were your duties, if any?"

"My day was structured, but it was by my choice. I would have gone mad otherwise, especially since I did not know what year or day it was. I only knew how old I was by asking my mother, but I do not know now since she has been possessed a lot. Cavaris would also communicate with me, but infrequently and often cryptically. Early on, he wanted me to train and learn combat, I assume so I could be another one of his servants, like Jovnelle and Sir Horuo," he explained. "In the mornings, I would train with combat. Around midday I would study or do what I chose, but there wasn't much to do. Sometimes I would paint or write but resources were few. In the evenings I would have supper with my mother, but she was often possessed and did not come, so she became very malnourished."

"What did you study, and with what?" Mr. Novet asked.

"Books. I have come to learn they were outdated, by at least a hundred years. I would study mathematics, sciences, languages, history, technology, magic, all which were very fascinating. Cavaris found I had books on magic. One day I woke up and they were no longer there. I think he had sent for my books to be hidden, though I found most of them after a few years. I never found the ones about magic, I can only assume they were destroyed. I never learned how to use magic past telepathy. Therefore I cannot fly."

"But why?" Mr. Novet asked. "Why study so much? Did you intend to leave Nojuni on your own terms?"

"Yes," Zandos admitted, getting a little shifty. "I always wanted to leave. I wanted to perfect my skills for when I would leave, so I wouldn't struggle to learn much more, but... that was not the case."

"Were you sent on missions by Cavaris?"

"No, he did not trust me with that," Zandos said. "He sent one man, under the name Reban, I think, three or so years ago, but he never returned. I think Cavaris knew I was against him by the time I was about twelve." Mr. Novet raised his eyebrows and typed into the hologram.

Turning to Jace, Mr. Novet's expression softened slightly. "Jace, you mentioned you didn't do much in Nojuni. Could you elaborate on what your routine looked like?"

Jace's jaw clenched, his eyes darting to Zandos before looking at Mr. Novet. "I… I tried to survive, 'cause life is hard in Nojuni and pretty much everyone knew I didn't belong. I mostly kept to myself. Sometimes Zandos brought me food, because—well, I couldn't leave—I—I would be seen as a threat since I look so different from everyone there."

"Why did you leave Esco in the first place? You are a Maligari, correct? Like Vasana and Pashano Maligari? Is that not your crown city? Furthermore, we have a known crown member of Esco here in the AHL, Sirani, I believe. Did you—"

—"Yes, I did, but I have reasons for leaving Esco. *Personal* reasons. As in, they don't concern the AHL and shouldn't matter to you." Jace could feel Mr. Novet's eyes boring into him.

"I will not say that this doesn't make me suspicious, Jace," Mr. Novet said. "This is necessary information for our assessment."

"Just say that I ran away," Jace said, angry.

"How did you survive before you arrived in Nojuni?" Mr. Novet asked.

"Surviving wasn't my plan," Jace said.

"Excuse me?" Mr. Novet said.

"I didn't want to… uh, I didn't really want to end up in Nojuni. I brought a lot of money with me, and I had been going north. I wanted to get to… to North Huzoril, any port city, or something, and get somewhere far like Elkostet or Dekerei from there, but I ran out of resources in Nojuni," he said, not meeting eyes with Mr. Novet.

Mr. Novet turned his attention back to Zandos, who was more compliant. "What information can you provide that would be useful to the AHL apart from what you disclosed during the group meeting?"

Zandos detailed information about guard routines, palace layouts, and weaknesses around the palace, all while Jace's eyes darted around, trying to find a way to leave. *This is hopeless.* He thought. The contrast between him and Zandos was stark.

They continued for another half hour. Mr. Novet put some notes into the hologram, then closed it by swiping his hand. "Thank you both for your cooperation. We will have to verify the information later, Zandos. As for you, Jace," he paused. Jace scowled. "We may need to have additional questioning later for your discharging," Jace squinted his eyes, worried about what he meant.

Mr. Novet gestured to the guards, and they stood up from their chairs. "The guards will escort you to the holding room before Ms. Belanis and that sophomore official group of yours comes to pick you up."

They walked out of the room and down a metal hallway. Zandos looked at the rooms as they passed by, which had small windows. Some people were on cots. He heard grumbling and screaming from a room without a window. He recognized the voice but didn't stop walking. They entered an empty room with bright, disorienting lights and a bench on either side. The room was sterile, white metal, and there was a security camera in one corner. As they sat down, Zandos let out a sigh. He knew that Jace could become a problem for their standing within the AHL, but he felt that he had cleared his own name by giving up so much information. He knew that Jace was unstable, but he was convinced that, like his mother, this wasn't his true self. But he could understand how Jace reacted.

"Do you want to go?" Zandos asked Jace in their pidgin. It was a garbled, inconsistent combination of Hakon, English, and Nojunian. Jace looked up.

"What do you mean?" he replied in the language.

"I'm offering to request for you to be brought back to Nojuni," he said.

"Oh, really?" Jace replied, a mix of relief and panic settling into his expression.

"I know that's what you want to do. You don't like it here," Zandos said. "You don't like anyone here. You don't like this city, this organization, and you sure don't like your sister."

Jace tightened his lips, looking at the ground, but didn't say anything. "Yes," he said after a moment. "I think we should go back."

"Not we," Zandos clarified. Jace looked up again, his eyes widening. "You. You can go alone."

"What?" Jace straightened, tensing his shoulders and pleading with his hands. "Why won't you come?"

"This is what I've always wanted to do. I've always wanted to leave. You can have all my things and my room. I don't intend to return."

"Are you crazy? You said you wouldn't leave my side, Zandos," Jace let his arms fall.

"Until you were ready," Zandos said. "I said I wouldn't let you go until you were ready. When you came to me, you were struggling. But you're very strong now."

Jace was pacing around the small room, cycling through different emotions. Sadness, anger, fear, until he finally reached desperation. He ran his fingers through his hair. "I don't understand, just…."

"You can go back to Nojuni. No one will tell you what to do, or how to feel, or who to interact with."

"But what if *Sir Horuo* finds me? What will I tell him about *everything* that happened? What will I do if something happens? What if Cavaris *escapes*, or something worse? I just don't...."

"You need to figure that out on your own. You've always wanted independence from everyone, is that not what you want?" Zandos pursed his lips. "The AHL has many resources. They have far more than Nojuni does. That's why I'm going to stay, since I finally have a chance to do what I've always wanted."

"I don't know what I want," huffed Jace, who sat down. "I thought I wanted freedom. Then I thought it was safety. And well, I suppose...." He clenched his fists and looked at Zandos. "I think I just want someone who would be there."

Zandos folded his hands in his lap. "I have felt that too," he said quietly. "But I cannot hold your hand forever. You are very strong, Jace. But many chances have been given to you and you rejected them."

"I'll change, Zandos, I just never knew it would come to this," Jace pleaded. "I want to stay. I don't want to be alone again."

"Well then you'll have to convince Mr. Novet," Zandos said, as clipped footsteps got closer.

Jace left silently and followed Mr. Novet out into the same room. He was joined by someone else in the room.

"You may recognize Officer Renee Rotura. I believe you two have met," Mr. Novet said. Jace said nothing but nodded. "This meeting will be to decide whether or not we should discharge you from the AHL. That is, let you go. You cannot return to Nojuni because of the information you have now, but we will send you to any nearby civilian zone as long as you sign an agreement of confidentiality. Now… according to your record, you have been someone… of note, for this organization, and only within the

past few days." Mr. Novet said. "And I hope you understand that we only have so much patience."

"Yes, Mr. Novet," Renee said flatly.

"I understand," Jace said, his voice lacking conviction. His eyes darted around the room. He knew he had to choose his words carefully. Renee sighed.

"Do you, Jace?" she asked kindly, in a way that made Jace's heart sink. "Shall we review your record?" Mr. Novet nodded, and Renee opened a hologram. "Assault on multiple officials. Failure to comply with guard orders. Four times. Failure to comply with officials, five times. Verbal harassment, two times."

"I didn't want to be here, it's just… so difficult to adjust," Jace said, standing up. He exhaled tensely, staring into Renee and Mr. Novet's eyes, looking for a shred of sympathy.

"Please remain seated," Mr. Novet said. "All of us had to adjust to challenging environments. We're not here to unpack your trauma, we're here to determine whether you're a threat or a hindrance, and we've concluded you are."

"But, I have information, don't you want that? I'll give it to you!" Jace pleaded.

"Frankly, anything you have to offer in terms of information we can retrieve from Zandos. Additionally, he has been more cooperative and had a better attitude," Renee replied in a firm tone. Jace straightened his neck, but didn't say anything.

"Well, Jace. We believe this is the end of the road. Gather any belongings you have here, and we will offer our services in transporting you to any civilian zone wherever you'd like within portal range or within Avukena State, if not accessed by portal." Renee said. "We will prepare an agreement of confidentiality for you to sign too."

"And from there?"

"You're on your own."

This was it. Jace looked around the room and slumped in his chair in resignation. Jace sat there for a few moments. He had failed to prove his point.

"Well, this leaves us with one question. Where would you like to go?" Mr. Novet asked. Jace thought for a moment.

"Esco," he finally said. "I want to go to Esco."

Mr. Novet and Renee exchanged a surprised glance. Renee opened her hologram to make a note of that, but stopped right before.

"Are you certain? You wish to return to your crown city?"

"Yes," he croaked.

"Any… particular part of the city? Esco is quite large," she asked.

"Vasana Square," he said, shuddering at his mother's name, which had not left his mouth in many years. Renee did not comment as she wrote it in the hologram.

"Alright, Jace," Mr. Novet said, his tone softening slightly. "Esco it is. You have two hours to say your goodbyes and gather your belongings—and eat, I'd recommend—before you will be escorted to the AHL portal room. You must remain in the AHL for that time. From there you will be taken to the Avukena Portal terminal, and from there Esco. The guard will follow you until Vasana square."

"Perfect," Jace said, his tone flat.

"That is all. Good luck," Mr. Novet nodded and smiled, but it didn't reach his eyes. He and Renee left, but Jace stayed behind for a moment. Soon, he'd be in Esco, though it hadn't felt like home for a while. He sat again, head bowed, and quickly formulated a plan. Surely Renee and Mr. Novet would tell the Escan police that he's no longer missing. He was going to meet his parents. Even if he failed, his conscience was clear.

I was inside Dewdrop with my group. We all sat down in our regular spots. The shop was cozy, with booth seats and hologram projections of the news on coffee tables. The air was filled with the scents of different types of teas.

"Did you see the news about Gosbon? The summer storms and Mahi attacks on warehouses caused a shortage in Lenton petals for tea," I said, gazing at my cup.

"That's crazy. So is the stuff here the real deal?" Reid asked.

"Yeah," I replied. "It takes a while to dry, so they say we'll see the effects in a year or so."

"No one drinks tea back in my hometown. I don't know why. It's so cold, I think it would catch on," Reid said.

"Yeah, tea is kind of a distinctive Avukena thing," I said. The Avukenans drank tea as much as the British or maybe even the Chinese. It was very unique to Avukena State, with a culture of both hot and cold tea. "Speaking of hometowns, what're you people gonna do in your guys' kingdoms when you get back for the festival?" I asked. We were all getting the next week off from work for the festival, and many people were returning home. International students from farther away often decided to just stay, since the festival was only observed in Avukena State.

"I'm gonna see some of my friends and then I'm gonna pack more stuff since I'm moving here soon," Reid said.

"Saku and I are planning on going back to New Kleth to help for the anniversary," Kairo said.

"My little siblings and I are from a small kingdom, Luzuma. Since it's so far away, we don't celebrate the flower festival," Levi explained. "It's kind of just an Avukenan thing."

"Why do we have it, anyway?" I asked.

"Hundreds of years ago a volcano exploded a few hundred miles east of here, and the winds carried ash over to Avukena City, Sjasa, and all the surrounding areas. It made the winter really long and difficult, it lasted a few years. and so when the first spring finally came and flowers were blooming again, they celebrated with a festival and a feast at the end of the night." Sirani explained. "It was sort of a dead tradition though, until Mother Everealm revived it about thirty years ago to try and gain public favor and talk about how amazing the AHL is."

"Has it worked?" I asked. Kairo shrugged.

"They don't make public polling information public. Who's to say. I'd guess not." Kairo said. We returned to everyday conversation until Levi's expression fell.

"What's going on?" Keya asked.

"Jace just got kicked out of the AHL," Levi announced, narrowing his eyes as he tried to hear the telepathic message. I turned to Sirani. Where I expected panic and maybe tears, she was silent and morose.

"Apparently it's 'cause of his bad behavior," Levi said. Kairo took the stack of our cups and put them in the trash, intently paying attention to Levi. We all moved out of the building.

"Got the full message yet?" Reid asked.

"Zandos says he's going back to... Esco," he said. "We have about an hour and a half before he leaves." Saku was wringing her hands and shaking her fists.

"Saku, what's going on?" Kairo asked.

"I have work in fifteen minutes," she said. "I'm really sorry, Sirani. I'm so sorry." She left running before she could say another word. The rest of us went to the AHL, beelining for the second subfloor.

Monday, 12:29 PM, AHL Central, Subfloor 2 - Mess Hall

Keya left to do work, leaving the rest of us to find Jace.

"Zandos said that he and Jace are in the lounge right now," Levi said as we quickly made our way there. Zandos was quiet and looked to be lost in thought. Jace as well. Levi, Zandos, and Jace discussed what had happened as we settled in with them.

"You did it," Sirani said flatly.

"Guess I did," Jace looked down. A thick pause settled.

"What part of town are you going to?" Kairo asked.

"Vasana square. Where the Bahana's used to be, but Renee says it's a bank now."

"You chose that?" I asked.

"Well, seems like everything's changed. Anywhere I pick is probably going to be different than I remembered."

"We'll see you off, then," said Reid. I watched Sirani, Jace, and Zandos's conversation. It was tense, emotional, and flat all at the same time.

"I guess questioning brought out a lot. Did you hear Mr. Novet ran the questioning?" I said to Reid, watching the three.

"Yeah. He's all alone now," Reid said. "Must be rough. They were all each other had for the longest time, it seems."

When the time came, the affair was quick; we didn't want to linger or dwell very long. We watched him and the guard walk into the purple and

130

blue portal, and he didn't look back. We went to the portal in the first subfloor that led to the main Avukena City terminal.

"You alright?" I heard Kairo ask Zandos.

"Yes, I just never be... without Jace. Is strange," he replied. Levi stood there the longest, looking at the portal where Jace disappeared. I turned back to see what was wrong.

"Doesn't take much to get forgotten around here."

"You think he'll be forgotten?" I asked.

Levi shrugged, staring at the portal. "Depends who's watching. If nobody's watching, then yeah. Someone'll outshine you eventually," he tapped on his scabbard strap, clearly uneasy. "I guess that's why you've gotta prove yourself when you can."

We dispersed for the day, even though it was early afternoon. Reid and Sirani followed me into the city. I opened my phone, seeing a reminder I wrote for myself: *Write Flower Fest Speech.*

"Looks like we gotta start writing our speeches and practicing them over the next few days," I said. "Should be simple, since they're not supposed to exceed three minutes. Marathene sent me a telepathic message earlier saying to expect about 20 million eyes and ears from radio and television."

"Are you doing one?" Sirani asked, pointing at Reid.

"Yes, but they told me not to write anything yet or prepare anything," Reid said. "It's really weird. Maybe they already have it written for me and want it to be said in a very specific way."

"They don't want you to come prepared? Do they think you'll disagree with what your speech should say?" Sirani asked.

"Yeah. They think I'm stubborn."

"You are."

"Thanks a lot, Isavna."

We took the portal terminal to walk around the north district for a few hours and check the stores we liked before heading back to the palace. I noticed Sirani, who had tear stains under her eyes.

"Are you alright?" Reid asked Sirani.

"Oh," she said, her expression blank. She focused her attention on the sidewalk in front of her. "I'm fine."

I gazed up at the clouds as they hung over the light blue sky, though I saw darker ones in the distance. We walked for an hour or so, only stopping once in a flight helmet store. I saw a small sheltered area with a glowing portal. They functioned sort of like bus stops; they were all over the city. I tapped Sirani's arm.

"I think you tried your hardest," I said, still staring at the clouds. I felt a quick sting inside my leg, a familiar pain. My thigh still hurts from the Jace-monster cutting it yesterday. I paused to take pain medication. I adjusted the gauze under my pants, knowing that it was absolutely going to scar.

I put the pills in my pocket and spared a thought for Jace.

IO

The portal terminal worked like a subway station or an airport. A main hub in the center branched off into more specific areas, not unlike a tree. We weaved between a few lines into the restricted area, where I tapped both my AHL ID and my Avukena Palace Ward ID before I could go inside.

Moving through the portal system almost felt automatic at that point. Sort of like typing or driving. The rush of air from the pulsing purple and blue portal spat us out in the palace's east wing.

By now, the wind had pushed the dark clouds over the sea, and it had begun to rain. Despite that, Mother Everealm was tending to the gardens. She was very protective of it. One would imagine the job would be left to landscapers or gardeners, but she insisted on tending to the whole court's flowerbeds, shrubbery, and topiaries on her own. She only left the small lawns to the care of more physically fit, young landscapers. Most of the court was gardens, anyway.

We went into the banquet hall for a rehearsal dinner. We residents were often the kitchen's focus group. There were white candles that filled the room with a warm, vanilla scent. I recalled Marathene saying she wanted to change the candles for a more floral scent to go with the theme. There were dark red drapes over the windows that overlooked the sea, with dark clouds hanging in the sky. We began to eat the first course, which was soup with what looked like little blue onions and tender cubes of felmine meat.

"So I heard about the situation back in your home kingdom," I said.

Reid scoffed. "Yeah," he said, frustrated. He went over the recent development of what was happening, which boiled down to disagreement on tariffs imposed by his crown city, Dekerei, on the neighboring city, Durio, which was very technologically advanced but through unethical means. It soured relations badly. "My parents are roping me back so I can serve as their unpaid therapist. I'll probably have to release some statements out to the city too. Durio has an heir too and they'll probably do the same with her."

"Oh, right, I think I read about it in my Current Events class," Sirani said. "The Seranoy continent always has some kind of drama because of their ores. Even neutral New Klethorog had to step out of domestic trade since Durio tried to force their hand." I thought about how similar it was to conflict in the Middle East over oil.

"It's a disaster. I don't even know why no one's paying attention to Durio's corruption," Reid said. "I'm gonna try to stay out of it as much as I can. Might visit some of the mountains, it's been a while."

"You should be careful," Sirani advised. "Your parents may have their own agenda, and getting tangled up in politics could be risky, considering Dekerei's trade plans have been controversial."

"Yeah, they absolutely have an agenda," Reid muttered. "But what choice do I have? I'll doom Dekerei to the reputation of a selfish runaway heir or be part of another generation of senseless bickering."

I tried wrapping my head around such world politics that we were expected to understand. I could hear the chatter of the other wards and the clinking of the palace china. The palace looked beautiful this time of day, with the rain creating a distorted image on the windows. Sirani departed to go on a date with some guy she had been talking to in the IT subdivision of the AHL. We would debrief the next day.

Reid and I went up the elevator, talking about whatever topic led to the next—old video games, Earth movies, and our favorite hot sauces.

I observed the buttons on the elevator, numbered one to twenty. There were offices, galleries, and ballrooms on floors one to sixteen, and the rest were guest rooms along with the entire east wing.

We always had a number of temporary guests and long-term wards, the bulk of which were Nojunian refugees. The AHL would transport them from Nojuni so the Mahis would have fewer magic surrogates. The wards had to work around the palace, cleaning, cooking, or doing some other thing to earn their keep until they could find a job.

Floor five was restricted to Mother Everealm and Marathene only; no one but them knew what went on there. Flying by was no use either because of the tinted windows.

Once in my unit, we began to open packages. There were various things I had ordered, like some skincare products I was going to send to Toniska that she liked, and a replacement pair of combat pants since my other ones got torn up in Nojuni.

"I heard Saku got payrolled," I said. I heard Reid ripping tape off packages.

"Oh really?" The cardboard tore as he flattened a box. "I guess we can't bully her for being a newbie anymore. And maybe she can finally quit her job at Bahana's."

"That's just so crazy to me, that a princess of a well-off state has to get a part time job at a grocery store."

"Kairo did too, so I'm guessing that's their parent's request, since they definitely *don't* need the money," Reid pointed out. "I'm sure glad to be Kairo's roommate. Even though our home kingdoms aren't friendly. But he makes really good Seranese food that reminds me of home, even if we use slightly different spices in Dekerei."

"I guess that means their kingdom values hard work. As airheaded as Saku seems, all the reports she's sent me to file away were excellently written." We finished with the boxes and left them outside my unit.

"Alright. Let's start cross-referencing the map and the data."

"All right." He tapped on his wrist twice, signaling his wrist projection to appear. He pinched outward with his fingers, which expanded the display. The translucent display grew and moved in front of us. In the meantime, I opened my wrist projection and logged into the file database.

We went over a plan to move people over to Huzoril State, east of Avukena State. There was a situation of civil unrest made worse by Mahis.

"So Mr. Makorod wants us to move 200 people to Huzoril, along with 25 hovervans and 15 armed hovervans." Reid explained.

"Those armed hovervans are beasts. It must be bad over there." I searched through the database. "Looks like we have enough operatives to send to Huzoril," I said, as I tried to find vehicle numbers. A pop-up appeared on my hologram. *Keycard Access Level 4 Required to view this data.* "That's weird. I guess I don't have a high enough keycard access level to see how many hovercars we have."

"Stupid," Reid scoffed. "I guess we should write a report to send to Renee instead." We spent about an hour writing her a report and finished our work.

"Well, you can leave now if you want," I said. "Since you have to leave so early tomorrow."

"It's fine," Reid replied. "The flight back home's pretty long. I'll have plenty of time to sleep on the plane." Portals had not yet developed the technology to cross oceans, so planes were still used occasionally. I stood up and moved to the sunken floor. There were some snack wrappers I hadn't cleaned up from the night before with Sirani and Saku.

"Well, what do you want to do then?" I asked. "As long as it doesn't have to do with AHL stuff I'll be fine."

"I dunno," he said, slumping into the sunken ground across from me. "We could watch *Death and Destruction Five*." He smiled, knowing my disdain for that series.

"If you want to waste three hours of time, sure," I said. "I heard they're screening *Death and Destruction Six* soon."

"Yeah, Kairo told me about that," Reid said. "It should be interesting. I'll probably wait until they release it on streaming, though. I don't think I can watch it all in one sitting." I stood up, went to my kitchen, and opened a snack cabinet.

"Well, do you want any snacks? I have some sodas and chips if you want. Actually, I have some of those chocolate pyramids that you like, Saku brought some yesterday."

"Oh, really? And the red cubes too?" he asked.

"Yep," I replied.

"I had some chocolate pyramids, red cubes, and candy geodes at home but they're all gone. I'm guessing Kairo went on a snack rampage or something."

"Someone did," I said. His expression fell.

"It was Saku again, wasn't it?" he said, laughing wryly. I laughed a bit, walking back with two sodas in glass bottles.

"Here," I said, handing him the large bag of red potato cubes. "Safe from Saku... for now."

"Thanks, Isavna," he replied.

"So what are you going to do back home? Or at least, hope to do," I asked.

"I want to gather the rest of my things to move out. I don't want to be there for too long. Maybe climb or fly around some of the mountains with my friends, go into the woods, mess around, the usual."

"Sounds like a nice trip," I said, sipping my soda, though here, they called it Jeya. It tasted like fizzy sweet tea with an undertone of vanilla, though the carbonation felt... sharper. They must've used a gas other than carbon dioxide. It was comforting, even though I knew true southern sweet tea couldn't exist in Avukena. I looked up from the label to him. He looked just as exhausted as I was. "You need one."

"Yeah," he said quietly. "It's just impossible to escape politics, no matter where I go. I can see why Jace wanted to leave Esco so badly." He stretched while holding the bottle, and I was worried his drink might spill. "I was never meant for this life of politics."

"Sirani hasn't said a peep about Jace since he's left, surprisingly," I replied. "I wonder how he's doing now. I mean, Esco's just down the coast a few hours flying. Portal fare's expensive though. They always seem to be in places where there's civil unrest."

"Yeah. People *hate* the king and queen of Esco. I heard there was a failed insurrection a few years ago."

"Gosh, really? I guess it makes sense. I tried to look in the news to see if there was anything on Jace being found—you'd think, 'cause he's the missing Escan Prince. But anything out of Esco seems to be either state media or heavily controlled. I hope our operatives don't get deployed there or anything."

He waved his hand dismissively and took another sip of his drink. "It's a municipal problem, so the police handled the civil unrest. But that state media stuff seems dystopian. Probably why Sirani isn't itching to go back or anything. They're part of Avukena State like us, but media laws are different there. I doubt our dear Mother Everealm will pass any media-transparency acts." He chuckled at the absurdity. I didn't understand.

"So then why are we deploying people in Huzoril then? That makes no sense." I asked. "Why not deploy people in Esco if there was a literal attempted coup?"

"What's a coup?" he asked.

"Oh, like an insurrection. It's a French-derived word, which is an Earth country."

"Oh, yeah. I've heard of French."

"France," I corrected.

"Whatever it's called," he said. "But to answer your question, it's just a matter of us picking our battles. Despite being in Esco, their problem just has to do with them having bad leadership, but in Huzoril, the protestors are protesting against Mother Everealm and the AHL. They think both entities are useless, make bad decisions, and drain resources." I squinted and stared into my drink.

"I see why we're so adamant about suppressing that protest, then. I… don't really know how I feel about that."

"I hate it. Those protests aren't violent, but the Avukenan media makes it seem like they are." Reid said casually.

"So, do you even, like, *want* to be in the AHL?" I asked. "Sorry, that sounds like a stupid question."

"You're fine. But the answer is no. I doubt everyone except Levi and maybe Kairo actually want to. Most of us are forced by our parents, since military service is the noble thing to do as children of monarchs."

"Zandos seems to want to," I said.

"I don't think he understands the full scope of the AHL yet." I finished the last of my Jeya and set it down next to me. I turned around and looked out my window. I saw people in the distance flying around the city, looking like specks of dust floating in a dusty room.

"Jace has about four hours of light left today. I hope he's at least found a place for the night." His green eyes caught a glint of the dying evening sun.

"He and Zandos were my next door neighbors. I heard them practice sparring at like 2 a.m. Now it's just Zandos though. Maybe you should go see him," I said, gesturing toward the room next door with my half-empty bottle.

"Alright." He stood up to go. "Are you coming?"

"I'm good," I said. "I wanna get to writing the speech."

"Alright," he replied. I saw him take his things and a brown messenger bag; I assumed he wouldn't return.

"Safe travels," I called. "Don't have too much fun without us."

"Bye," he smiled, closing the door.

Monday, 8:28 PM, Avukena Palace, Floor 20

Reid walked out of Isavna's room. Directly to the right was a door left ajar. *This must be it.* He peered through the crack and saw Zandos's leather coat on a small table. It looked clean and shiny; a small bottle of leather conditioner and a used paper towel were next to it.

He pushed the door open slightly, inspecting the room. There was a full bookshelf, and empty bookstore bags around it. He saw the titles of some, about Hakon, English, magic, and technology. *I guess he's studying hard now.*

"Zandos?" he asked tentatively. Reid looked around cautiously. The room's scent was thick with leather, musk, and a faint body odor, like Nojuni Palace. "Zandos? You in here?" Reid continued in Hakon. Trying not to be too invasive, Reid didn't go too far in.

"Reid?" A voice said from the bedroom. This unit was structured differently, with a small living space and a separate bedroom. It looked opulent and perhaps a bit dated.

"Is that you?" the voice said in Hakon, with the notable accent. Reid sighed, knowing this was surely him.

"Yeah, it's me," Reid said.

"What are you doing here?" Zandos said with clear apprehension, stepping out of the room in different clothes, probably given to him by the AHL.

"I'm…" Reid said in Hakon, barely above a whisper. "I'm just here to see how you're doing. After Jace left, and stuff. And also to apologize for what I said yesterday." Zandos nodded. "It was wrong. And I… I saw your memories when we tethered." Zandos's expression was hard to read. "I get it now. I felt what you did." Silence hung in the air, in a way that made Reid slightly uncomfortable.

"I understand. I saw some of your memories, too." Zandos's speed and fluency of Hakon had greatly improved, even though it had not been that long.

"Which ones?" Reid asked, hoping it wasn't anything too embarrassing.

"I believe it was your parents," Zandos said thoughtfully. "They were telling you to focus on school and AHL. They did not want you to have friends here, because they said Avukena City people are too soft."

"Yeah," Reid said, messing with the lint in his pocket. "They still don't know. They really only just sent me here because the education is so good. They even gave me an English name to fit in with the others, since Avukena City has so much Earth influence. But they still don't *really* like this city, and especially not Nojuni. Honestly, I used to believe them."

"Hm, yes, it is cultural," Zandos said thoughtfully. "I read about it in one of my new books. Wars are fought over beliefs."

"Yeah, that's still true," Reid said, looking aside. He knew that his parents would be very unhappy if they knew he spoke to Zandos.

"I was just about to go walk on the beach," Zandos said, pointing to the sunset in the west facing the bay. "I've never seen one, and I didn't have the chance to do it yesterday."

"Oh," Reid said, still too nervous to look him in the eye. "That's… that's nice."

Zandos went to the entrance and put on his AHL-issued combat boots. "Are you coming?" he asked, tying the shoelaces.

"Yeah," Reid replied. They made their way downstairs and out of the palace. He didn't know what to talk about with Zandos. They stepped into an elevator.

"What did you do today?" Reid finally asked. "In the afternoon."

"I went to a bookstore with Levi," Zandos said, looking at the city outside the elevator as they descended. "He got me some books about magic and language that I read for most of the afternoon after he left."

"Oh, that's nice," Reid replied, shifting his position. "Have you read about flying at all?"

Zandos nodded, eager to share what he learned. "Yes, I have. I haven't learned much about magic, but flying was something I always wanted to learn."

"Well, flying feels really freeing," Reid replied. Zandos was looking at him intently. "Without practice, it can be pretty hard to start. But it's mostly about trusting yourself." The elevator finally stopped, letting out a gentle ping. They walked out, exiting and taking a path through the gardens to the beach.

"I can hear the ocean," Zandos said. "I never heard it until I left Nojuni. I saw maps today. Apparently there's an ocean past the mountains in Nojuni, but the crossing looks dangerous." They made their way to the beach. It was somewhat empty, save for a few bonfires down the coast. Zandos went up to the water and touched it. He felt the wet sand, watching it crumble between his fingers. He saw a seashell and put it in his pocket. Reid stood several paces back, watching him.

"Look!" Zandos exclaimed as a water felmine breached the water and began to fly with a person on its back. "Is that a person?"

"Yes," Reid replied, shouting a little over the sound of the ocean. "They're water people, the Batrans. They live just off the coast of Avukena. Sometimes you'll see some of them in town."

"I never knew people could live in the water," Zandos said, walking back to Reid, nearly tripping in the sand.

"You know," Reid said. "Maybe this is the perfect time for you to try to fly."

"Really?" Zandos said, still catching his breath.

"Yeah," Reid replied, his hands in his pockets. "There's barely any wind. And if you fall, well… can you swim?"

"Yes, of course," Zandos said, excited to try. "There are many snowmelt ponds in the summer. They're cold, but pleasant."

"Have you been able to invoke wings yet?" Reid asked, putting his messenger bag in the sand.

Zandos shook his head. "Almost. I can't tell if I'm crazy, but I can just feel that I almost have it."

"So you're going to try and push your shoulders down and then back, as if you're stretching." Reid demonstrated, and Zandos mimed the movement. "Then… how do I explain this… try to send a telepathic message to yourself to invoke them."

"Like a thought?" Zandos asked, practicing the movements.

"A bit more powerful than a thought," Reid replied. "Like a belief. Convince yourself that you have them."

"I feel something," Zandos narrowed his eyes and stood still, as if he had a spider on his nose.

"Good. Just let it happen."

"Nothing's happening," Zandos replied immediately. He bent his legs and spread out his arms. He looked as though he was trying to balance a tall stack of books on his head.

"Don't force it," Reid advised, amused at Zandos's stance. "It's fine if it doesn't happen today. You'll have a lot of time here in Avukena."

"Is it okay if I keep trying?" Zandos said.

Reid looked around at the setting sun. *I have to go soon.* He looked back at Zandos, awaiting his answer. *Eh, what the hell.* "Sure," he replied, surprised at his own willingness. "We've got time."

The two were on the beach for maybe another half hour, until the setting sun made it too dark to see.

"I'm content," Zandos said, smiling, as he relaxed his shoulders. "Thank you."

Reid nodded and smiled sincerely. They walked back, leaving only their footsteps to be washed away by the rising tide.

II

Tuesday, 6:37 AM, AHL Central, Subfloor 7 - Laboratory & Medical Ward

Brev observed the footage projected on the holotable. It looked like an infrared camera video, but was instead measuring magic the naked eye couldn't see. It was a looping video of Zandos tethering to a mouse, taken during a research session an hour ago.

"There," Brev said, pausing the footage on a moment when the magic threads shot out of his chest. "It spreads from him like a spiderweb. Mahifers only shoot from one point."

"Well, we can't tell HQ about this," Mr. Novet said quietly. He finished the last of his coffee. "They'll be forced to talk about it to Mother Everealm, and she will *not* be receptive to her grandson's magic, or even his existence. We've still got him registered as an ordinary Nojunian refugee."

"I heard about that," Mr. Makorod said. "About HQ having to doctor his eye color in pictures."

"Well, what did the tests say?" Renee said, turning to Brev. She described the results to the group.

"Well, to sum it up, this magic lines up with both Mahifer-type tethers and divine-type tethers. This is extremely anomalous." Mr. Novet rubbed his temples. A spark of worry crossed his eyes. He checked over his shoulder, then looked between the others.

"Summarize plainly. What does Division Three want us to do?" he asked.

Brev forced the technical jargon into plain Hakon. "Zandos and I figured out a way to prevent the outbursts, but the incident and his magic signature point to divine magic being involved. The data resembles that of a child who hasn't learned to use their magic yet. As for what needs to be done, we've cleared him to be in public with supervision. He has been using brown contact lenses to hide the red for now. Renee, make sure that you or the SO8 keep Zandos supervised when in public. We can't let Mother Everealm see him either, or she'll have him killed on the spot. Her omniscient powers have disappeared already, but we can't take chances."

"Why keep him close at all? If he's dangerous, we quarantine him in subfloor five and move on. Why assume all this risk?" Mr. Novet said gravely, his hands folded. "We should keep him as an asset and use him before we lose this chance."

Brev's jaw tightened a bit. "Mr. Novet, this is not about us in this situation. The data points to Zandos being a fledgling god. We need to figure out his paternity, too, if it's, well, human at all. His DNA is in near perfect condition considering the stress on his body, and even for a twenty-year-old—"

—"Then he could be a valuable tool for us," Mr. Novet said, as if it were obvious. Mr. Makorod looked at Renee nervously.

Brev sighed and continued. "The way we treat him now could lead to his stabilization or his failure. The tether he had with that sophomore official almost killed him, and I'd rather he be an ally than a threat and liability."

Renee leaned back in her chair. "From an operational standpoint, keeping him intact is more useful than wringing him dry."

Mr. Novet crossed his arms. "I suppose a short leash may be better than keeping him in a cell. I can accept that argument."

"The ledger won't look good for this," Mr. Makorod said, opening his wrist projection and looking at a financial spreadsheet. "Mostly in human resources, there's going to be a lot of overtime if the magic and science engineers work with Zandos every morning."

"I won't have the interns and hourly workers working on this," Brev clarified. "This is just me and Zandos, and we'll be monitoring him on a monthly basis."

"What happens when HQ starts to demand a return on investment?" Mr. Makorod asked.

"We will give them controlled reports if they demand an ROI. We'll frame it as progress. Renee, get him the soonest possible appointment for a wrist projection implant. I want to train this guy as a weapon," Mr. Novet said without hesitation.

Brev turned off the holotable. She looked with ill-disguised malice towards him. "He's a person. If you forget that, you won't get anything useful from him in the end."

Mr. Novet didn't look up. "Do what you must with him, then. But know that we're also expecting results."

Tuesday, 9:26 AM, Avukena Palace, Isavna's Unit

I heard my phone buzz as I finished revising my speech. It was a text from Toniska, my sister. *Hm. I didn't know she was in town today.* The journey, with Avukena's space pod technology, was only about twelve hours. She came to visit for about a week every few months, though, and between AHL work, it would be the first time I'd actually see her in about six months.

"Levi is here. He wanted to return something he thinks is yours before he goes back to Luzuma," Toniska said in the text. I replied and made my way down.

"What's up?" I asked him, quickly trying to fix my hair in a semi-presentable way. He passed me my Mahi blaster.

"Is this mine?" I asked, appalled that I would forget it.

"Yeah, I found it in the mess hall and decided to bring it to you before I forgot," he said. "I thought I recognized the AHL ID on the bottom of it, so I typed the numbers into the database, and sure enough, there you were."

I thanked him, and we settled into the firm couches.

"So, uh… how's Zandos doing?" he asked. "I ran into Reid in the morning when I was going to Salia and Taren's dorm." Salia and Taren were his two youngest siblings. "He said they hung out yesterday."

"Yeah, they went to the beach right outside of here. I didn't hear from Reid after that, but Zandos seemed pretty happy when I saw him in the corridor afterwards," I said. "Thanks for taking him to the bookstore, by the way."

I saw his younger siblings approach. He had a little sister who was Toniska's age, a tenth year, and an even younger brother, a seventh year. Salia walked over to Toniska and began chatting with her. Taren stayed at Levi's side, having no one to talk to. The three sure looked like siblings, sharing their straight black hair, bright yellow eyes, and fast accents.

"So how long are you guys going to be there?" I asked.

"Like two days. We're not even waiting on a plane, just waiting for our mom to be ready at the portal terminal since we're not too far," Levi explained. "She's gonna wanna know what I've been up to." He stretched. "Hear anything from Renee or Mr. Makorod about another mission?"

"No, why?" I asked.

"I dunno. Gives me something to do. I think they're fun, even though Keya gets super worried every time I go out for one." He tugged at the slightly worn black leather of his back scabbard, as if it was just itching to be used.

"Salia, are you looking forward to going home?" I asked her, but she was deep in conversation with Toniska. I repeated my question.

"Oh," she said, chewing gum loudly. I couldn't tell the expression on her eyebrows behind her thick black bangs. "Yeah. I mean, I was like, there last week, but I totally forgot my favorite sweater there, but I'm thinking I might leave it there, 'cause it's like, summer now," she said, waving her hands around. I nodded tentatively because she spoke maybe twice as fast as Levi. *I wonder if their native language is also as fast, or maybe even faster.* I saw Salia wearing flared leggings, a style I had only seen on Earth.

"Hey Levi, is there much Earth influence over in Luzuma?" I asked.

"Yeah," he replied. "I guess that's why my parents gave me a name from that one holy text on Earth. Many noble families give their children Earth names, mostly English ones. It's 'cause those noble families send their kids to Avukena City for school, and there's crazy Earth influence here, so they give us these names to fit in better." I nodded. *I was starting to wonder that too.*

He, Salia, and Taren stood still for a moment, no doubt receiving a telepathic message.

"Alright, well, bye, Toniska," Salia said, picking up her pink and black designer purse—*expensive taste.*

"See you later!" Levi added, picking up his AHL-branded duffel bag. They went to the east wing lobby, where there was a portal that led to the main terminal in the city.

"Do you have food?" Toniska asked, typing something on her phone.

"Um, no, I was kind of rushing down here," I said. "I could cook, but it might be a little while."

"Nah. I'll just go to Dewdrop for something. Can I have five fancuna?" she leaned back, her hair falling over the edge of the sofa.

"Sure, I guess. You can come in later, too, because your order for that cleanser you like finally came." She always brought an empty bottle of her cleanser on Earth to transfer the product into. I passed her a coin, and she went out without looking back.

When we were younger, I didn't really think about being an adult and being in a world where we didn't share a room or fight over who had to do the dishes. Mother Everealm took a lot of things from me, but she especially took away my family. Our relationship had stretched thin, and for a while, I just convinced myself that we're all too busy, and it's just a normal part of growing up.

A small part of me had a feeling that Toniska was wondering the same things that I was. Did our parents know something about Avukena? They gave us these strange names that make it seem like we'd fit in on paper, and allowed me to be taken here without a big spectacle. I wanted to know so badly if they planned for this, the same way Levi or Reid's parents gave them Earth names to fit into Avukena City. I wondered sometimes if Toniska knew the answer, if she asked them over dinner or something.

We used to be close enough that before I gave her the coin, perhaps she would have told me to sit down and told me outright how much our parents knew. But now we watched each other from a distance, wondering if we're still the same people from all those years ago. I was too nervous to ask. It seemed like a heavy topic to discuss among strangers.

I walked back up to my unit. *I wonder what I'm even going to do today.* Everyone was gone. I contemplated shopping in town or going on a day trip. I liked the restaurants in Huzoril, but those portals were shut down for now, and I didn't want to run into a protest. I thought about Esco.

I sat up in my bed. If someone were to go visit Jace, it shouldn't be me. *Maybe I should visit Zandos.* I put some water in my kettle and set it on the stove. I was trying to save up for an electric kettle, but my other expenses made it less of a priority.

I heard the water come to a rolling boil, and I took it off the stovetop right before it started whistling.

I put the hot cherry tea into an insulated cup and left my unit, locking the door behind me. I tasted it. It was tart, in a way that dried my mouth a little, but wasn't unpleasant.

I lingered outside of Zandos's door for a moment, trying to see if I heard anything coming from the inside. I felt my pendant get a little heavier, just enough for me to notice. Finally, I decided to knock.

"Hey, Zandos, are you here? It's Isavna," I said, embarrassed about my extremely broken Hakon. I decided to try to meet him in the middle regarding language. I heard no response. I knocked again. "Hello?"

Finally, some footsteps came. The door opened, and Zandos was there.

"Yes?" he replied, looking a little surprised to see me. It appeared he had gotten a haircut since we brought him here. And a bath.

"I, um, wanted to apologize about lying to you," I said quietly. "About how the AHL's been trying to kill your mom...."

His expression darkened, but only a little. "I understand all of that now." He said in Hakon, slower than I had heard him speak with other people. "No one truly wants to kill my mom but Mother Everealm. Or, well, no one that I have met so far."

He invited me in and we sat in the sitting room. He had a few books open, but he unfolded a paper map of Avukena State to show me. He pointed at Esco, right south of Avukena.

"He's not far," he said. His finger hovered over Vasana Square. "Have you ever been there?"

"No," I said. "I've only ever heard about it through Sirani."

"Jace told me little about Esco. He said that it was where he was from, and that was all I knew." He leaned back on the couch. "I was reading about it today, it used to be an industrial city, but Sjasa became more powerful only recently."

"Yeah, Esco's been on an economic decline in the past thirty years or so. I doubt your books will say much about this, but the Maligari dynasty has been running on fumes for a while."

I looked at an open book about law. There were annotations in Hakon and question marks. "Are you trying to become a lawyer now?" I asked, pointing to them.

"I'm trying to figure out what's allowed," he said. "Nojuni has no laws. Order is nice, but also confusing." He closed the map. "The person at the bookstore also gave me this," he held a copy of *Avukenan Etiquette for the Nojunian*. "It's in Nojunian so it's very nice."

I recognized the pamphlet; there was a stack of copies in the lobby of the east wing.

He set it down and rubbed his eyes. They were somewhat bloodshot and had pronounced dark circles that reminded me of a raccoon. "It doesn't feel like enough."

"I understand," I said. "When I first came here I didn't know how to use magic at all. I wish I could've spent my whole life preparing like you did, it would've made all of this so much less embarrassing. Avukena moves so fast."

Zandos nodded vigorously. "Yes. This place is so confusing. I thought everyone spoke English because I saw you speak English. And when I came here, people were scared of me. I feel like many people pretended to like me, until they realized they could use me. When I was at the AHL this morning it felt that way."

"That sounds about right," I said. "You get used to being used. My whole existence here is to serve Mother Everealm's pursuits. You're still a secret to her; she doesn't know you're related to Jovnelle."

"I don't like her," Zandos said darkly.

"You're not the only one," I said. "The AHL pretends to. That's why they've kept you around. They're keeping the secret."

Zandos traced his finger on the spine of the pamphlet and thought. "They are treating me like a tool and they seem slow to do things. You all have worked for seventy years and only stopped invasions with no counter-offensives?"

"The AHL's upper generals are afraid of doing any big moves because no one wants your mother dead. We're all stalling. That's why I'm here," I explained. "They expect an Earther with no emotional ties to suddenly be okay with everything and be loyal to Mother Everealm." I finished the last of my tea. I felt a short flicker of anger. "That's my whole assigned purpose. They say I'm the last one, that they can't replace me, but I know they'd find a way."

"I understand," Zandos said, sounding somewhat confused. "Am I only still here because I'm useful too?"

"Yeah," I said, not sugarcoating it. "No one really knows what to make of you, either. Not after your tether with Reid. You're not what the AHL expected." Zandos looked down. "It's a good thing," I added quickly.

"I don't want them to treat me like a strange animal," he said. "In the morning I went to the AHL. Brev and Renee did tests on me, but it will probably be more time until I can control my tether." He was far more fluent in Hakon than English, but he still spoke slowly enough that I could understand. He folded his hands together and pressed his head to his thumbs. When he lifted his head, his undereyes were darker, and his skin was paler. "Isavna, how did *you* arrive here? You are from a different planet entirely, no?"

"Mother Everealm and Marathene essentially abducted me. I went to bed one night then woke up in a space pod. I was horrified."

I saw surprise cross his eyes. He then nodded thoughtfully and squinted. "That sounds... terrifying. I came here by my own choice, but you were taken, and from a different planet. How did you deal with coming here?"

"I tried to survive. Like you. I forced myself to figure everything out and come to terms with the fact that no one here would mourn my death, at least in my first months here. This world treats me like I'm disposable."

"Why not allow yourself to die?" Zandos asked as if it were obvious. It felt strange, but I knew he had to have contemplated things like that in his past.

"I wasn't ready. It felt like the easy way out."

"And you didn't choose to go back to Earth?" I laughed dryly at the absurdity of the question.

"How? Literal *gods* took me. I have things on Earth that I loved, it was my whole world. I hated it here for the first year. I did want to go back, but I didn't have it in me to defy Mother Everealm. I don't know how I could possibly hide from her, even if I tried." A warm wind entered the room.

"It's too hot out. I've never been in a place like this." He said bitterly. "It feels like I'm on the sun." His comment made me wonder if there were places where the cold stung, even in the summer.

Tuesday, 11:03 AM, Dekerei Mountains, South Ridge

Reid landed under a large and ancient pine tree. The snow had gotten bad, causing them to need to land early. He was with his friend, Nagon, and Nagon's girlfriend, Madina.

"We've had a really mild spring and summer so far. I don't know why it's stormy all of a sudden," Nagon said, pulling a blue scarf over his nose. He was speaking Dekeren, the local language.

"Fine by me," Reid replied. He looked over to Nagon and Madina. He couldn't make out the faces of either of them since they both had their flight helmets on over their beanies. The mirrored visors reflected the snowstorm.

Madina shook her white wings to get rid of excess snow and retracted them, making them disappear. Reid didn't know Madina very well; Nagon had started dating her after Reid left.

"We're not far from Durio if you guys want to stop there," Nagon said, checking his wrist projection.

"You sure?" Reid asked. His voice was muffled under the scarf. "What are the chances of this storm letting up soon?"

"Let's see," Nagon replied, checking the weather on his wrist projection. "Looks like fifteen minutes. It'll be too dangerous to fly." Madina sat on the frozen dirt, her boots caked with dirty snow. Nagon sat down next to her. Reid used his wand to invoke a large heat orb. Nagon wiped the snow off his shoulders.

"So tell us about Avukena City," Nagon said. "While we wait."

"Well, everyone there drinks tons of tea," Reid began. "And the city's very clean. The dorms are really nice, you can tell it's the capital of the world."

"Have you ever been in the palace?" Madina asked. "I saw pictures of it online the other day, in an article about some local festival going on there soon."

"Yeah, I've been in there," he said, crossing his arms and retracting his own black wings. "I was there last night."

"Really? What were you doing?" Nagon asked. He held his hands over the heat orb. Reid thought about the best way to explain Zandos to them.

"So there's this guy who came to Avukena like a few days ago," he began, trying to find the right words. He knew they would flip out if he mentioned he was from Nojuni. *No one* was supposed to interact with Nojuni. The opinion of Nojuni in Dekerei was not a positive or open-minded one.

"And what about him?" Nagon asked.

"Well," Reid said. "There's a lot of stuff he doesn't know about magic, so I was spending time teaching him how to fly, and well, he's staying in the palace so that's where I saw him."

"Wait, doesn't Isavna live there?" Nagon asked.

"Who's Isavna?" Madina asked quietly, leaning into Nagon.

"The new Earther. You know the ones that Mother Everealm gets to try and dismantle the whole Nojuni empire?" Nagon said, hinting at the absurdity of the task. "Those ones. She says it's because they're more 'pure' and uncontaminated by Jovnelle's shadow magic and her agenda. She thinks Avukenans are too involved and biased."

"Yes, I remember the imports."

"Well, she's one of them."

"Oh, that's sad," Madina said, lowering her voice even further. "You know it's only a matter of time before there's a new one."

Reid listened to their conversation, acutely aware of their underlying feelings. They were critical of Mother Everealm's ideas, but not sympathetic to the Earthers. If anything, they probably viewed them as helpless, magicless, and pathetic. "Isavna's been working in the AHL for a while now and we've been doing a lot of missions. In fact, one of her missions was where she met Zandos."

"Who's that?" Nagon asked.

"The guy I mentioned earlier," Reid said, trying to recover his accidental slip. "That new guy in the palace who didn't know a lot about magic or anything."

"Where's he from?" Madina asked. "I can only think of a few places where people don't commonly use magic."

Reid hesitated as the storm howled around them. "Well, he's a new correspondent, from a place not far from Avukena City. We found the missing Escan prince there too, if you remember that whole deal—"

—"Yeah, but where was that?"

Reid hesitated. "Not far, really, just across the sea for us—"

—"Reid," Nagon interjected. Reid heard him scoff under his scarf.

He took a breath, knowing that this would be the hard part. He felt a bit of responsibility to change their minds or at least let them see the other side.

"He's from Nojuni," Reid finally said, his voice quiet. Reid could feel the shock from the two, even behind their heavy winter gear.

"Nojuni… Nojuni? You sure?" Nagon said in disbelief as he sat up straighter. "Are you serious? They actually let someone from *Nojuni* into the city, let alone the palace?"

"Oh, Reid, that isn't safe at all, you know what goes on in Nojuni," Madina said. "People from there are these horrible, corrupted monsters who go and destroy those other towns and… oh! Makes me shudder. He could be possessed or something."

"Listen," Reid began, holding up his hands placatingly. He winced internally at her lack of understanding of how possession actually worked. "We receive hundreds of refugees a month from Nojuni, and none of them have been an issue. Also, that's a myth; if he were possessed, we would know by now. This Zandos guy is really just another refugee."

"I'm all for being open minded, but Avukenans… they're really something else," Madina said. "To think how they let one of *them* be among you?"

"Who is he in Nojuni, like, is he important? Or a regular guy?" Nagon asked. "Just give it to me straight this time."

Reid tightened his lips under the tall collar of his coat.

He had been friends with Nagon since childhood, and he felt like, even with this, he could trust him, but Madina was another matter entirely. Information like this in the wrong ears could spiral into something horrid. Zandos's secret was a personal thing, but it was a political one too; something that was being kept away from even Mother Everealm. He could feel the confession to Nagon rising in him anyway, but he clamped his lips and lied.

"He's just an ordinary refugee. He's barely got a handle on magic and Hakon."

Nagon let out a big sigh, shifting his position.

Reid held his tongue about the tether incident, too. "He's got a little bit of inside knowledge, so we keep him around in the AHL. He's currently in our operative squad."

"Wait, wait," Nagon said, sounding alarmed. He stood up. "You mean this *Nojunian* is just prancing around the AHL like nobody's business, and he's your *coworker* too? *And* you hang out with him too?"

"He's under strict orders to always be accompanied when he's out of either the palace grounds or the AHL base. And, well... *hanging out* is kind of a strong word right now. More like... acquaintances? It's complicated," Reid said, looking outside anxiously.

"I don't know about this, Reid," Nagon said. As they stepped out from under the tree, the storm let up slightly.

"Yeah. I get it. Either way, my hands are tied. Everyone else around me is already friends with him to some level. He's been through all the protocols and stuff, and... it's not like I have too much of a problem with any of it, it's still kinda strange for me. I'm getting used to it." Reid used his wand to make the heat orb disappear. Nagon opened his wrist projection and showed them a picture of a cafe in Durio, which they were near. Everyone else nodded in agreement.

"And the Earther? Is she friends with him, too?" Madina asked the two telepathically. During the flight, talking out loud was impractical, so they resorted to telepathy instead.

"I'm not entirely sure, to be honest," Reid replied. *"She was the one who first found him, and she's been helping him get used to Avukena. It's interesting to see. She doesn't have the same thoughts about Nojuni that we do."*

They landed in Durio. Madina and Nagon took off their flight helmets since it was warmer there. The snow wasn't nearly as dense. They also pulled down their scarves, revealing their reddened noses. Reid kept his scarf and beanie on, hoping not to be recognized in Durio.

Levi looked at a wall covered in paintings of members of his family tree in one of the sitting rooms of his palace. Luzuma wasn't large by any means, nor was its palace. He let his eyes wander around the portraits of his family members.

For a moment, it seemed like the portraits were alive, all watching him, even though most of the relatives in them were long gone. Still, he felt this nagging sense of eyes on him. He picked at a section of the maroon and ochre-patterned wallpaper next to him; it was peeling off the wall. He looked over at the opposite wall, where the portrait of his first ancestor stood. *There it is, your first ancestor, who came here from Huzoril.* Levi sighed, left with nothing but a lingering memory of his distant father. He circled the room, digging for any memories of him in his mind.

All he could remember was his father's disappointment when Levi first learned to fly, at fifteen. It was a skill people learned young, and in situations like those, he often fell short. It reminded him of Zandos. *Maybe we are kinda alike. Weird parent relationships, magical ineptitude, not good enough, not smart enough…* he knew he had some value, but the portraits were a tangible symbol of valor. Something concrete and real.

Levi traced the empty spot on the wall. He pretended to be satisfied with progress, but he wanted *results*. Truthfully, he hadn't flown in years, not only for his disdain of magic, but because of his awful experience doing it. He paced back to his room. His mind was already racing with contingency routes and other plans. He looked at the portraits again as he left, colored white and golden in the mid-afternoon sun. If he was ever going to do it, he had to earn it.

I had been teaching Zandos how to cook for a while, and we were eating the blanched vegetables and white rice we made. Suddenly, I received a telepathic message from Renee, at the same time as my wrist projection pinged, about a mission briefing on Wednesday. I glanced at Zandos to see if he had received the message. He looked at me with confusion.

"Why is… Renee want to speak with us?" he asked. He rubbed his eyes, which were still bloodshot. "No, *does*, why does Renee want to speak with us?" he said in English.

"Looks like we're going on a mission." I listened to other telepathic messages to see if anyone else got it.

"Anyone else get a message from Renee?" Reid asked me and some others. Zandos and I replied.

"No, what do you mean?" Kairo asked. *Saku agreed.*

"Never mind," Reid said.

"I got it," Levi said.

"What?" Sirani asked. *Strange that she's not coming.*

"That's really weird. It's this mission meeting that Renee sent out. I wonder why only some of us got it," Levi messaged.

"Maybe they want a smaller team?" I added.

"I guess," Reid said. *"I don't know why there aren't actual task ops."*

"Stuff like this doesn't come around twice. It's our chance to get promoted," Levi replied.

"Whatever it is, I guess we'll find out Wednesday," Reid said. *"I'll be back by then."*

"Please tell me what it is when you find out," Sirani said. *"I'm curious now."*

I checked the time. It was only moments past noon.

"So, have you managed to fly yet?" I asked Zandos. I was impressed by his progress so far, so my impression of him wouldn't change regardless of his answer.

"I practice yesterday with Reid," he said in English. We had been working on English since we began eating.

"Practiced," I corrected him.

"Yes. I practiced yesterday with Reid. On the beach."

"Were you able to fly?"

"No," he replied, looking a little sad. "But… I feel so close, so close to do it."

"Doing it," I corrected.

"Yes," he said wistfully. "I want to do again."

"Do *it* again." We agreed to try again on the beach. As I left my unit, I saw Sirani in the elevator.

"Well, fancy meeting you here," I said, gently pushing her shoulder. She had on one of her big straw sun hats and a flowery dress. She had a picnic basket in one hand.

"Well, I was wondering if you wanted to go to the courtyard or the beach," she said, smiling.

"Actually, we were just going to the beach to help Zandos fly," I said. "This is perfect." We went outside and onto one of the more secluded beaches, one of the private ones for palace residents only. Sometimes, when I came here, I would run into Marathene or Mother Everealm.

"So what did Reid tell you to do?" I asked Zandos.

He explained his methods, like the shoulder motions, while Sirani and I nodded.

"Yeah, that makes sense," Sirani said, biting into a finger sandwich she made. "You should try to do it quickly. If you do it enough times in rapid succession, it should work."

I thought it was similar to a two-stroke gas engine, like a lawnmower or weedwhacker, where you had to pull it sharply a few times to get it to start. I didn't mention it since I was sure neither of them knew what that was.

Sirani and I sat at a picnic table while we coached him on his technique. We were out there for a few hours until the wind picked up.

"Are you sure you want to keep doing this?" Sirani asked, holding down her hat. "It's getting a little windy."

"Yes," Zandos said, a hardened look of determination. He didn't seem so tired anymore. Or, he just wasn't showing it.

He did it a few more times until suddenly and forcefully, two large, black, leathery dragon wings unfurled from his back. His eyes widened, and we began to cheer for him. Maybe it was painful, it often was for the first time, but he didn't seem to notice.

"You did it!" Sirani said, running to him. I left the sandwich I was eating on the table and ran up to him.

After some celebration, he looked at us.

"How do I use?" he asked.

"Think of them as another pair of arms. Try to stretch them and move them down forcefully," Sirani said. The wind was still strong. He faced the ocean and spread them. They were maybe fifteen feet on either side of him. They were black like his hair, but they were tipped with a bit of gray or silver, which was uncommon. I was astounded to see he had dragon wings; those were very rare. I had never seen them in person.

"It might help to get a running start," I said.

He walked back about twenty feet or so. "I feel much balance," he said.

"When you get up there, it's like swimming. The more streamlined you are the faster you'll go. Try to put your legs in front of you when you want to slow down," I explained.

He began to run, and he took off. He went maybe twenty feet high before the wind put him off balance and caused him to bank left and splash into the water sideways. I saw him swim to the surface and begin to cheer. Sirani was clapping. Zandos got out of the water, sopping wet. Sirani cast a small drying spell on him. After some more tries, he could fight the wind and return to the ground.

"How do you feel?" Sirani asked him.

"Strange, like try to fight in dream," he replied.

"Yeah, I get it," I answered. "When you first get wings they're pretty weak."

"I am happy can finally fly," he said, looking out to the ocean wistfully. The breeze carried the salty, slightly decaying smell of the ocean. "I not believe… could do it, ever do it."

"It only gets easier from here, the hard part's done. You'll get stronger and faster," I said.

He pointed to a group of water Batrans riding felmines, taking off into the city.

"One day I fly… like them."

12

I tapped my breakfast order into a screen at the end of the mess hall table, then waited around as the rest of my group did the same. Everyone around me had the same tan blazer as their uniform.

"This could be our big opportunity, guys," Levi said, running his thumb along the black leather of his back scabbard, like a sash over his shoulder. "Before we get promoted and stuff."

"You seem to care about it a lot," Reid said. "Why's that?"

"I've just got some people at home who should know I did this." The sounds of clanking forks, knives, and spoons reverberated through the echoey mess hall. "They won't believe me otherwise." I didn't quite understand what Levi meant, but he seemed serious about it.

"What did you get?" Reid asked inquisitively.

"Oh, just one of their small salads. I'm not even that hungry, honestly," I said, tapping my fingernails on the table. "I had brunch with Sirani earlier. She wanted *all* the meeting details, but we haven't even had it yet." The food came almost instantly. I poked around the lettuce of my salad. Reid dug in as soon as he saw it was acceptable to begin eating.

"Maybe Renee's forming some kind of all-star sophomore official group," Reid suggested.

"Doubt it," Levi said, finishing his soup. "I still think this is the test to see if we're worthy of being promoted."

"Gosh, how final," I said. "Makes me a little nervous."

"Looks like we only have five minutes until the meeting, guys," Reid pointed out. "Let's go, all-stars."

We went up the elevator, up into the first subfloor, and made our way down the bland office wing to the meeting room. I looked at the clock hologram above the door once we sat down. Renee was waiting for Mr. Makorod at the head of the table. She looked as anxious as any of us.

"Last-minute theories?" Reid asked me quietly. Renee shot him a look. Suddenly, Mr. Makorod finally entered, looking a bit inconvenienced. Renee opened a hologram with notes. Without a preamble, Mr. Makorod dove right into the meeting.

"We have a situation in Nojuni that will require a stealth mission to be carried out," he began, his voice grave. I didn't know what he was doing before, but he had beads of sweat covering his forehead. "Counterintel suggests that Cavaris is preparing for something big. The Mahifers attacking North Huzoril have been found to have high concentrations of magic, which we've observed are produced right before a large-scale siege." I heard Renee's finger tapping the hologram as she took notes. "Our mission is to infiltrate Nojuni Palace, with help from me and Renee, and capture Sir Horuo, the palace chamberlain." I felt an immediate unease. He was the most terrifying and hideous man I had ever seen, second only to Cavaris. The way Zandos acted around him made me confident of this.

"We believe he plays an instrumental role in reporting incidents and carrying out tasks given to him. Eliminating him would remove that barrier. Normally, Renee and I would be able to handle this independently, but we trust your level of experience and believe that this would be an invaluable opportunity for you all." He paused. I looked over at the others; they seemed to want to do it. "This is strictly voluntary. The risks are not insignificant for a mission of this scale, but Renee and I believe you are all ready for it. This mission will be carried out tomorrow. I will continue with further details once you confirm. If you decline, we have more operatives lined up to take your position." He said, looking at us to answer. We looked at each other again, and we all nodded.

"Well then, let's begin with the details." Renee said, opening a hologram to project onto the whiteboard. She swiped to an overhead map of Nojuni Palace.

"The palace is very old and considering the level of possession the civilians are under I have no doubt they will be easy to bypass, and of course, any advanced technology on their part would be out of the question," Mr. Makorod began.

"We found some low-traffic routes to avoid the possessed. They're generally slow to act, but you know the drill; non-lethal take-downs unless instructed otherwise," Renee said. "It would be helpful to memorize these, but considering this is tomorrow I am not concerned if you don't."

"Once inside the palace, we will need to be very quick in finding him. Except for approved instances, do not separate from the group," Mr. Makorod said.

"Excluding you, Zandos," Renee said. "At the moment, you would be our most effective distraction. For that reason, please wear the clothes you would wear in Nojuni, the rest of us will wear stealth gear and servants' cloaks."

Zandos nodded at her explanation.

"After we locate Sir Horuo, we will need to find him or move him someplace empty so we can capture him more easily," Mr. Makorod said.

"How do we handle him then?" Levi asked.

"With extreme caution," Renee advised. "He's dangerous, but he's not invincible. We've developed a special restraint system with a more potent version of the chemicals found in Mahi blasters. Your jobs are to subdue him, distract him—anything you need to do to buy me and Mr. Makorod about fifteen seconds, which should be enough to contain him. We need him alive."

"What's the exit plan?" Reid asked. "Once we have him, I imagine he won't be happy. I doubt we'll have much time."

"Precisely," Renee said, swiping to a new image on the hologram of the route to and from Nojuni. "The hover van will be waiting outside for us, the same one we will use to get in. We will place Sir Horuo in a small holding cell trailer attached to the back, with a camera we can monitor." *Seems like a solid plan.*

"And what if things go wrong? Do we have a plan?" Levi asked.

"Escape with our lives," Mr. Makorod said. "We and Counterintel have been working very hard to make sure this mission is a success." Despite his confidence, I felt uneasy.

We adjourned the meeting not long after and headed back to the palace. Zandos had to go since he was getting the procedure to get his wrist projection implanted, and Levi went with him. That left just Reid, Sirani, and me since she had joined us. We decided to stay in the AHL a little longer, practicing some combat with each other and target practicing our Mahi blasters with empty cartridges. They were shotguns with a foldable stock. They used different kinds of ammunition, like slugs, birdshots, and the kind we used on Mahis, filled with a liquid toxic only to them. A little bulky, but useful.

We did some training with wands for some time as well, though we knew we couldn't use them in Nojuni. They were sort of a crutch, used only for advanced spells or if someone had weak magic.

We spent some time cleaning and fine-tuning our weapons, the main four: our wands, which we had cleaned of any dust and scuffs, our combination knives, which went through routine sharpening in knife and short sword form; our Mahi blasters, which we loaded with filled cartridges, and our modified pistols.

I put my weapons in a shoulder bag. We were allowed to bring them into town and the palace, but we had to unload them and have the ammo in a separate container. It was mid-afternoon, so we decided to go into the palace.

Levi and Zandos were in the east wing's lobby. Levi was explaining to Zandos how to use his wrist projection. Zandos looked excited, if not a little bit freaked out. I saw the fresh scar on the inside of his wrist, where they usually were.

"Can I… telephone people?" Zandos asked as my group came to sit with them.

"Yeah, you can call people," Levi said.

"Does Jace have a wrist projection?" I asked.

"I think so," Zandos said. "If no, then he use telepathy."

"He does; he gave me his contact right before he left for Esco," Sirani said, pulling it up.

She stared at it for a few moments until she finally called him up. The hologram turned flat, and there was a loading icon on top of it depicting two geometric felmines chasing each other's tails in a circle. Suddenly, the two images expanded, and Jace was there. The hologram flickered before stabilizing. I saw a city in the background and assumed it was Esco. He looked to and from the call; it appeared like he was walking.

"Hi," Jace said, surprised to have received a call.

"Hey," Sirani said. We all gathered behind her to see. "Sorry for the cold call."

"That's okay," he said. His background stopped moving, and it looked like he was sitting down somewhere. Even though Esco was just down the coast, it seemed so far. "How's it going there? You guys look like you just came from the AHL."

I nodded. "Yeah. We've got a mission," I said. "Can't discuss too many details where we are right now."

"It has to do with Sir Horuo," Sirani whispered. "How is Esco?"

His expression fell a little bit. "It's been a lot of adjusting to the local culture. It's not like it was when I left. I haven't built up the courage to go to the palace yet... but I've been recognized."

"Well yeah," Sirani said, as if it were obvious. "The police are still looking for you. You're a *missing person,* Jace. I think our parents would like to see their estranged son."

"I dunno," he said, pursing his lips. "Public perception has changed. People don't forgive their policies as much. They think they should move on, or step down entirely, it seems. I nearly got jumped yesterday, but I didn't want to tell the police or anything. That old supermarket in the south end got abandoned and it's really dangerous now."

"Well then now's the best time to see your parents," Levi added. "Maybe they do actually wanna see you again. And, well... y'know, worse comes to worst, it'll be a distraction from whatever's going on and you can just come back here. Least you tried."

"I suppose you're right," Jace said, sighing. "It's gonna take some serious courage though. I've been staying in a hotel, but I don't want to use up all my money. I hope it goes over well with them."

We chatted for a few more minutes before we decided to leave, not before Zandos spoke.

"Jace, look!" he said, showing him the fresh scar on his wrist. "I gotten my wrist projection!"

"Wow, good for you," Jace said, slightly surprised.

"*And* I can fly now!"

"You've been doing a lot," Jace said quietly. It sounded almost as if he was sad he couldn't be there. "Use your powers for good. See you all… sometime." He hung up suddenly, not giving us enough time to respond. *What's his deal?*

We went into the formal dining hall. They were setting up some features in the main dining hall for the flower festival dinner service. The waitstaff was practicing, so they served the other palace residents and us.

The first course was a salad with sour preserved flower buds. Sort of like capers, but more mellow. Something about the salad, maybe it was the fake Avukena capers, reminded me of the sandwiches in the Italian deli down the street from my house on Earth. My heart hurt for a moment. *I have to go there when I visit.*

I observed the people at my table, finishing the small plates quickly. Reid seemed to be getting along well with Zandos. Or, at the very least, they didn't seem uncomfortable. *I miss Saku and Kairo.* They had been gone the longest, planning to return the following day.

The next course involved large soup pots in the middle of the tables, with each of us having our own serving plates. It was brothy and tasted like sweet ginger, with carrots and steak sliced so thin that it appeared like a flower on top of the large bowl.

"I think I'm starting to see a theme here," Reid said.

"Yes, many flower things. In Nojuni, there was flower, millin, and we boil it to make soup," Zandos explained. "It taste horrible. Like if you boil and eat old book."

By the main course, I felt satisfied, but I kept eating.

"Ugh-ack!" Sirani gagged, her face twisted in disgust.

"Are you okay?" I asked her.

"Yeah," she said, her face pale. "I just didn't realize this had alicorn meat in it. I *hate* alicorn meat. Unicorn meat I can stand—but *alicorn*… is disgusting," she said. Alicorns were winged unicorns. They were distinctly leaner and had darker meat. Both animals were commonly eaten in Avukena.

When we were done, a server brought us a hologram with feedback questions on the dinner service and the food. Upon completing it, we separated for the evening. Zandos and I went upstairs into our rooms while the others went to the dorms.

I spent the rest of my evening preparing my food and clothes for the morning. I decided to take a bath, too.

I let my mind wander as I sat in the warm and bubbly water. *This feels useless when I know I will get sweaty and gross tomorrow.* I sank my back into the water and blew bubbles with my nose. *I wonder how Jace feels about not being there for Zandos anymore. I mean, he flew, he got a wrist projection; all these milestones.* I rinsed my hair with the handheld showerhead. I levitated some water in a sphere that was suspended above the bathtub. *At least I can still do this.* I lathered some soap between my hands and rubbed it on a small rag I used to wash my body. *I guess it's kind of impossible for Reid and Zandos to become 'besties' or anything.* I thought. *It would make it weird with Jace when or if he comes back.*

I drained the tub and rinsed my body off with the showerhead. I dried myself with a towel and then put on my robe since I forgot to pick out my clothes for the shower.

I began brushing my short damp hair after changing. It was no longer than my chin, so brushing was easy. *I wonder if Jace will come back at all.* I thought. I didn't even really believe the AHL would accept Jace back, not after how he was. I looked at my bed behind me as I sat at my vanity, pushed against the wall. I climbed into it. I put a towel over my pillows since I didn't care to dry my hair. I didn't have a care for a lot of things right then. Maybe I just felt lazy.

"Are you still awake?" I heard telepathically from Reid. It caught me by surprise; it was about ten by then. I blinked, pulling up my blanket. I had taken off my glasses, so my vision was blurry.

"Yeah, I'm awake," I replied. *"Did something happen?"*

"Nothing," he messaged. *"You just seemed a bit off today during the dinner service. Usually you have a lot more to say."*

"I'm fine. I was just kind of watching everyone, and you seemed a little caught up with your new friend," I said.

"Sure," he messaged. *"Still wouldn't call it that. Are you sure you're alright, though? You didn't even seem to talk with Sirani much."*

"I'm fine," I said. *"Really. I am. Something happen?"*

"Something is making me feel a little weird about Jace. His abrupt hangup and everything."

I pushed my head on the pillows. My hair felt cold and wet against the back of my neck.

"Yeah. If talking to his parents doesn't work and he comes back I don't know what he's going to do. I mean, Zandos seems to be caught up with other things, and I don't see what Sirani's going to think. He'd probably have to get a regular job; he can't

work in the AHL, and he probably won't be able to freeload with Zandos for very long. I don't know him super well, but I can sense he's had a change of heart."

"He means a lot to Sirani and Zandos. And I know the AHL isn't one for second chances." Reid replied.

I yawned and turned in my bed. *"What's Levi's deal, too? Have you noticed how twitchy he gets about our missions and stuff?"*

"Yeah, like he's trying to prove something to someone."

"Or maybe to himself. I don't know," I said. *"Well, see you later."* I could sense him hanging on the line for just a little longer, then he left without saying anything else.

I3

Thursday, 4:16 AM, AHL Central, Subfloor 1 - Command Center & Office Wing

The AHL was dead silent this time of day. Some of the corridors' lights were still turned off. The elevators were unusually quiet. As usual, we landed on the first floor beside other portals.

Zandos and I went straight to the conference room from the day before. Renee looked at us intensely as if waiting for us to do something. That, or she was stressed. I glanced at the clock. It was about a quarter past.

After stopping for extra weapons, we got Sir Horuo's cell, got in the van, and left for Nojuni. The ride was silent, except for Reid and me chatting telepathically. We parked somewhere inconspicuous, where there weren't any possessed sentries. Considering our failure last time, we assumed they'd be on high alert. We took to a known broken window on the palace's west wing, the same area that Sir Horuo's quarters were supposedly in.

We entered slowly, and I scrunched up my nose. The horrible, familiar scent was back. I looked over to Zandos, and he seemed mostly unbothered.

"It's real bad, isn't it," Reid said, quietly letting out a wry laugh. "How can anything survive in this place? Besides mold?"

I shook my head, widening my eyes. We settled into a corner by a fallen picture frame.

"This is where we will meet. If you ever get lost, return here. Avoid using telepathy or magic," Renee explained. We put on our cloaks, which had scent-masking technology that had been recently developed. I put my hood back on, and we went to Sir Horuo's quarters. My necklace became so heavy it almost bothered me, though I didn't know why. *Never mind that.*

I noticed how many more servants there were walking around the palace. The palace smelled more foul, and I heard groaning and whining from possessed servants that gave me goosebumps on my neck. When I came to Nojuni, I rarely looked at their faces, but the noises they made sounded so human it scared me more than any Mahi ever could.

"Where did all these people come from?" Reid asked quietly. "I know they come from cities, but there's so many here right now."

"Dunno," Levi replied in a whisper.

"These are likely the people from Huzoril that the Mahifers brought," Mr. Makorod said. "Mahis will possess them and bring them back to Nojuni Palace. Sir Horuo dresses them all in cloaks using magic." I observed Zandos, who was in his regular clothes. His head was on a swivel; he looked everywhere for the sentries and servants wandering.

The thought of the people roaming this palace as ordinary citizens from Huzoril made my stomach twist in a way I hadn't quite felt before. In my head, I had always compartmentalized possessed people as something uncanny, as in not quite human. But the fact that they were from a state so close to Avukena made me realize that perhaps I encountered these same people in one of my weekend outings in their capital. Or maybe I saw them at a sports match between my school and theirs.

Mr. Makorod held up his hand, signaling us to stop. Renee turned around.

"There are some guards up ahead that might be hostile. Remember, don't engage, and only go for non-lethal take-downs if we say so."

"Unless, of course, your life is in danger," Mr. Makorod said. "In that case, do what you need to do."

Levi, Reid, and I nodded. I tapped Reid's hand and pointed at an especially beautiful stained-glass window. There was a lot to love about the palace, if one could ignore… everything else about it.

Zandos was ahead of us a few paces. The guards didn't seem to mind him. The door to Sir Horuo's chamber was only slightly beyond where we were.

The guards didn't seem to mind us, either. They were all crowded around a corner of the room like zombies. The door was slightly ajar. Zandos knocked quietly while the rest of us waited in the corridor. We could hear them quietly conversing until Sir Horuo exited the room. We knew we had to get the other guards to go away or eliminate them somehow.

Renee gestured for us to move in. We proceeded to the small lobby before Sir Horuo's chamber door. Four, maybe five guards stood huddled in a corner, their movements jerky and disjointed. They began to notice us and became hostile. Mr. Makorod signaled with his hand. I understood the task; we needed to take them out quietly. The air felt suffocating, made even worse by the gurgles of the guards.

Mr. Makorod instructed us to choke the guards from behind and use our combination knives if the Mahifer tried to escape the body. I hastily put on my gloves, grabbed the shortest guard, and wrapped my fingers around their neck. I didn't even want to look at their face. I tightened my grip, but I felt the guard's fingers clawing at my hands. They squirmed, weakly but aggressively, until they tired out and went limp. It made me feel uneasy, but I knew dying was more merciful than anything else that could happen now; the person was already beyond saving.

"Well, I hate to separate like this, but you two, go dispose of the bodies. Sir Horuo can easily detect them and will come out if we don't dispose of them first. See if you can find an open window," Renee tossed Reid an instrument. "And take DNA samples so we can see if they match missing person reports." Levi and Reid nodded. I wish we could have saved them, but when people were possessed for longer than two days, it was impossible.

The four guards were extremely emaciated, making them light. I assisted them in loading the possessed people into an old curtain we fashioned into a stretcher. They disappeared into the corridor with the four bodies. I could see the impression of Levi's broadsword under the cloak. I glanced at the feet of one of the guards. I felt the hairs on the back of my neck stand up when I realized they were wearing blue high-top sneakers that were popular with the Academy students in my grade. *They really are just like me.*

I turned my attention to Renee and Mr. Makorod, who were waiting for the right moment to strike from the corridor. Renee told me to fall to attract Sir Horuo.

I entered the small lobby where the guards were before and fell, obscuring my face from his view. I was pretending to be the dead guards we killed the moment prior.

I heard footsteps approach me. For a moment, I doubted whether it was right for me to put my trust in Renee and Mr. Makorod. The footsteps intensified and got dangerously close. I had to try to calm myself somehow. I clenched my fists, feeling the moisture of my clammy hands under my gloves. As he approached me, I held my breath, trying not to move.

Finally, I heard a faint beeping followed by a hiss. A bit of mist settled to the ground, but I didn't turn to look. It smelled cold, acidic, and metallic, like the lab.

"You can stand now," Renee said. I rolled over on the ground to look, and then I got up.

Sir Horuo was cast in a pile on the ground. *Thank goodness it worked.* I stood up slowly, unsure of what to do. My pendant suddenly became lighter. I thought about Sirani's words from our sleepover. *Maybe this is some kind of magical item.*

Zandos, Renee, and Mr. Makorod were tying him up in a restraint position that looked painful. Mr. Makorod had severed the long part of his cloak that dragged on the ground. His upper body was folded over his legs in the fetal position, and his arms were handcuffed under the inner part of his knees. He wasn't dead or anything, not even unconscious. His eyes were fully open and blinking, and he was still breathing. I could even see his horrifying white irises. *I thought he would be a lot angrier. Maybe he is, and he just can't do anything about it.*

Renee and Mr. Makorod carried Sir Horuo in a curtain stretcher, much like the one Levi and Reid used. They also covered him with an additional curtain to hide his body. Zandos was behind us, ensuring we were safe from other servants. We made our way down the stairs.

"Now to find Reid and Levi," Renee said. "They should be at the meeting spot if all went well." We descended the staircase. I was still scared, but I felt a sense of success. This mission had gone off without a hitch and relatively quickly compared to other missions. *I can't wait to go home.* I felt a little bit of happiness and hope as I went down the stairs. I lifted my hood as we reached the first floor.

I suppressed a scream as my hands went cold. There were dead guard bodies shredded to pieces. Over in an alcove of the room, Levi, or at least what I thought was him, was slumped over Reid. *Why is he lying down on the ground?* I moved a little quicker to catch up. Zandos did, too.

"What's going on?" The words tumbled out of my mouth louder than I would have wanted to. Every possibility I thought of was worse than the last. I knelt next to the two bodies. I began to smell blood. I turned over one of the individuals.

It was Levi. His face was pale and frozen in a mask of anguish, and had not yet gone cold. His cloak was stained with blood. It was still fresh.

I was so shaken I forgot to breathe. Zandos ran up to me, while Renee and Mr. Makorod, obviously stressed, had to move Sir Horuo to the cell; he could regain control of his body at any moment.

"So?" I asked Zandos, who had his fingers on the pulse of Reid.

"Reid is alive. But Levi… he is not," he stammered, sounding just as shocked as I was. *How could this happen?* "We should bring Reid to a safe place. He is alive, but we do not know how bad he is hurt." I pursed my lips. I looked over to Levi's pale hand. He was still gripping his broadsword.

I turned my attention to Reid. He was out cold but alive. *I can't let it end like this.* We wrapped his wounds to stop the bleeding with our emergency first aid kits. They weren't deep like Levi's, but there were many. I worried about any internal hemorrhaging, but inspecting for that would have to wait. Zandos and I carefully carried Reid over to the van first, and Levi second. I took pictures of the scene to report to the AHL, trying to hold back tears once the realization of the situation dawned upon me.

As I took pictures, I lingered near the spot where we found them a little longer than I should have. I kept hearing the distant groans and gurgles of the possessed servants, but that hardly mattered now. No thoughts passed through my mind. I forgot to blink until I felt my vision blur with tears.

"Did you take pictures?" Renee asked in a gentler voice than I had ever heard her speak. I didn't even notice her arrival. I nodded, keeping my eyes on the small alcove with blood smeared on the dusty ground.

Renee pressed a button inside the van to open a compartment below the bottom frame, where we often stored weapons.

Mr. Makarod laid Levi's body on the bottom of the compartment. I took a shaky breath and stepped into the van. I tightened my lips and swallowed hard, trying to be okay with putting Levi in the compartment below the van. It just felt so wrong to think that he had now become an object.

We reclined Reid's seat as far as it could go as we put him there. Renee took off Reid's bandages to get a better look at his wounds.

She fumbled with the van's first aid kits, then sanitized the wounds and replaced some of the provisional wrappings of the deeper cuts with the proper dressings. Zandos sat in the front seat while Mr. Makorod drove. He stayed silent.

I opened my wrist projection to make some unfortunate calls. I needed to contact Levi's family and his girlfriend, Keya. I first dialed Salia, his sister.

"Hey, Isavna," she said. "What's up?" she noticed my expression and reddened eyes. "Oh my gosh, are you okay?"

"Get Taren here, and your parents if they're there."

"Oh, I'm in the dorms but—"

—"Okay," I said, preparing to drop the news. "Your brother… he's passed. Please get your parents to join you." I waited about twenty minutes as she took a portal home. Levi's mother picked up the wrist projection hologram from Salia, her brows knitted in worry.

"What? What's wrong?" she asked.

I tensed my throat, trying to maintain composure. "We went on a mission…." I blinked away tears. "He's gone. Levi just died."

Thursday, 8:22 AM, AHL Central, Subfloor 7 - Laboratory & Medical Ward

I heard faint, consistent beeping. I started to wonder if it was only in my head.

"We need a transfer to the Crystal Grove Hospital," I heard one of the medical workers say to Renee. Her voice was almost as sterile and bland as the environment around us. I hated hospitals. Nothing good ever happened in one. Mr. Makorod was explaining to Keya and Sirani what had happened. Keya had tears in her eyes, her hands cupped over her mouth. I turned my attention back to the medic. "They're the only ones around here who aren't bogged down with refugees and disaster relief efforts." She left, handing Renee a report. While Reid's injuries were certainly bad, there was nothing the medical ward hadn't encountered before. The ward was loaded with more urgent patients who were also fugitives or Nojunian refugees, so they decided to transfer him. His injuries, from what I could overhear, were mostly blood loss, and there wasn't much internal hemorrhaging going on.

The thought of Reid dying made my stomach churn in a way I hadn't felt before. I knew a lot of death was going to happen around me—it already had, but this felt a little different. I trusted the medics' judgment on the situation. Plus, even if I was wrong, what could I have done?

Renee stood up silently. I picked up my bag of personal items and followed her, not thinking about where she was going. A sense of emptiness settled in the pit of my stomach.

Renee and I reached the garage, and she sat in a small hovercar. It looked like it was her own; there were a few scuffs that the AHL repair people would fix, had it been part of the fleet. Additionally, the car was muted blue, a color that the AHL would never pick. I sat in the passenger seat, and she didn't seem to mind. She started the car while waiting for something to happen. Songs and ads played on the radio.

I saw medics exit the elevator, wheeling a stretcher with someone covered in a white sheet. There was an IV bag hooked up to him. *Must be Reid.* They loaded him into an ambulance and left. Renee shifted her engine to drive, preparing to follow the vehicle.

"Set destination to Crystal Grove Hospital," Renee ordered. The dashboard hologram loaded a map.

"*Veshta* district," I muttered, noting the unfamiliar name. I looked at the map. It appeared to be on the south side of town. To me, it looked like the middle of nowhere. Anything farther south or east than the city center was generally considered seedy.

"Yes, it's a bit of a drive, considering we're coming in from the north." Renee said.

"Why not take the portals?" I asked.

"My off-duty clothes and my personal items are in here. I don't want to startle people so far from the base by showing up in military clothes. And when Reid recovers, I don't know how well he'll be able to walk, making it difficult to travel back through the portal terminal." I looked outside and let my vision blur.

I felt like I had too many things to think about. Even though I had known Reid for as long as I'd known my home here, the thought of him or others so close to me dying used to feel so remote that it didn't even make me feel anything. But now, it was overbearing. I also had a feeling that Renee knew precisely what I was going through.

We merged onto a highway. Since most vehicles were hover cars, it didn't matter what material the roads were made of as long as they had the proper markings. On this highway, it was smooth white metal. Or at least, that's what it looked like.

I saw Sjasa's cityscape float by as we drove. Morning steam rose off the tops of buildings as the sun slowly warmed them. There was a lot of reconstruction, more than Avukena had at the moment. Sjasa was flatter than Avukena City, with fewer skyscrapers. To my right were barges moored in the distant coastline. There were also fewer cars on the road than you'd encounter in a normal city of Avukena City's size, because so many people flew or used the portals.

"Have you ever been to Crystal Grove Hospital before?" I asked Renee.

She pursed her lips. "A few times. Veshta is a rich elderly community, so the hospital is nice and well-equipped. A number of years ago we tried to send some badly injured task ops there, but they declined, instead sending them to a public hospital that didn't have enough trauma equipment. That was before most of the Mahi problems occurred, and back when hospitals could be picky. Far before you were here."

"So, was it really worse when there was a bump in Mahi activity a few years ago?" I asked, furrowing my brows. "Mother Everealm and Marathene made it seem like the end of the world. Like Avukena City was on fire or something."

"You've been here for… what, three years? Four years ago an attack completely wiped out some villages north of Sjasa, which sent widespread panic in the city. Mother Everealm exaggerated it to generate public support for the AHL. And, well, I wasn't the one who told you, but some people even believe that Mother Everealm knew the attacks were coming and allowed them to happen so we could have an incident to scapegoat. And the attack wasn't quite that bad by today's standards, but for many younger people, it was the worst they had seen." I leaned back in my chair. By now, we were in a tunnel, crossing over to Avukena City.

"Y'know, I don't know if it's crass for me to say," I began. The tunnel's white lights poured into the car's slightly dusty dashboard in a strobe pattern. "But I feel like Mother Everealm and Marathene are holding something back from me. Like, I know something bad is going to happen if I don't complete my mission, but it's not like I fully believe her plan might be the best idea."

"You wouldn't be wrong in that assumption," Renee said quietly. "Mother Everealm is known for being cryptic, if not just strange."

"What do you mean, strange?" I asked.

Her eyes remained steady on the back of the ambulance. "Well, her plans are a bit faulty at best," she said, hesitating. "And there's been a lack of results."

"Like nothing comes from her plans?" I ventured, noting her distaste. "That sounds awfully vague."

"Well, Isavna," Renee surrendered. She exhaled. "Frankly, this whole thing of bringing Earthers over here from Earth to defeat Cavaris is ridiculous in basically every aspect. The logistics, the cost, the time—it's incredibly half-baked. No one knows why Mother Everealm does this, really. She says it's because Earthers aren't as influenced by 'Jovnelle's Agenda.'"

"Honestly, I feel less sympathetic to Mother Everealm than to Jovnelle."

"Exactly. That's exactly my point. The Earther before you was too. Everyone thinks the real reason might be some kind of grudge Mother Everealm holds against Jovnelle. Something that's preventing her from getting out there and killing her and Cavaris herself."

"What do you think it is?"

"Oh, I don't know. All I know is that we don't need to keep bringing Earthers to do it. And none of this is your fault, Isavna. But you probably know better than everyone that this isn't exactly an easy task for an Earther to do." I was silent. The only sound was cars passing. I looked straight ahead. "Not to say you're useless, you've made a tremendous effort and helped us as much as you could," she said. "But I know that just sounds like a platitude."

"I mean, yeah," I said, crossing my legs. "It's kind of hard not to feel pointless when the world makes sure you know how replaceable you are. I'm quite literally just another 'cog in the machine.'" We exited the tunnel, the brightness making me squint. I glanced at the map. *Great. Another hour to go with traffic.*

"I'm not going to tell you that you're wrong," Renee said. "Everything is replaceable. Mother Everealm's universe has a really weird way of making things happen."

"Do you think we succeeded today?" I asked Renee. "On our mission."

"That's not for me to decide," She said, gripping the wheel. "We completed it. Sir Horuo is in subfloor five right now, awaiting interrogation, imprisonment, or whatever they plan to do with him—I don't know. Our duties ended once we turned him in."

I stared at the ambulance in front of us. I didn't have any way of knowing if Reid was alive or dead. *Maybe both. Like Schrodinger's cat.* I believed that Levi was alive for a few moments until he wasn't. It made peace feel like an illusion.

"Isavna, does knowledge comfort you?" Renee asked me.

I thought about it. "Oh, I don't really know," I replied. "Sometimes it feels like a big burden, other times it feels calming."

"In the AHL line of work, especially in my position, knowledge is a powerful tool. It has advantages that even the most skilled of task ops can't replicate. However, it can also drag you behind. I'm sure you've heard about Reban by now," she said quietly, her voice softening uncharacteristically. I looked at her. She stared straight ahead with glassy, orange eyes. Her nose, with a soft peak in the middle, was outlined with sunlight.

"Yes, I have," I said quietly. I thought about the story that Reid and Sirani had told me about. Reban was Renee's husband, the double agent.

"Well, he's in subfloor five at the moment. I don't know what they're doing to him. I don't know if he is alive or dead. Much like I don't know what's going on with Sir Horuo or Reid." She loosened her grip on the wheel. "It's the price we pay for the work we do."

"How do you deal with it?" I asked quietly. "Not knowing what's going on with Reban?"

"I just let go. I've given it a lot of time, but I still don't know if I can love a bad person, or someone who's done bad things, so I just… I just don't think about it. I just focus on what I can control. The missions, my life, my health… even the SO8, by extent." I heard her exhale heavily. "You learn to live with the questions."

We drove in silence for a while longer. I questioned my ability, as an Earther, to fulfill my mission. I questioned Renee a little bit, and whether she was right. I at least found a shred of peace knowing that she did care about us, because otherwise she wouldn't have driven all this way just for one guy and would have just delegated the task. One thing was for sure, though. If I wanted anything to change in my life, I had to stop letting things just happen around me.

"Destination is on your right," the car said. We got out of the vehicle and proceeded. I exhaled, as if I could breathe out my worries.

14

Renee and I stopped in the bathrooms to change into our off-duty clothes, and then we continued into the hospital lobby. It was far smaller than the one in the city center. We were here on personal business, so we didn't announce ourselves.

We waited in silence for what felt like forever. Renee was staring straight ahead, like a cat looking out the window. I couldn't have tried to guess what was going through her head.

Finally, a doctor came out of the hallway. He was talking to a nurse in Hakon. Most of the billboards and signage in this part of town were in Hakon. The doctor came a few paces our way and gestured for us to come to him. He began talking. Though he spoke fast, I gathered most of it, words like "alive," "Something happening," and "seven." Renee nodded sharply.

"Reid's fine for now. They want to keep him until Seventh Day, but he thinks one of us should stay in town in case his condition worsens," Renee translated for me telepathically. The doctor handed us a paper. Half of it was in Hakon, and the other was in English.

"I understand that… west side of Avukena is speak a lot of English," he said.

"Thank you for being considerate," I said slowly.

"I will stay," she told me telepathically. She instructed me to go home. I went to the nearest portal stop, a bit of a flight from the hospital. I navigated my way through the system.

"How's Reid doing?" I asked her once I was home.

"As fine as he could be," she replied. *"I've heard nothing yet. I'm going to stay in a hotel here today."* I opened my wrist projection to see how far the Veshta district was and converted it to miles. I had barely begun to understand kilometers, so the Avukenan measurement system was far beyond me. *Wow, it's nineteen miles out.* Avukena's roads between the city center and the Veshta district seemed especially rough after I looked at them on a map. The outline of the streets looked sort of like spiderwebs.

I tried sending Reid a few telepathic messages in case he was lucid. Something stupidly innate in me thought this was a good idea or would work at all. I heard no response, but I lingered on the line. I sat slumped on my bed, staring out the window. I felt anxious, mulling over the few moments where I was utterly confident that Levi was alive right before I discovered his body. *I need to talk to someone smarter than me. I can't sit here rotting forever.*

I went to Mother Everealm's throne room. I didn't fully expect her to be there; it was most often Marathene doing paperwork or enjoying the view. She did most of the work these days; Mother Everealm and her omnipotent abilities have been severely diminished due to several hundred years of tethers and other taxing uses of magic. After all, magic is finite on Avukena.

I walked into the hall, a bit larger than my junior high's gym. It faced the ocean; I could hear the rumbling.

"Hello?" I called out. "Is someone here?"

"Yes?" I heard in an enchanting voice. I saw Mother Everealm come out from behind her throne, where she had a table and often did work while enjoying the view. She had a light pink cloak over a white dress that trailed behind her. She was about eight feet tall, and her crown probably made her even taller. She had shiny hair the color of white-blue clouds. "Do you need something, Isavna?" she smiled, the corners of her mouth folding into storied wrinkles.

"Well, I don't know if you know this yet, but we went on a mission to capture Sir Horuo," I said.

"Did the mission succeed?" she asked, inviting me to the small sitting area behind her throne. The way she said it made me think she knew. The chairs were tall; I had to climb to get on, and even so, my feet dangled for about two feet or so. They were clearly made for Mother Everealm and Marathene's height.

"Yes," I said, hesitating. "But something else happened too." Her expression darkened a bit. "We lost someone."

"Was it someone important?" she asked, sipping from a teacup, though her eyes remained on me. There were purple curls of steam rising.

"Important to us," I said. "He was a sophomore official in the AHL like me, and part of my operative squad. I… I don't really know how it even happened." Her expression shifted from worry to… indifference, almost imperceptibly. "We captured Sir Horuo, and when we approached the meeting spot, me and Zandos…" I said, trying to keep my tone steady. "We found Reid and Levi just lying there." My mind returned to the image.

I didn't want to remember it. "Zandos checked their pulses. Reid's in the Crystal Grove Hospital, on the other side of town, and Levi's dead." My face felt hot, and my vision was getting blurry. My eyes stung a bit, even if it was just from eyeliner seeping into them.

Mother Everealm's ethereal presence seemed to fill the room. She set down the teacup. "I understand. What troubles you most? Is it the uncertainty, the loss of Levi, or Reid's condition?"

"I think it's all of it," I said, wiping away tears with one of the fancy paper napkins on her table. "I wish there was something I could have done. I… I just don't know, I don't understand, why it had to be this way instead of any other way. They tell me Reid's fine, but I thought Levi was fine before when he really wasn't."

"It's natural to feel that way," she assured me. "Loss is a part in the natural cycle of anything existing. Nothing can be permanent, and while it's unfortunate to have it happen to those we hold dear, it is inevitable that we will lose important things. One day, you will lose what feels like everything. I don't know if that has already happened or is yet to come, but the sun will always rise tomorrow. Those who bear witness to it will change, but the sun will continue to rise." She shifted position, her crown sparking in the light pouring in from the window. "You may carry that truth lightly some days, and heavy during other days."

"Yeah," I replied quietly, unable to say much else. I decided that she must be right. I noticed an engraved plaque on the back of her throne, which was facing the door. *The sun shines brightest in its latest hours.* I likened it to the light spreading around the throne room, stretched thin, as if trying to last as long as possible. Marathene arrived with some paperwork, coming to greet me before sitting.

Mother Everealm gestured at Marathene, just as I was about to take my leave. A moment passed. Marathene glanced at the table, looking morose.

Mother Everealm spoke. "I heard of the Mahifer attack in the northwest district. Chilling, isn't it? My, how far the plague has spread." She paused. The sudden shift in mood put me on edge. She paused, looking at me. "I believe I sense unease from you."

"Um… yes," I replied apprehensively. I suddenly remembered another detail. *Might as well ask now, to change the topic.* "Oh, by the way, I meant to ask you something about my magic, actually."

"And what's that?"

"Well, how do I explain this… it's sort of failing now. I get tired when I try to cast light orbs or heat orbs. I can't levitate heavy objects anymore either. I'm worried that at some point I won't be able to fly or use telepathy," I said. "By any chance, do you know why this is happening, or… um, how to fix it?" I had a thought. "Like something to do with the tether magic?"

"No, it's not the tether magic," she said, looking aside. I tilted my head slightly, not enough for her to notice. *Is she… lying to me?* "And as for solutions… let's see… I don't believe there's anything immediate—not quite." She looked out the window. "I suppose that fixing your magic can be arranged, after you complete your mission." She let her words hang in the air for a moment, like the lingering steam over her teacup. She folded her hands on her lap. Something about this felt very off-putting. "And Isavna, I hope you understand that you still must eliminate Jovnelle."

"I thought my mission was to kill Cavaris. He is the root of this whole issue, is he not?" I said, my tone firm yet placating. "Isn't she your daughter?"

"Oh, I loved her as much as I could," she said, her voice dripping with contempt. My necklace felt heavy under my collar, like it was listening. "No amount of love can change who she is. I gave her clear instructions so she would not spread shadows everywhere, yet here we are." She looked away, as if this wasn't all her own fault. Marathene's eyes were glazed over. She looked like she wanted to disappear.

"What if she felt wronged, or vulnerable, and… maybe that's why she made the pact with Cavaris?"

I saw her jaw tighten, and then she turned her head slowly. Her eyes locked on me like a predator. "I will not let my world be contaminated by her rot and ruin the beautiful flowers that have grown. The world will not bleed for a minor mistake from ages ago." I felt scared to break eye contact, but I could see Marathene out of the corner of my eye, looking tense and stiff as a board.

I excused myself, pretending to understand and comply. I stood, falling a bit from how high I was. I felt like a mouse in comparison to her furniture and her hall, and perhaps just as insignificant.

I lay down on my bed and closed my eyes, trying to make sense of it all. The tension had not yet left my body. I felt a knot grow in my stomach.

I had these duties, these herculean tasks, from a world I hardly knew. *I must be useless here.* Renee made me feel sure of that. It was a tragedy how all my memories were being replaced with awful ones, while the world and life I used to know slipped further and further away. How *dare* they take my peace from me? I wasn't selected for this mission because of fate or destiny; it was because of convenience for those in charge. And all because of one individual.

I felt a flicker of hatred as my attitude towards Mother Everealm suddenly shifted. *She* was the reason that the AHL focused on making

Nojuni inert, not on actually killing Cavaris or Jovnelle. *Her* ideology made the higher-ups in the AHL treat unusual people like Zandos and me as tools. Because of *her,* Levi had to die, and *she* didn't even care.

I still remember how her expression became so indifferent and callous after she realized Levi wasn't important to her plan. *Her stupid plan. No, not even; her cruel, torturous agenda that led to all of this.*

Hours passed, where I felt so resolute in my opinion and so sure of myself that for a moment, I didn't feel so useless. But I couldn't do anything. I was instead compelled to cry.

Saturday, 12:04 PM, Luzuma, Luzuma Royal Crypt

I stared blankly at the casket. The service had gone on for about thirty minutes by then. Light yellow millin blossoms decorated the top of the dark blue casket, and his AHL medals sat on top. Because of the Luzuman culture, the funeral called for all light yellow, which had a distinct name: *Ajani.* I borrowed a dress from Sirani, which fit snug and long. It was tight and loose in all the wrong places. Makeup also wasn't permitted, since it was seen as a sign of vanity; the Luzumans thought it to be a mask during someone's most vulnerable moment: death.

Sirani was beside me, looking down, and Keya on the other side, her hands covering her mouth the entire time as if she could physically hold back her sobs. Levi's mother was present, but his father was not. She sat alone in the first row, her shoulders stiff, trying to stay dignified. Sheer *ajani* fabric covered her dark black hair. None of the other half-siblings seemed to have cared to make it, however many of them there were.

In the back were Mother Everealm, Marathene, and some AHL officials, like Mr. Makorod and Renee. It was the only time I had ever seen her in a dress. She wore it like it was foreign; no doubt borrowed from someone else. Mother Everealm looked neutral and unaffected, which annoyed me. I honestly couldn't tell why she was there.

Currently at the podium were Salia and Taren, lamenting and crying to the audience. Salia stood behind Taren's lanky frame. I saw Levi in their features.

She was mad. She looked beyond the crowd, at the yellow millin gardens behind us, her neck tense. "He was annoying," she said. "But he always cleaned up after himself and others. Always got jobs done. He enjoyed AHL work, somehow, but I suppose it gave him purpose." She seemed angry that he had died at all. There wasn't much grace in the way she spoke, but she stood like she had been trying to suppress sobbing for hours. "Anyway. He wouldn't have wanted much of a eulogy. He was just the dad we never got and the brother I'll never get back." She left the podium promptly.

A few more people continued with creatively bankrupt speeches, his mother's being the most bland. Perhaps she just had difficulty putting her thoughts into words, or maybe it was because her accent was hard to understand. The angry, spiteful part of me thought she must surely be uncaring. We proceeded outside to the burial grounds. Levi's family had a crypt, but those who weren't family were instructed to wait outside.

I could hear the wails of family members echoing in the crypt. I saw Saku and Kairo, their expressions reminding me of wilted flowers. Jace had come back from Esco for this and was joining Zandos. Their expressions were hard to read.

Keya was still crying. She looked inconsolable.

"Keya, it's—" Sirani began.

—"Will you please just let me be sad?" Keya wailed. "Please." Sirani stepped back.

I saw the family members begin to exit the crypt. We didn't say anything to them, and they didn't say anything to us. They passed back to the main area where the service was.

"It may be the end for him, but it doesn't need to be the end for our mission," Mother Everealm said quietly, with what felt like feigned empathy. I scoffed in my head—it was more so *her* mission than ours. *The nerve to remind us about your god-forsaken mission right now.* I wondered why she was even there at all, if not just to remind me why I'm here.

I thought back to the engraving in her throne room. *The sun shines brightest in its latest hours.* If Levi's death taught me anything, it was the fragility of life. How lucky it made me feel to survive so many missions. How I needed to be firmer if I was going to save myself from grief somehow.

I thought about Renee, who looked like she was forcing herself to be firm and neutral. After the car ride, I realized that she must have had some kind of difficulty being vulnerable. That ride was the first time I had seen her that way, and it sort of changed the way I saw her. She was always forcing herself to be so resolute and authoritative, and for a long time, I believed that's how she truly was. I used to think she was so efficient and practical. Was that what maturity looked like?

More likely, she was like Zandos: hurt, afraid, and left to protect what little he had left. Maybe it was better this way.

Saturday, 3:12 PM, Avukena Palace, Isavna's Unit

I kept my mind on the banquet set for later in the week, despite anxiety clawing at my thoughts. *Was it Wednesday or Thursday? I don't know.* I tried to distract myself by digging through my closet for something to wear.

I passed by a mirror and saw my pendant. I stared at it for a moment, spinning it between my fingers as it caught the light. *What's the deal with this thing?* I heard a knock on my door. I was already on edge, and it surprised me. Thinking it was Sirani, I picked up the light yellow dress she lent me.

I opened the door, seeing Reid.

I dropped the dress and hugged him. I felt a sense of relief, which seemed hard to come by at the moment.

"Come inside," I finally said. "I can make tea." I set a kettle with water on my stovetop and looked at him. He had dark circles under his eyes, but apart from some bandages and lurid bruises, he seemed fine. He was wearing regular clothes. I assumed he went to the dorms before coming here.

"So what happened?" I asked him, Levi's death still fresh in my mind. "Well, we don't have to talk about it right now if you don't want to. Did the doctors say you're going to be fine? From what I remember it was just cuts on your chest, right?"

He pulled down the collar of his shirt to show the bandages on his upper chest.

"The doctor said I was going to scar permanently. But honestly, they look cool as hell." He smiled softly, but it didn't reach his eyes. "At least my dad can't call me a scarless weakling now."

"That's certainly one way to look at it," I said, noting the apprehension in his voice.

"I heard Levi's funeral service was earlier today," he said, his hands folded on the table. "Felt horrible that I couldn't go."

"I think he'd forgive you," I said. We sat in silence a few moments longer. I could only hear the dull rumble of the city, the ocean, and the kettle beginning to boil.

"I can tell you what I told Renee on the drive back," he said as I set a mug with tea on his side of the table. We moved to the sunken floor. I gestured for him to tell me. "So after Levi and I disposed of the bodies and took DNA, we ran into some guards."

"Were they hostile?" I asked, covering my legs with a black plush blanket.

"We didn't think they were," he said. "But they became aggressive quickly, and Levi didn't realize his gun was empty. I took them on, but there were five or six of them and they were pretty massive. One of 'em sunk a liver punch in me, and by the time I was down, Levi had no choice but to take them all on. I only knocked down one or two. He used his broadsword once he was out of ammo and sliced up another guy. I got up and fought a little more," he said, taking a deep breath. "But… one of them grabbed hold of a sharp, rusty spear and started hacking at Levi's chest. It didn't go deep, but it cut him up real bad." His description lined up with the aftermath I remembered seeing. "One of the guards tried to kill me with the same spear, but by then, I had bled a lot, and I had passed out. I guess they thought I was dead already. Renee showed me the pictures, and we have no way of knowing what happened afterward."

"They were completely shredded into pieces. He quite literally fought to the death, then probably collapsed by you to die. I can only imagine he thought you were dead already, too."

"We can only guess now," he said. "It's my last memory of him. It's not like we were best friends or anything, but it still hurts. It scares the hell out of me. I… just can't believe this happened. How he died thinking I had died too." The tea had brought back a bit of color to his face, but he was still anguished.

"And Kairo?" I asked. "How's he doing? He didn't seem too well in Luzuma. I know they were really close in school and work."

Reid leaned back. "He's not doing well. He's been really quiet. I thought that it would be best to just leave him be for now. I've only seen him come out of his room a couple of times. What about Zandos?"

"Jace is back with him. They're living together again. They're… different, they don't, like, cry or sob like Keya does, they just become real quiet, like stone statues."

"I guess we all grieve differently."

"Do you want to stay for dinner?" I asked him. "I can make something if you don't feel like going down to the dining hall or going home."

"Yes," he replied. "That would be nice."

Tuesday, 6:11 PM, Avukena Palace, Formal Banquet Hall

It was almost time. By now, everything had returned to a normal rhythm. It gave me a sense of hope, like a small sprout, but it was also just as fragile. Plates clattering, faucets running, and the voices of many could be heard as an air of excitement buzzed around. The wards, servants, and some of my friends were setting the dining hall for tomorrow.

"My biggest brother's gonna do a speech for the banquet!" I heard a small boy say to his friend as he pushed a cart with plates on it. His friend was sitting on the cart, passing plates to the tables. They were set a bit haphazardly, and one of the older maids was fixing them and adding neatly folded napkins.

"Be more careful," she called out to them. They obliged.

"The banquet's gonna be really boring. We can't go to it though 'cause my brother says we make everything dirty and we're going to ruin it," the other kid said.

My mind returned to Levi as I heard them discuss their older brother. I shook my head. *This isn't going to happen again.*

"Did you finish your speech?" Sirani asked me as she set a crystal goblet on the table. Reid was across from me, setting dessert spoons. I was snapped out of my nervous trance and forgot how sweaty my hands were as they gripped a pair of forks.

"Right....yeah. Yes. I've spent some time on it. I heard it's going to be televised," I said.

Reid nodded in approval. "For real?" he asked, not looking up. The bruises on his hands were mainly yellow by now, almost blending away into his skin color.

"Yeah," I said, nodding. "All the major cities are reporting on the state of their region so that the whole world can know their involvement, invasion rate, casualties, and so forth," I explained.

"I heard some big investors are going to be there. They're thinking about buying AHL bonds or something," Reid said.

Sirani looked at me, concerned. "I wish I could do one. Maybe next year or whenever we do this again."

Thinking about Esco made me think about Jace. *It would be wild if he did one.* Since the days of the mission and the funeral, I hadn't heard from him. Sirani hadn't said anything either.

"This is all out of order!" I heard the maid's rough voice say. She sounded like a smoker, but I had never seen any kind of cigarette usage in Avukena.

"What's the matter?" I asked, looking at her.

"Dessert spoons must be placed with the handle facing right," she scowled.

"Oh, that's my fault," Reid said quietly. The maid returned to her work as Reid quickly flipped all the spoons.

"What about you, Reid?" I asked.

"What?"

"The speeches," I said. He looked at me for a moment, expression blank.

"Oh," he said. "I'm doing one. AHL North, Dekerei Base, gave me their blessing to do it. I had a meeting with region reps and we came up with a speech."

We finished setting the silverware, and we began with the place cards. Many of them were names of monarchs of nearby places. Sirani, Reid, and I moved to the main table when we finished.

The main table was a giant ring, with openings on either side to access the giant middle table, which had an area for a chocolate fountain, which was filled with water at the moment, while technicians made sure it worked. On the inside of the ring table, there was a river of purple magic, sparkling gently to float the food around and around in circles, like a sushi conveyor belt back on Earth. The conveyor belt was currently empty, except for some leaves, sticks, flowers, and toys the children had left.

"When does the actual festival start? Do you know?" Sirani asked. Like Reid and I, she was setting down place cards for the main table.

"Like at one or so," Reid answered.

"Well, we better get this place ready," Sirani said brightly as we set down the last place card.

Wednesday, 8:00 AM, Avukena Palace, Isavna's Unit

My curtains whirred, splashing the early summer sun in my unit, though I was already up. I felt little rushes of excitement that tingled my fingertips. My clothes for the evening banquet were strewn over my poorly made bed. I finished my makeup for the festival, and I looked outside my window. I could hear the city noise; it was louder than usual. Zandos was practicing flying outside my window, going against the breeze. He had a new flight helmet. Kairo and Jace were also with him, showing him how to stay steady with the fickle winds.

I opened my phone and looked over the itinerary. Set-up began half an hour ago for people operating booths. The festival in the east square, near the palace, started at one. Processionals for the important people and bigwigs from other cities for the dinner began at six. The Avukena Regional Marching Band would play some rigid, stale march for them. The band was a recent thing. Marathene and Mother Everealm, along with other high-society members of the region, were really into the big hats with feathers and stately marches that they played, so the band was formed about fifty or so years ago. It was jarring, thinking about something so Earthly and, to an extent, American being adopted and paraded by the Avukenans. But I supposed it made sense; Mother Everealm had spent a lot of time on Earth when she brought humans, Earth commodities, technology, foods, plants, and animals from there.

I was told the procession would be full of other monarchs with failing cities, while everyone gave hollow claps. *I'm probably not going to that one.* I thought. *Sounds incredibly boring.* The actual banquet began at seven and was set to end at two or three in the morning. *Maybe I should take a nap before the banquet.* I looked outside. They were testing the lights and screens in the courtyard for the procession. A lot of people looked happy, but it was hard to tell from a distance. Whatever the case was, I pretended they were.

Maybe today will be different.

15

"Come on, just start already!" Sirani said as she held a tote bag in her hands, squeezing it tightly. She wore a green, yellow, and orange dress with two ornate pins. Some people dressed normally, but most wore their region's traditional clothes, like Sirani, which was a big point of the festival. There were booths around the square, selling different things and games in the middle.

"My mom gave me, like, 200 fancuna for today," I heard a girl behind me, maybe about sixteen, say to her friend. She had a tube dress that was irregular and puffy from the hip down, like a cloud. It was typical of the southern island regions. They were really into asymmetry. She had rose gold and green makeup that had vertical lines going down her face.

"Oh, for real? My sis gave me 100 but she said I would have to give her back whatever I didn't spend."

I looked from the back of the festival to the front. Some officiants sat around, waiting for 1 p.m. to open the gates and let us in. The chatter slowly crescendoed, and we were packed shoulder to shoulder, waiting for the gates to open. Zandos looked around in pain and wonder. The square was beautiful. I heard the chatter diminish, and everyone focused up front, so I craned my neck to look.

"Hello everyone!" the official on the stage at the front of the festival called out. He was pudgy and wore a purple hat, making him look even more rotund. "Welcome to Avukena City for our folks from out of town... yes, it is wonderful that you all have come! Please enjoy what Avukena has to offer! The processionals shall begin at six, and the banquet at seven, for the state of the issue speeches."

"Just open it already!" a young teenage boy shouted.

"Ah yes, of course, yes." The official huffed under his scruffy walrus mustache. "The festival is duly open!" the official proclaimed as he waddled out of the way.

I pushed and shoved to get past. Sirani was behind me, gripping onto my purse strap so she wouldn't lose me, and Reid did the same. I was shoulder-to-shoulder with everyone around me. I wore my own "traditional" clothes: cowboy boots, a big buckle I got from my uncle the last time I visited Earth, a flannel, worn jeans, and a cowboy hat. That was the only thing I considered quintessentially American, though I wasn't from the American Southwest. It was a little jarring to me. It felt like a part of my *old* identity. It was either that or something from my Mexican heritage, which I felt was too far removed to wear anything from it. Now in Avukena, I was someone else. I didn't often notice what I lost because Avukena always asserted I was meant to be someone else. They didn't care, so long as I was from Earth and I did what I had to do. Looking around at all the others, I couldn't help but wonder who else felt the same—wearing clothes that weren't theirs—more of a costume than anything.

We explored the stalls. It felt somewhat like a state fair back on Earth. I flew up with Sirani and Reid to survey the colorful park. I could hear some sneezing, the scent of flowers almost cloying. I looked around my group, making sure Zandos didn't get too far, but he was with Saku and Kairo, enjoying themselves. I tried a dessert from an Angeten Island stand. It was the spongy flesh of a fruit toasted in a pan like tofu and drizzled with something salty. I had some honey eggs that I didn't like quite as much, but the stand was popular.

In the central park near where I was, Reid, Zandos, and Saku were kicking around a ball with Kairo, playing some kind of Avukenan sport, somewhat similar to soccer. They had bulky northern clothes cast in a pile under a tree to make it easier to play in. I watched them as I ate my snacks and sat on the green plush grass. The present summer climate had summoned a small gust of wind, the sounds of which weaved in and out like people's voices, bells ringing, and wings flapping. A group of university students clad in flowy white and red garments were trying to find a spot to land. They went as far as to decorate their flight helmets with rhinestones that matched the jewels on their shoes. I thought about Dorothy's ruby slippers from *The Wizard of Oz* and how much they reminded me of that. At that moment, I felt like Dorothy, swept away into a fantasy world. *We're not in Kansas anymore.*

I heard my phone buzz. It was Toniska.

"Heard there's a flower festival. Why did it have to be exactly as I left? Ugh. Send me pics, have fun." Her message concluded. I took a picture of Kairo and Reid kicking around the ball and sent it to her. I also took a picture of the beach and palace in the distance.

I sat for an early bonfire at the beach before I went to get ready for the banquet.

"Did you like the festival?" Sirani asked Jace. He had stayed in Avukena since Levi's funeral. I hadn't asked him how Esco went, nor did anyone else. He didn't ask questions and tried to stay out of the way. The only thing I heard from him was how he was seeking employment now that the AHL wouldn't take him back.

"Oh yeah, it was nice. I liked the food, I think I overate though."

"Jace!" Sirani said. "You know we're eating more food later today."

"I'll make room," he insisted. The waves lapped gently on the shoreline as the evening birds and felmines flew, squawking and yapping. The lighthouse on the far island shone gently, casting light onto the land under it. Time seemed to escape quickly.

For the first time in a while, we were all together again, apart from the funeral for Levi a few days prior. Zandos and Jace were finally together again, joking and having fun like they had a few weeks ago, although Reid now joined in on the banter. I felt a sense of security sitting next to Sirani and Saku. Kairo, who would usually be with Levi, was now staring into the fire. His eyes looked watery, either because of the smoke of the fire pummeling his face or because of the events of the past few days. I felt sorry for him, considering that he had just lost one of his best friends, and I couldn't even give him a proper goodbye. What troubled me the most was that every day, I felt a sense of unease; there was a feeling of uncertainty that always promised to keep me on edge. Like how *today* was one of those days. And tomorrow. And the day after.

The banter died down, and we focused on the ocean creatures jumping in and out of the water, as well as the birds—or people, it was hard to tell—circling the bright sun. I checked my Earth phone and felt surprised.

"It's already four forty-five! The banquet starts at like, six!"

"Oh my gosh! I won't have time to shower!" Sirani said in alarm.

"You'll be fine," Saku said. She looked somewhat dazed.

"Are you okay?" I asked, smiling, my brows furrowed.

She flapped her hand dismissively. "I think I got a sugar crash," she said, smiling. "I wasn't very smart today."

I looked over at Kairo, who I would usually expect a playful retort from, but he was silent. He didn't even seem lucid. He was just focused on the fire, crackling and burning. Saku noticed, but all she did was sigh and avert her eyes. Reid approached him, and I saw them talk, too quiet for me to hear. I saw Kairo's expression remain fixed on the fire, as he shook his head slowly.

"Well, I better get going," Sirani said. I followed her, leaving my group and heading up to my unit.

Wednesday, 5:00 PM, Avukena Palace, Isavna's Unit

Sirani swept a big, fluffy brush on her face while sparkling powder evanesced into the air nearby. I fixed the lifting edge of my false lashes, bordering my purple eyes. They were brown before I came here, but must have changed in transit, since I have no recollection of it happening.

Considering the brevity of my speech, I didn't feel nervous. Sirani wasn't either. She hummed a tune while she pinned back flyaways. She was going to give a speech about the effects of the local AHL base on the

Avukena-Sjasa region. I was going to give a general speech, one of the first ones of the night, about the fight against Cavaris as a whole. It was meant to be introductory, with broad numbers about the war.

I considered bringing my combination knife. Then I scoffed at the idea's absurdity. *How paranoid can I be?* Sirani, in her champagne-colored dress with gold flowers, smiled at me.

"Isavna," she said. "I can't believe it. I think this is my first true banquet where I'm giving a speech."

"Yeah, are you nervous?" I asked.

She shook her head. "No. Just some excited butterflies."

We made our way down the elevator and walked to the banquet hall. At the far end of the circular table, with the floating magic river bringing food around like a sushi belt, I saw Mother Everealm and Marathene beckoning for us to come over. Looking at Mother Everealm, all I could think was how deceptively nice she looked. Her crown gleamed in the banquet lights. Marathene's crown, just shy of her mother's, sat on her shiny brown hair. I took a seat near them, alongside Reid and Sirani. I greeted them and sat down.

We picked up food from the magic conveyor belt and put it onto our plates. I could see the smart-looking investors on the other side of the table, with ritzy suits and dresses. Nearby, a camera crew was getting ready for the speeches that started at six.

"The Prime Minister of Gosbon sent us this," Marathene said, passing me sausages. They had a rich, smoky scent. "I spoke with him recently."

"About the tea crisis?" I asked, cutting open the sausage.

"Yes. The whole island chain got hit really hard with the north wind storm last year, so most of their crops are failing at the moment, like tea."

"Is everyone okay?" I asked.

"Well, the northern islands aren't doing too well." She brushed back her brown, wavy hair. "That's why the prime minister stayed. We sent them supplies, and their economy should recover in a couple years."

"Years?" asked Sirani as she listened to the conversation. "It must have been *really* bad."

Before I knew it, Mother Everealm blew a ceremonial horn. Immediately, all chatter waned, and the attention was on her.

"Esteemed guests," Mother Everealm began. "I am pleased to welcome those who have journeyed from great distances and those who reside within these very walls. Tonight, we will commemorate those who have remained steadfast in the valiant fight against Cavaris and Jovnelle, and honor those who have given their souls for the cause. Most importantly, we have speakers here who will share their stories and report on the state of the issue in their regions. Following the initial addresses, speakers from Avukena's southern provinces will convene in the next room. To those joining us on hologram or radio, the stations APR two for radio and DPB three for hologram will have the southern region speeches." People from the next banquet hall had moved into this hall to listen to Mother Everealm. "I shall now invite sophomore official Sirani Maligari to the stand." She gestured to Sirani, who stood up, invoked her wings, and flew to the raised platform.

"Thank you," Sirani said. The camera people were also perched on a ledge, focusing their cameras steadily on Sirani. She introduced herself and went over the numbers for our region. She set the ledger down on the stand and looked at the cameras gravely. "These numbers hide some gaps. They don't show that we've had to cut thirty task ops, and that we were barely able to deliver aid to Huzoril state during their civil crisis." She stared straight ahead, as if too scared to look down at Mother Everealm and us.

She finished her speech, trying to wear a slight smile. The banquet hall gave apprehensive but sincere applause.

"You're next up, Isavna. Good luck," Sirani said. I nodded, feeling a surge of adrenaline. I got up from my seat and tried to invoke my wings. I felt immediate panic, realizing it wasn't working. *This can't be happening.* I tried a few more times, and finally, it worked, painful as it was. I felt I did a good job hiding that with a fake sneeze to cover my hurt. I flew up to the ledge. I looked down and saw everyone looking at me. Everyone was dressed to the nines. More people poured in from outside, too.

"We gather here today because of our work, not because of chance or accident. We have done necessary things to protect our planet and everyone in it. Doctors work late into the night and supervisors plan until their eyes go dry. It's because of them that our restaurants serve dinner late into the night. And still. There are many empty offices and few names on the sign-in sheets. We have lost people and places that should not have been lost. I see institutions that allow their prudence to calcify into complacency, not because of laziness but because of fear to defy those above us. What I ask for is simple. Pass on your skills, knowledge, and time to those who need it most to protect your community against Mahifers. Invest in AHL bonds. Know the signs of possession and know where Mahifers lurk. Without fuel, the Mahifers will die. Now, for the next portion of the banquet, I will be calling out names of outstanding Avukenan citizens for their work in technology and science that will help us defeat Cavaris. Senior officer Askard Novet will be handing out the awards." For another thirty minutes, several individuals flew up to receive medals. Afterward, I looked over at the audience to gauge their reactions. They looked tired. I was tired, too. I gave them a courteous nod and flew back to my seat.

I looked at the quiet investors in the back, gauging their reactions. Reid gave a speech, followed by Kairo. There was a water Batran who spoke about the Gosbon sea. Zandos or Jace would have done a speech, but we didn't trust the people, especially not the older foreign investors, to accept them without bias. People from Nojuni were still seen as mostly evil, so it was better to just not mention it, at least for now. Some other people did their speeches, but the ordeal ended quickly. We kept on eating, moving on to flower-themed desserts as investors approached tables with booths for the AHL and different regions.

Wednesday, 8:03, Avukena Palace, Formal Ballroom

The room was decorated with flowers of all kinds, and as we moved into the ballroom, chairs were spread out near tables with smaller finger foods and sweets. There was a pit orchestra on the other side of the hall.

"May I have this dance?" I asked Sirani, half joking. She laughed and took my hand as we both whisked around the ballroom and spoke, trying not to bump into the crowd.

"I think we did a good job," Sirani said loudly over the music and chatter as we circled the ballroom. "Because we do need recruits and interns to replace the graduates." Our long, slightly fluffy dresses brushed the marble floors as we waltzed around.

"I hope you're right," I replied. "'Cause most of our group isn't staying local." I glanced around the ballroom, looking for potential candidates. There were people from different places and backgrounds talking to staff at the sign-up booths at the door, looking excited. "Maybe we should talk to some of them," I suggested.

"Maybe later," Sirani said, exhaling and half rolling her eyes. "Right now, I just want to have fun." She smiled, spinning me around. Looking around, there was no shortage of fun around the room as Jace and Zandos stood off to the side, snacking on finger food, even though they had just eaten.

"There's like a fifty percent chance that Jace is eating something whenever I see him," I said to Sirani.

"Yeah. He's always been like that, even before Nojuni."

I felt so compelled to ask what happened, if he was okay with his parents. "So what happened in Esco?" I asked Sirani casually.

"What?" Sirani asked.

"With Jace," I said, my voice low.

"Oh," she replied. She looked unusually morose. "Well, Jace tried to talk to our parents and they said they would only accept him back if he never left again."

"Never?" I said, brows raised.

"Never. Not even to Avukena or to say hi to Zandos or anything. So, well, he rejected that."

"I don't know whether to feel happy or sad about that," I said. "I'm guessing you'd be presented with a similar proposition."

"Yeah," she said, casting her gaze aside. She didn't look sad, just serious. "But I think I'm ready to move on from them."

"Really?" I asked. She and I didn't talk much about her family, but she seemed to long for Esco in this weird way since she came to Avukena City. *Something is odd about her parents.* I thought back to how Jace and Sirani were fighting back in Nojuni when we first found him. The topic of their parents seemed to be a heavy one. I could tell that she wanted to be at peace with her family, though it appeared she had finally given up on the Esco dream.

"Yeah. The more I think about it, there's just nothing I have to go back for besides them, and, well, why? To feel loved? Like I belong? I feel more of that here than I would in Esco. A few years ago, maybe, but not now."

I looked for my friends among the crowd. Kairo was talking to a mustached man dressed in fine silk, and Reid was talking with Zandos and Jace. It almost felt like a dream to be in a fairy tale princess ball. The song ended, and the crowd dispersed as more people moved in for the next dance. My friends reconvened by the jelly-filled cakes. Saku had taken off what looked like uncomfortable high heels and put on some flats. Zandos looked a little on edge, and we all seemed to notice that. He was shifting his fingers, and he had a slight twitch in both eyes, which caused them to narrow.

"What's wrong?" Reid asked, approaching him. Jace looked concerned, his eyes darting between Zandos and our surroundings. I felt my necklace get heavier and tug down at my neck, like someone was pulling on it. *What the hell is wrong with this thing?*

"Did you see it?! I saw something fly outside window. Something is not right," Zandos said, his brows furrowed. Sirani and I paused our dance to walk to them. I stared at my pendant, a teardrop shape. I removed it and put it in my dress pocket.

"How? We're incredibly well guarded," Sirani said.

"That is exactly why. Everyone is inside right now. We are an easy target," Zandos said blankly.

"That's impossible," Saku said, convulsing a bit, trying to shake off the feeling.

"Well, there's a lot of people here. If there's a Mahifer, then security would probably take care of them immediately. We should alert security just in case," I told Sirani.

"What are we even supposed to tell them? One of our friends has a feeling there might be some evil *something* around here?" Sirani pointed out.

"I'm really sure about this," Zandos said.

Kairo came over. "What's going on?" he asked. Sirani explained the situation to him, trying to keep a low voice. Jace nervously offered Zandos a ladyfinger with millin icing on top, trying to console him. Kairo had a look of concern.

"I cannot forget what I saw," Zandos said, as he looked out a window and his eyes widened. "I see it—it is gone now, but—was there."

"What are you on about?" Reid said quietly. My necklace in my pocket had gotten so heavy that it made me feel unbalanced.

"I think we should do something about this. I'm getting a similar feeling," I said, trying to interpret what my pendant was trying to tell me.

"I'll go tell security," Kairo said, looking at us for any objection. He left and went to speak to a guard. I walked to a table that had little pink macarons that looked like flowers. Reid, Sirani, and I stayed close to Jace and Zandos in case something happened.

Reid and I began to chat, while remaining uncomfortably alert. Most of our focus was spent on scanning our surroundings.

Out of the corner of my eye, I noticed something flying outside the glass roof that looked too big to be a bird but too small to be a felmine. I looked at Reid. He saw it too. What could it have been, a Mahi? A really large flying person? I gestured to madeleines arranged like a large carnation, and Reid passed me one. Before I could thank him, my pendant got so heavy that I fell down.

As I tried to get up, the glass roof shattered into a million pieces, catching light and glittering like stars, before the chandelier came crashing down onto the guests.

16

Wednesday, 8:58 PM, Avukena Palace, Formal Ballroom

Silence, then disaster. People began to scatter and run as guards entered the hall to investigate what had happened. Guests who tried to fly away began to plummet to the ground. I knew what was going on, and Reid seemed to know as well. At that moment, we were the target of a full-scale Mahifer invasion. I attempted to regroup with the others. Reid, Sirani, and I hadn't gone far from the snack table, but it would be nearly impossible to find them now.

"Please remain grounded," a guard shouted as people tried to fly and dodge the falling bodies. "If you become possessed midair, you *will* fall to your death."

A big, voluminous black dress flew over the open roof, with a burgundy cloak trailing behind.

"Isavna, are you okay? Are we under a Mahi attack?" Saku cried out as she approached me. My group had managed to reconvene by the entrance between the main hall and this ballroom. Jace, Kairo, and Reid struggled to retain Zandos as he drew his combination knife and began slashing at the air madly. We all put on our flight helmets, as did all the guests.

"What is Jovnelle doing here?" Sirani pointed, horrified. Her eyes were wide and her mouth agape as we ran for cover. "I... I... can't believe," I looked at her, and at Jovnelle. Her neck was limp, jaw slack, as she hovered around the room, and for a moment I thought she was dead.

"Whatever Cavaris wants her to." A chunk of the roof began to fall, right where I was standing. I screamed, and we all dove aside. A group of Mahis swarmed like bees, heading in our direction. Sirani struggled to run in her heels, so I ran up to her and fireman-carried her with me.

We stopped in a corridor, and I put her down. She beat a small Mahi with her shoes until it turned into a puddle of acid. I decided it would be better to just do without my own impractical heels. I quickly kicked them off and proceeded barefoot, with nothing but my thin decorative pantyhose between me and the cold marble floor. It wasn't a perfect plan; I got a cut almost instantly, but it was better than risking a broken ankle. I ran close to Reid and Zandos, and Sirani and Jace followed as we formed a group.

"The portals are down," I heard some guests saying. "And so are the elevators. How do we get out of here?"

A few Mahifers approached us, their long, ghostly black tails whipping side to side like fish swimming upstream. Reid had his combination knife, luckily, and was able to fend off some of the Mahis. I grabbed a metal bar that fell from the roof and thrusted it firmly at the Mahi that was trailing me, one of a small swarm of four. I hacked at them with my metal pipe. It didn't work as well as a combination knife would've. *Why didn't I just bring it?* I lowered the pipe into what looked like its throat. It tried to swallow the pipe, but it began to choke as I forced it further down. I could sense its tether magic trying to possess me, but it died before it could. I reached for another pipe, which was significantly heavier. My arms and chest felt weak from exertion as I lifted the pipe up to stab into another one of the Mahi's horrid forms.

I looked behind the Mahi once I had killed it, resting my arms on the pipe. Jace was running towards me in a panic, and Sirani was on the ground, with a purple aura surrounding her.

"Sirani, are you okay?!" I shrieked, lunging towards her. The purple aura meant that a Mahi was trying to possess her body. There was a purple trail of magic leading somewhere, like there was a tether too. I saw Jace pursing his lips and tightening his fists. He seemed indecisive, like he didn't want to risk killing his sister. He exhaled sharply and started running towards Sirani, who had begun to morph slowly into a half-human. It felt like the start of a bad dream, and all I could do was watch.

Reid dragged me away into the next room, which was a smaller corridor. This one had even more Mahis blocking the exit. Among them were possessed partygoers, turning into monsters of all kinds. Zandos was fighting them. He seemed crazed, like whatever mania he was experiencing earlier had manifested in his fighting. The Mahis also didn't seem too interested in fighting him; they were acting like they were trying to run away from him, despite their hostility towards everyone else.

The same black-dressed figure from before moved through the halls. Jovnelle was nearby. Her harrowing presence hung heavy in the room like the dust of her palace.

"We can't hold them for much longer," Reid said as he stabbed a Mahi with his short sword, panting and sweating. A few small fires had broken out, which caused a haze in the hall. People tried to put them out with magic, but the steam generated made the visibility near zero. "We have to either block them out or get moving." I worried about Mother Everealm and what would happen if they found Jovnelle.

I fought the Mahis until I was too tired to go on, but I didn't need to. We had managed to kill the group and blocked off the two entrances of the corridor with knocked-over bookshelves.

"What is the plan?" Zandos asked, panting and slumping over on a chair. Color had begun to return to his face.

"Isavna, you have some equipment in your room, right?" Reid asked, sweat beading up on his forehead. "We should regroup there and get what we can. Especially since we don't know if this building's going to collapse soon."

I nodded in agreement, trying to use my sweat to slick my bangs out of my face. "I don't have a ton of equipment," I said through ragged breaths. "But Zandos's room is there too. We can at least get a few knives, patch up our cuts, and drink some water while we're up there."

The lot of the Mahis seemed to have moved elsewhere in the palace, and we knew we were running out of time. I knew I badly needed my combination knife and Mahi blaster. I carefully ran over the cold marble floor, covered in broken glass, trying not to cut my feet any further. I led Zandos and Reid to the quickest route up to the staircase, since the elevators were down. Many guests sprinted out of the building. Guards and AHL members tried to stave off the Mahis whose auras drove out the guests like smoke in a beehive.

My feet ached. I tiptoed as carefully and quickly as I could as we went up the fire escape staircase. We stuck to the right side as palace tenants, woken up by the commotion, evacuated on the left. Pallid faces of children were just barely illuminated by the wall sconces, which had begun to flicker.

The last of the tenants left the stairwell, but the children's cries of fear still echoed. I could only hear the panting breaths of Reid, Zandos, and my own as we ascended. We had made it to the thirteenth floor in ten minutes, with only seven floors to go until we reached the corridor where I lived. Suddenly, the lights went out.

"The power shut down. Of course," Reid said, grunting in frustration. "There must be fire reaching this wing, or it's a preemptive measure." I used the small flashlight on my wrist projection to illuminate my path, as did the others. The dim light shone on the door's silver plaque, indicating the seventeenth floor.

"We're almost there. Come on. I have candles in my unit," I said. I wish I could've sent any telepathic message, but that would surely attract Mahis and give away our position. I couldn't feel my feet. They were cut from the broken glass, leaving a light trail of scarlet blood behind me.

"I'm worried about Sirani. I don't know if Jace was able to take her on or anything," Reid said as we continued walking.

"Yeah. She is possess now. If we learn anything of what happen to Jace, we know removing the Mahi takes much time and precision. We must trap her to have… success," Zandos said.

I felt shocked all over again, thinking about the purple aura I saw surrounding Sirani. *No,* I thought. *This isn't happening. No way.* I tried to forget what I saw.

"Are you okay?" Zandos asked, noticing the falter in my step.

"What? No yeah, I'm fine," I said sardonically, as my vision blurred, trying to continue walking through it all. "My best friend didn't just die in front of me."

"She didn't die, Isavna. She's just possessed," Reid said, poorly hiding his own concern.

"As if that's any better," I replied bitterly. I held out my wrist projection to the door we passed. *Nineteenth floor.*

The ground shook lightly as I heard distant rumbling. We crouched close to the ground. Reid gestured for me to shut off the light.

"Do you guys sense anything?" I asked.

"If there is a Mahi, we will know," Zandos reassured me. I reached around me, trying to gauge how close the others were and if they were still there. I flicked through the settings on my flight helmet to see if any of them would help me see better. A thermal camera allowed me to see the others. Night vision would be helpful, but the technology was expensive and primitive in flight helmets. After waiting another minute, we proceeded.

The rest allowed us to move more quickly, so it was only half a minute before we reached the twentieth floor. I looked around once we reached the familiar corridor, reorienting myself since it wasn't the usual elevator entrance. I inhaled sharply, noticing the door to my unit was open. The thermal detection didn't pick up anything around me except in my unit. *Seems everyone else has evacuated.* Except, as we entered my apartment, it sounded like people were there, gathered in the sunken floor of my living room. Reid drew his combination knife and moved slowly, going first. Zandos went behind me.

"... I don't think I do, but she probably knows where to find some. Or at least, I'd expect her to know," I heard a voice say.

"Saku?" Reid whispered as we entered slowly. The shape of the heat signature rendered on our flight helmets seemed to resemble her and some others.

"Reid? Is that you?" Kairo asked.

"Yeah," he said, walking slowly because of the darkness. "I'm with Isavna and Zandos. Where are Jace and Sirani?"

"We don't know," Saku said, letting out a squeak. "Last I saw, Jace was running away from Sirani and some guard had tried to contain her with a net or magic." I could tell she was scared. I quickly ran to the bathroom to clean my feet and put on a pair of fresh socks. It still stung, but less so.

We were all crowded around my battery-powered lamp in the middle of my sunken floor, trying to prepare a game plan. Candles were scattered around the room. I patched up Saku's feet before giving her a pair of socks. Bandage wrappers littered the ground. The stairwell and elevator door were barricaded with my table turned sideways, a couch from Zandos's room, and my chaise lounge. Kairo, Zandos, and Reid had left for Zandos's room to get any weapons and change into more usable clothing as quickly as they could. Saku and I did the same, though she was silent the whole time.

Eventually, they returned, and we finished changing into whatever was the most practical. We discussed equipment, our plan, and whether or not to loot the other units.

We all talked except for Saku, who was borderline sobbing.

"Saku, you're going to be okay. Sirani and Jace will be fine," I said, trying to console her.

She tied back her hair. "How do you know? There's more Mahis than us. We shouldn't have left them," Saku said. "We're such horrible people to leave behind friends who really care about us."

I saw Reid's expression glaze over as he stared into one of the candles. I felt my palms get sweaty. *Levi.*

Kairo slowly spoke to Saku in Klethoris, trying to comfort her. Zandos interrupted him to speak.

"I have seen many terrible things in my life, living in Nojuni… many of days I go to sleep and the mornings I wake up seemed more useful and enjoyable if I was dead. It is something I am numbed to… but life has always gone on. The only reason why I am here today is because I know killing myself is worse than whatever will happen if I keep going. I know that Jovnelle feel the same, she would be dead by her own means if she did not believe in us," Zandos said. Saku huffed. I could feel her cynicism. "If we wait any longer, the lives of our friends are not guaranteed," Zandos said in Hakon.

"The building might collapse if possessed people don't find us first," I said. "Let's go back down. I have some extra weapons in my dresser." I ran into my closet and got them. Zandos and Reid were fully armed, so I gave Saku my extra sidearm—a nine-millimeter pistol—and an extra combination knife. I gave Sirani my biggest kitchen knife, as she didn't have her combination knife on her, though most of us thankfully did.

"How are we going to get out of here?" Zandos asked, as the elevator clearly wasn't an option. The stairs would take too long. I walked into Zandos's room, looking to see if his unit had an emergency exit.

"Maybe we should just go up two more flights and fly down," Reid said, putting on his flight helmet. I nodded.

"Zandos, how do you feel about flying?" I asked. He gestured with his hand.

"So-so. I might be able to glide down safely."

We made our way up to the roof, a place I didn't often visit. The altitude made it especially cold and windy. Looking down at the ground, there were AHL buses and vans already there, and they had corralled a lot of the possessed monsters. To our right, a spire creaked as a burning Avukena State flag fell towards the gardens. Blinking pink and green lights, Avukena's emergency colors, could be seen on the ground beyond the haze. There was no immediate sign of Jovnelle. She still had to be in the palace. We all put on our flight helmets and invoked our wings.

A strong crosswind threatened to blow us into the tallest spire on top of the palace. Zandos kept steady, and we began to descend. We chose to land a bit far from the main area, in a corner of the park, to avoid any falling debris. We sprinted towards the palace, reached the main door, shuffled past the crowd, and headed into the main ballroom.

There were pieces of Mahi carcasses strewn across the ground, but no sign of Jovnelle; at least not in this room. Disaster relief workers were cleaning up shattered glass. As I looked back, the streetlights in the courtyard seemed engulfed by the haze and Cavaris's presence. The possessed partygoers seemed taken care of, for the most part, except for a stray Mahi here and there that we quickly killed with a short sword. We went to where we suspected Cavaris and Jovnelle to be: Mother Everealm's throne room.

Upon our arrival, the room was still intact. Jovnelle stood, zombie-like and possessed, looking at Mother Everealm and Marathene. I felt like I walked in on a situation I shouldn't have, but my presence had already been noticed.

"What's going on?" I asked, trying to do something. My friends came in shortly after me, having to first save some people from Mahis. Marathene's face contorted into fear, but not for herself.

"Stay out of this, Isavna," Mother Everealm said grimly, her face cold. "You are not needed here."

"But I *have* to complete my mission," I said, gritting my teeth, still focusing my eyes on Jovnelle, who was hovering around the room. Pieces of her long, decrepit dress were falling off.

Jovnelle fell to the ground, like whatever magic was holding her up had suddenly extinguished. Her eyes turned white, though I barely got a glimpse as she tried to sit up. She hardly had the energy to keep her eyes open. Her face and figure, from what I could tell under her dress, looked incredibly emaciated and pallid, more so than when I saw her on the mission. I had to make a plan.

A piece of the building fell, kicking up debris. I wiped the dust off my flight helmet. I ran back several yards as I tried to pause and think. I knew I had to get close to Jovnelle, break whatever tether was happening, and get her out without Mother Everealm knowing.

Saku shrieked as she spotted a figure dashing in the sky, covered in white plaster dust from the hall. *Cavaris.* There was a trail of purple magic that anchored him to Jovnelle's back. I knew it had to be Cavaris' tether, because the only other person with tether powers was Mother Everealm, and hers was invisible. He flew about, knocking down vases and infrastructure. The sensation of the black, translucent creature flying around overwhelmed my mind and my senses. He looked like a horrible storm cloud, as wisps of the black magic extended out from his form like tendrils.

He looked at us and let out a horrifying, reverberating bellow that rang throughout the building, spattering bits of acid around the room. The noise in my head swelled into a terrible crescendo. He launched out an appendage from his translucent, ghost-like form, which released a flurry of magic, smoke, and fire. We all dove and hit the ground to avoid it. The once-pristine marble floors became a blackened battleground of rubble. Cavaris whipped his black, smoky tail around, knocking down large wall fixtures and shattering the precious glass window.

"I think I see some kind of tether," Kairo told our group telepathically, which I could barely hear amid all the noise in my head. The others around me grimaced, feeling the mental pain too. I got closer to the ground, behind a piece of rubble, trying to force all the other noise out and find a solution. I could barely see Jovnelle on the other side of the throne room.

Cavaris hurled another flame. I turned around to run, but someone was in my way.

Sirani stood there, eyes blackened, with an inky sludge leaking out of her eyes, mouth, and nose. She was half-transformed into a frog-like creature. The purple tether from her back, like a leash, was attached to Cavaris. He was attached to multiple monster-people at that moment, with more tethers forming by the minute. I stopped breathing for a beat before beginning to pant and trying to run away, but quickly, she hobbled in my direction, letting out a gurgle from her throat. I couldn't see Jace.

Everyone else was focused on fighting Cavaris, so Sirani was left to me. She began to slowly transform, her flesh stretching and contorting unevenly into a huge, black, frog-like creature. The jaw grew unnaturally large and split; I could hear the bones crunching. Sirani, or what she had become, was bleeding from several places.

"I… savna, just… do it…" she gurgled right before she entirely took monster form.

She let out a scream. I lunged at her with my sword and slashed it at her, but the monster dodged it and positioned herself behind me. She spattered black goo everywhere, which burned the marble floor. AHL members came rushing in, trying to help contain Sirani. She thrusted towards me, trying to bite me with her uneven, mismatched teeth coated in a thick layer of slime. I rolled to the side, scrambling to get back up. I tried to reload my Mahi blaster, but I was out of ammo.

"Come on, come on!" I yelled at my blaster, which failed to shoot. The ejection port was open and empty. I grabbed my nine-millimeter pistol in the other hand and shot at her haphazardly, as I tried to get back. *So am I supposed to hit vital points or what?!* I thought. *I still want her to live, but this pain has to be agonizing.* I shot at her knees, trying to contain her somehow.

I looked at the monster's eyes, and Sirani was still in there. She let out a shriek of pain as black ooze dripped from her broken, bumpy skin with sludge-filled ulcers. She roared and spat out a stream of the goo as she fell to the ground. I dodged most of it, but some of it splashed and hit my right leg and arm, burning through my clothes and a bit of my skin.

"Someone, knock her out somehow! Then we can remove the Mahi!" Brev shouted, holding a tool of some sort that looked like a small vacuum cleaner. I knew I couldn't hit any vital points, or I would kill Sirani forever. Instead, I used my remaining energy to hurl a piece of stone at her head. It wasn't very effective—a distraction, more than anything, but it bought enough time for someone to shoot her with the tranquilizer.

"Renee!" I shouted, recognizing her flight helmet. The light outdoors had begun to fade, and the power was shut off, making the room dark.

She nodded without losing focus and shot the creature a number of times. Brev quickly followed, installing the small machine onto its head. My knees buckled under me as I tried to process everything going on. I watched Brev fumble on the straps and administer substances with a needle. Quickly, the purple aura disappeared, and Sirani lay there, in her human form, with broken and bloodied knees. I could only look on in horror, too stunned to even cry. My hot breath and spit covered the inside of my helmet, and worse, my glasses were all smudged. I wanted to vomit.

Brev and Renee dragged Sirani away, careful not to hurt her knees. Somehow, the rest of her bones were intact. I turned to see the others still fighting Cavaris. He summoned waves of Mahis that didn't let up and used his corrupt magic to blast around the room, leaving craters. He launched loud, vibrating screeches which made the ground rumble—I hopelessly ducked, already down, trying to shield myself from falling debris.

I heard another explosion, and more Mahifers came rushing in from above. The constant noise of the AHL's automatic rifles made my head spin. I heard the horrifying screams of someone burning alive. I stared ahead, not strong enough to look.

The now-decrepit hall was painted in the setting sun's angry red and yellow colors, which mixed with the fire's lurid glow and the blood on the ground. We were running out of time.

In that moment, I felt utterly defeated. I watched everyone around me fight with barely contained rage towards Cavaris, the sheer adrenaline superseding any need for rest. And here I was, unsure of who to be mad at, and which mission to fulfill—Mother Everealm's or mine. Jovnelle's body was still cast in a pile on the west side of the hall, but she was clearly alive. *This is my chance to do something.*

I hobbled towards her, keeping to the wall. Her dress was torn and ripped as she lay motionless on the ground, though her tether to Cavaris was visible. Having regained some energy, I was able to move quickly. I huffed, reaching under my helmet and wiping away sweaty hair from the front of my face. I dragged her aside to an alcove and inspected her wounds, also searching for whatever anchored her to Cavaris. I followed the light trail of purple magic, but much like a rainbow, it was hard to see from up close. I wrapped Jovnelle partially in a curtain, as she was cold to the touch. As she warmed up a bit and fell in and out of consciousness, Cavaris seemed to get even stronger. Then it hit me.

Cavaris drains life force. If she is stronger, then he will be too. The only way to weaken him is to weaken her.

I unwrapped her from the curtain and slapped her across the face. Not hard enough to hurt her, but hard enough to shock her.

She gasped and fell unconscious—but in the same instant, Cavaris roared. His obedient flow of magic had suddenly been interrupted because the key was not to strengthen her, but to suddenly weaken her so much that she didn't have energy to give.

I looked away and open-palm hit her across her sternum, and her gaunt body spasmed. It was just hard enough to shock her, but not too hard that it would hurt her badly. She was clearly too weak to cry out. I looked at her face, feeling panic and worry. I couldn't let her die, but I had to get her weak enough that the tether would break. *Zandos will never forgive me if she dies.*

The purple aura of magic dimmed when she jolted. Her breath was ragged and shallow. Her face had turned purple as she began to cough, choking on her spit. The tether looked like a taut string but started to fray as she coughed. I watched as she shook violently, nearing death, and the tether frayed. And just as it finally disappeared, and Cavaris howled, she stopped moving.

I worked as quickly as I could to resuscitate her, flipping her over to try and force the spit out of her throat.

"Come on," I hissed, feeling my hands go cold as I panicked. *I don't know what will happen if she dies.* I held her body and hit her frail back with the heel of my palm until a wet cough came out and blood dribbled from her mouth. As Cavaris howled and cold air from outside blew around me, I could barely tell if she was breathing at all. I laid her on her back and started doing compressions on her sternum. I coughed, trying to shield Jovnelle from a cloud of dust that suddenly billowed from a falling column.

"Damn it, *breathe,* just *breathe,* Jovnelle!" I seethed, trying to keep my cold, shaky, sweaty hands from compressing her sternum too heavily. I looked up to Cavaris, who was screeching and flying around. All the Mahis had disappeared, and the purple tether that had once connected Cavaris to her was now gone.

I felt Jovnelle twitch under my hands. *Was I imagining things, or was this real?* I paused, and she twitched again. She drew a weak breath, and her eyes fluttered open. I let my hands fall, and I folded over her, letting out a raw, shuddering laugh that was partially relief and partially exhaustion.

I tried to stand up but fell on my knees beside Jovnelle. Her breath had steadied, though she seemed weak. She vomited something that looked like purple bile. Saku ran by and tossed me three water bottles, moving quickly to share with others. I fumbled with the lid of one of them and poured some into Jovnelle's mouth. I winced, hearing a semi-automatic rifle being shot close to me.

"He's gone. You're safe now." I said in Hakon, not caring that I butchered the words. I was certain she couldn't hear me, for it was too loud, but the way she held my gaze told me she understood.

I turned on the light of my wrist projection to get a better look at her. Her dress was torn, with her dirty, bloodstained chemise visible. Her pure white hair was knotted with a mix of dirt and blood. Her face had wounds, and vomit covered her chin. And yet, she was beautiful. She wasn't perfect—no human, no creature, no world, nor divine being ever was. And yet, there's beauty in crooked trees, unrefined gems, and Jovnelle.

I forced another laugh that came out half-sobbing when I realized Jovnelle was truly alive.

"Zandos would've killed me if I let you die," I said in English, the words tumbling out of my mouth like the avalanches in the cold Nojuni mountains, which I would never have to visit again. I sat against the wall, still panting. Cavaris was still flying around the room, growling like a thunderstorm. He was looking for Jovnelle.

I covered her and myself with a torn curtain and played dead. I let my body go limp, but peeked out of a small hole in the curtain to see what was happening. Cavaris was attempting to produce more Mahis, but it caused his physical form to shrink. I watched him chase the Mahis and reabsorb them into his body. He circled the hall like an angry captive fish. Mother Everealm and Marathene distracted him at the other end of the hall.

I knew I had to get Jovnelle somewhere safer. I took off the curtains and saw Zandos and Jace. I tried getting their attention, waving my arms wildly since yelling would be useless. Both of them noticed me and came running. Zandos kneeled by Jovnelle and broke down in tears.

He had known her all his life, but it wasn't until today that they truly met without Cavaris possessing her, even Jace, whom Jovnelle had also treated like her own son. Zandos wrapped the curtain around Jovnelle's frail body and carried her out of the palace as quickly as he could. Mother Everealm and Marathene were together fighting Cavaris, along with a large group of operatives. He was more conservative with his attacks, except for a large fireball he launched at the westernmost wall of the building.

The sudden collapse of the wall was barely audible from the din of the rifles, roars of Cavaris, and the crackling fires. Reid had narrowly avoided the glass window shattering.

Kairo and Saku had retreated to a corner, leaning against the wall. Keya was with them. *But Reid… where's Reid?!* I tilted my head to see the glass window where I thought he was, and he had gone. I stood up, regaining strength, and changed the setting on my flight helmet to a thermal camera. All it picked up was fire, which was getting worse. Far worse. I needed to find a way out of there or end this now.

I thought about Levi, and how he could have lived if I were a little quicker. I was not about to let it happen again. I stood up, circumnavigating what was left of the hall, searching for Reid, dodging rubble. I spotted him in another alcove.

"What are you doing?!" he shouted at me as we both ducked and dodged a part of the wall that caved in.

"I couldn't let anything happen," I said, rolling over to a safer area.

Cavaris had turned into a horrible maelstrom, sweeping up objects.

"Do not allow him to escape!" Mother Everealm shouted at the task operatives.

He roared and flew towards the foyer, leaving a cloud of debris in his wake. I wiped the dust off my helmet's visor and ran after him with Reid. He was going towards the courtyard, where everyone had evacuated.

Outside, sirens wailed, and several dozen emergency service vehicles were parked in the courtyard, flashing pink and green. I dodged medical equipment and evacuees crying to emergency service workers about their newly lost loved ones. The warm summer air was contaminated by anguish and dust. We all looked around to try to find Cavaris, but he was seemingly gone.

"Never mind Cavaris, where is Jovnelle?" Mother Everealm seethed.

"What the hell is she thinking?" Reid told me. "Isn't Cavaris the whole goddamn point of the AHL?!"

"Exactly, but she's got some personal business with Jovnelle, it seems." I spotted Zandos holding her in the millin garden. We ran over to them, where an EMT was trying to nurse her back to health. Mother Everealm went after us and stood at the other end of the garden. Reid and I ran behind a bush for cover; we didn't know what Mother Everealm was about to do.

She took a half-filled automatic rifle from a task operative and pointed it directly at Jovnelle.

"You!" she began, her tone filled with ire. "You made a deal with Cavaris! *You* destroyed our world! What you have done is unforgivable!" Her voice crackled like the fire in the palace.

"Wait..." Reid whispered to me. We were both crouching on the ground behind the bush. Jovnelle began to cry, overwhelmed with everything.

"This... I... you... I didn't do anything to you..." Jovnelle said, surrendering. Only a few dozen task ops and disaster relief people remained.

"Mother, no, you can't be doing this!" Marathene said, trying to take the rifle from her. She was shorter and weaker than Mother Everealm, but still pulled with all the strength she had. "This is my sister! Your own daughter!"

Mother Everealm yanked the gun away, not after a stray bullet fired and hit the ground. Marathene recoiled. She inhaled sharply and went after her again, this time taking out the magazine. She pressed it between her hands and vaporized it using her magic.

"The gun's not empty though," Reid whispered. "I can't see the open slot." He was right. Even without the magazine, the rifle still had one more shot.

Marathene panted. She stared at Mother Everealm, her body convulsing as if unsure what to say. "You just… you just want an excuse to kill her! After all this time, pretending she's a nuisance so you can throw away your worries!" Marathene said, stepping in front of Jovnelle. Zandos held her tighter.

"No. She was always a weakling, and you knew it! She never would have amounted to anything. Her dark magic is a hindrance," Mother Everealm insisted, still holding up the rifle. "You should have listened to me. You, Marathene, were meant to shine. Jovnelle's darkness has no place in our world!"

"You don't get to decide what is good or bad." The fire sister shouted. "Why are you so sure that you're right? Because you're too consumed by your own guilt?"

Mother Everealm looked distraught, as if she was going to either break into tears, violence, or laughter. She lowered her head, staring at the gun. It was a machine with a simple purpose, yet she couldn't bring herself to do anything with it. "I have done so much for this world—"

—"And that is what you tell yourself every night, and every morning that you chose yourself over Avukena," Marathene growled.

Mother Everealm dropped her gun and screamed. "I *love* Avukena!" she screeched, her voice surging like a flame. She stepped close to Marathene. "I would have done *anything* to keep it from rot."

I peeked over from behind my bush. She looked behind herself, seeing me. Reid quickly pulled me down, but it was too late.

"Isavna," she said, calling me forth, but not turning to look at me.

"Don't do it," Reid insisted, holding me down.

"I don't know if I have it in me to defy her right now," I rapidly whispered. I stood up. "Yes?"

"It is time for you to finish your mission."

I felt thorough panic as I began to glow and levitate above the ground. I screamed in terror, as for the first time I felt a sense of evil coming from Mother Everealm.

She levitated me over to her and handed me the semiautomatic rifle. My knees collapsed under me as the magic faded. I kneeled on the ground across from Jovnelle and Zandos. Mother Everealm pulled me up forcefully and gestured with her arm towards the rifle and Jovnelle. The other onlookers were looking at me, horrified.

The gun felt foreign in my hands. *What should I even do right now? Pretend it's empty? Pretend I don't know how to use it?*

I had to make a choice. It was either my mission or everything else along the way.

"Isavna, I do not have a lot of time," Mother Everealm urged. She looked away from Jovnelle. "Do it," she said. Her voice had quieted, as if giving a bit of mercy. Marathene looked at me in horror. I began to panic and quickly weighed the risks.

I had made it this far by sheer luck. I didn't believe in a god, but I knew I was still here for a reason.

"Marathene is right," I said. I stepped away from her. "This is why you sent me, because you couldn't do it yourself, huh?" My whole body tensed as I held the rifle to my side. I heard Mother Everealm's sharp, vicious inhale. I didn't dare look.

"She chose Cavaris." Mother Everealm said.

"She chose the only person who wouldn't reject her." Marathene interjected.

"She is not blameless! She wanted what Cavaris could give her: power, riches—"

—"You have never been to Nojuni palace if you think there are any riches!" Zandos shouted.

"You made Jovnelle believe that she was broken, that darkness was evil. Cavaris just offered her what you wouldn't," Marathene added.

Jovnelle stood up and ambled towards Mother Everealm, her shoulders heavy.

"I will not shout, I am too weak now," she began, as she stood with the last energy she had left. Mother Everealm diverted her eyes. "But you… wanted to kill me. You sent people to kill me."

"I needed them to end what you had become," she seethed, not looking up. "I saw what you did, with the possessions, destruction, and all the strain on Avukena's resources and people. You corrupted the balance, and I was left with no other choice."

"You saw what *he* did, but you never saw me. You never looked at me long enough to know the difference. But I am not evil. I am not the source of imbalance, yet you made it seem like I was," Jovnelle said, heavy with her emotions, brewing for centuries.

"You brought shadows into the world I was still planting," Mother Everealm said, her voice fraying at the edges. "Oh, how one mistake can unfurl into thousands, I…."

"Then say you were wrong," Marathene said plainly.

"No, I will not," she protested. "I did what I had to do, it was all too far gone."

"You conflated her existence for everything she represented to you; all that you couldn't control," Marathene said quietly.

Mother Everealm's breath trembled. "Was I the villain?" she wailed. "Was—Was I—*Am I* the villain for trying to save my world?! *My* world that I created and built from nothing?!" Her fingers quivered like leaves in the wind. "I love Avukena and everything in it more than you can imagine! I cannot believe... my love for you never changed!"

"Then why did you do this to me?!" Jovnelle cried out. Their eyes met for a moment.

"I was afraid of what you could become, but... I... I became a monster." She looked down at her hands, her rings reflecting the fire of the palace. A small blue diamond with white edges. But now, the blue reflected bright yellow. I heard the sirens wailing as people tried to put out the fire.

"I was wrong." She looked older than I had ever seen her. "My, how I was wrong. I have never... been wrong before. I thought... I was preserving balance. I was—" she looked down at her hands again. "No, I wasn't."

Zandos huffed, still angry. I felt my pendant, still in my pocket, become less heavy.

She closed her eyes for a moment, as if seeing a vision. "I believed —that, well... if I could've just held on...." She opened her eyes again. "And Cavaris is rising now because... I'm holding more power than I'm meant to."

The admission left her exposed. She didn't stand quite as tall and proud as she did before. She walked closer to Jovnelle and kneeled, holding Jovnelle's hand in hers.

"As long as I live, the world will continue to correct itself through war and Cavaris trying to rise to match my power."

"What are you implying?" Jovnelle asked, confused but neutral.

"That I should have died long ago," Mother Everealm said. "I gained more power than I should have, and now Cavaris is trying to match it and restore balance."

Marathene made a small, choked sound. I looked around me, my body flush against a bush as I tried to inch away.

"You want me to kill you," Jovnelle stated.

"You will choose," Mother Everealm said. "Because I have made enough choices."

Jovnelle's face was unreadable. She was staring at the mother who rejected her, blamed her, and sent her to her death. The mother she once loved.

"Will this stop Cavaris and the war?" she asked.

"He wants balance too. If the light side is weaker he must match that. As for the war, that is for you all to decide."

Jovnelle pulled her hand away, and for a moment I thought she might refuse. But then, it began to glow violet. "You will give me one thing first," she said, her voice firmer now.

"Anything," Mother Everealm replied, closing her eyes.

"The truth. Why did you neglect me before I was even born?" Isavna

"Because of what you represented," She opened her eyes again. "I was afraid of what wasn't light, and what I couldn't control. I was wrong. I am sorry."

Jovnelle's magic flare glowed brighter. "Yes, you were wrong."

Mother Everealm nodded once, then smiled weakly. "Thank you, my daughter."

The spell released like a comet. I braced on the ground.

Mother Everealm's body turned into a flurry of stars that compounded into a blinding mass and sent a small shockwave across the palace courtyard. I was already on the ground, but Reid, by the bush, fell. The mass floated far above the sky and became a bright star. The only thing left was a gust of blue magic that quickly went into her crown, the only thing left of her. And like that, she was gone, and a horrid pain struck through my body.

I7

As the spell struck through Mother Everealm, I felt a surge of something raw and violent tearing through me. My pendant felt like it burned white-hot in my pocket. I was already on the ground; had I not been I would have fallen.

My vision whited out, and I couldn't breathe. All I could feel was an overwhelming sensation, like I was thrown into a volcano. My pendant felt like it was searing against my leg, and then, it all stopped.

I pulled it out from my pocket and stared at it as I gasped for air. It looked the same, being small and unremarkable, with a new scuff on the edge of the stone. I looked closer, and it looked like it was glowing. Like it had some kind of heartbeat.

Reid helped me sit up as Marathene ran over.

"Isavna, are you wearing the necklace?!" she asked, her eyes crazed with fear.

"Now I am, why? What was—what just happened?" I asked, fumbling with the clasp as I put it on.

"That necklace," she began. "It—well—now that Mother is dead, don't *ever* take it off." Her grip on me tightened.

"What's the deal with it?" I demanded, panting. "Why didn't I know this before?" she looked around, at the smoking remains of the palace, at Zandos holding Jovnelle, and the crowd of stunned onlookers. She and Reid dragged me aside, away from the others.

"Your tether just transferred," she said, her voice quiet. "That pendant is not a diamond or some kind of natural gem. It's a piece of Mother herself. It could come with dangerous powers you don't know how to wield." She took another pause to make sure no one was watching. "It was inert while she lived. That is why your magic faltered; it weakened as she did. It's active now, so if you lose it or it's destroyed, your tether will reroute to the next strongest source.

"Cavaris," I said, my mouth dry.

I looked up to the star Mother Everealm had just become. Both of them were gone now. She was dead and Cavaris was… somewhere.

The AHL buses were loading the injured. Sirani was among them. Medics shouted instructions, and someone's voice shrieked, high and shrill, until it gave out.

"Wait, so why wasn't I ever told about this sooner? I'm lucky I happen to be wearing it now." I asked her angrily. Marathene grimaced.

"Your magic faded as Mother's did, since she only had so much life force to give." Marathene's bottom lip trembled as she stared above me. "When you came to the throne room after Levi died, and you asked her about your fading magic," Marathene said, finally kneeling to meet my eyes. She was biting down on both of her lips, trying to hold back a sob. "I'm sorry Isavna. She was lying to you. You didn't have to kill Jovnelle. You never should have been told you had to kill her, or been brought here to fulfill a mission that was never yours." she trembled. "I'm sorry I didn't say anything. Maybe if I had said something before it got worse, then she would still be alive… I'm sorry, I should've stopped her from taking you from Earth when I had the chance…."

I didn't say anything. I was too mad at the world and mad at Mother Everealm for everything that had happened, even if she was gone now.

"So then what's the truth?" I asked her, after she had caught her breath. "About the pendant. Why didn't she tell me the truth about it sooner?" she took a deep breath as she steadied herself. The tears on her cheek reflected the pink and green lights of the emergency vehicles parked around the court gardens.

"Mother used to be a ghost-like figure like Cavaris, during the birth of this world, but then took human form to live among her people. One of the tradeoffs was that her powers became finite."

I squinted, wondering why this had anything to do with my pendant, though it was news to me. *I suppose it makes sense. Why would she be human and Cavaris not be?* Marathene continued.

"Her magic was running out far before you got here. When she told me she wanted to bring an Earther to finally finish the job, I kept asking her, 'Mother, are you sure? Do you have the energy left?' and she would always tell me she did. But just enough for one more. That pendant had a large portion of her life force—more than enough for any human lifespan. When your magic started fading, it was a sign that hers was finally going to give out."

"But my magic stopped fading," I said. I levitated my Mahi blaster next to me with ease.

"That's because the tether you had with her no longer exists. You're running on the pendant's magic. Mother was worried that you might try and kill her to stop your fading magic if you knew that being on the pendant would bring it back."

I remained there, stunned, hearing a support beam somewhere within the palace suddenly give out. I finally pulled off my flight helmet. The cold air made me realize how much I had been sweating. My short hair stuck to my face.

"Why would she think that of me?" I didn't even see how it could have been possible for someone like me to successfully kill her. I took off my smudged glasses and hung them on my shirt collar.

"Probably because that is what she would have done." I looked at her, and her eyes became watery again. It must have been difficult for her to come to terms with the kind of person her mother turned into. A group of operatives called for her help and she left hastily, and I was left on the ground alone.

I looked at the rifle next to me. I opened the ejection port and took out the last live round, intended for Jovnelle, but never used.

Reid came up to me as I pocketed the round. His face was pale and blank. He didn't say anything. We stayed until the truck left and the building stopped burning. We walked to the dorms with a crowd of other guests.

And after that, the world kept turning. The star that Mother Everealm became gleamed on the firehose runoff on the sidewalk, guiding her people one last time.

Thursday, 12:40 AM, 3rd Floor, Everealm Academy Residential Community, Elkostet Hall

The door to Reid's dorm room clicked unlocked as he opened it. Inside, it was still just as Reid and Kairo, who also lived here, had left it. Their festival clothes were cast in piles beside an already-full laundry bin.

I closed the door behind me and took off my AHL boots. Only my second pair in four years. I set down Mother Everealm's crown, which I had taken with me, but it was wrapped in a torn curtain. I shed my jacket and left it right beside it, not before taking out my phone.

"Do you have any phone chargers in here?" I asked Reid as he collapsed onto the couch.

"What do you think?" he asked dryly. *That's right. People don't use cellphones here.* I tossed my dead phone onto the rest of my things and sat on the couch. My body ached in many places. I felt gross.

Reid let me use the bathroom, where I showered and changed into borrowed clothes. The room was plain, with bits of shaved hair in the sink and a stain on the ground.

I finished, and Reid went in after me. The lumpy pullout couch in the living room was already dressed in some stiff, rough, gray sheets. I collapsed onto it, and the springs squeaked in protest. I closed my eyes and heard the shower start. I tried to let my body rest, but my mind wouldn't.

I listened to the hum of the refrigerator, the shower, and the occasional siren outside. I began to think.

Is my mission over now?

My mission, not Mother Everealm's, has been to survive as long as possible and retain my identity as an Earther. And to save Jovnelle. But now, was I supposed to return to Earth? Stay here? I ran my fingers over the lumpy bed, suddenly feeling a deep sense of unease.

The shower stopped. A few moments later, he emerged. I shifted on the bed, and it made such a loud squeak that it made both of us flinch.

He went towards the old refrigerator and took out two green sports drinks, handing one to me.

"Goodnight." He said with finality as he headed to his room, stopping for a moment to stare at Kairo's door.

"Are you going to sleep?" I asked him, opening the bottle.

"No. I'm going to be calling Saku. She's in the hospital with Kairo and Sirani," he said.

"Okay," I replied, too tired to say anything else. I felt a little guilty, like I should be with Reid, calling my friends. But my body and my mind ached so deeply I couldn't bring myself to stay awake any longer. He retreated into his room, closing the door. I turned off my lamp and pulled the rough sheet up to my chin. The hot Avukena summer night reminded me of what Zandos told me a week ago, about feeling like he was on the sun. I turned over and tried to fall asleep. *This sheet feels like sandpaper.*

I fell asleep staring at the light spilling out of Reid's room from the gap under his door.

Thursday, 10:21 AM, Avukena Palace, Courtyard

Reporters and cameras were swarming around the palace like wasps. The police were controlling a small crowd. As I came with my group, most wearing the clothes from last night, a horde of reporters came, stuffing microphones in our faces. I felt a flicker of panic and anger as I pulled Mother Everealm's crown, wrapped in a torn curtain, tighter against my body. I was not interested in talking. Many of them followed me as I walked over the stone steps of the courtyard. *I should've expected there to be a crowd today.*

"What would you say happened last night?" One reporter of *Avukena Now* yelled at me, a boom microphone hanging over my head, nearly touching my glasses. I pushed my way through the swarm of reporters. I gave them a cursory glance. The loudest and most annoying groups were celebrity tabloids. The news seemed to spread quickly overnight, as correspondents from as far as Elkostet were there.

"What happened to Mother Everealm? Did Jovnelle kill her?" A reporter from *Avukena Daily* shouted, flashing a camera in my face. I felt a surge of anger and annoyance. I had to shake off the emotion they were trying to make me feel.

"No, she didn't. And it doesn't matter now, since she's already gone," I snapped, trying to sound confident and unaffected. I turned away coldly, still trying to evade the reporters. They gasped and murmured.

"Rumors say Jovnelle was spotted here last night. What do you have to say about that?" someone from *Eye on Avukena* said.

"Yes, she was here," I answered bluntly.

"Was she really the one who killed Mother Everealm?" A reporter from *Avukena Pop Magazine* asked, sounding incredulous. I stopped and turned to face the reporter. I felt a lump in my throat and tears in my eyes.

"You're pathetic, can't you understand the severity of what just happened?" I said, with more aggression than I should've, though it was probably the reaction the reporters wanted. "Do I look like I'm willing to give you information right now?"

My home was in shambles. Mother Everealm was dead. My best friend couldn't walk. I invoked my wings and flew towards some islands. I was sure the reporters would be flying too if they didn't have equipment. I'd rather they were Mahis than reporters. Then I could at least kill them.

I took a deep breath, having landed on the island. The sea was quiet. There was a small village of expensive vacation homes on the other side, but I was alone for now, except for the crown I was leaning on.

I tried messaging Sirani, but she didn't say anything back. I thought about talking to Reid, but his door was shut when I left. I threw a small pebble into the water and sighed.

I saw the palace remains, the entire middle section seemingly gone. It looked like a cake that was stomped on. Both the east and west wings were preserved, but we weren't allowed in yet due to the risk.

I couldn't dream at all last night, and I supposed it was due to the overload of everything in my life right then. It was too much to even think about. But seeing the palace in its condition gave me an indescribable feeling in my heart. With it all being over, at least I hoped, I had the opportunity to reflect on what had happened. But I couldn't. That palace was what gave me what I needed to possess a life I enjoyed with friends I loved, while in a strange world with a leader I despised. It was honestly too much to see it all just... gone.

A few minutes later, Reid reached out to me telepathically, and we talked a bit, and he decided to join me on the island. I sat down on the beach and stared blankly at the sky, waiting for him to arrive.

Reid landed about thirty yards away from me, retracting his black wings and breathing a little heavier. It was windy, and he flew against the airstream. He walked over to me, hands in sweater pockets. I didn't say anything.

"Hey Isavna," Reid said softly. The waves lapped gently on the gravelly shore. The tide had gone down a bit, revealing some tiny seashells and colorful crabs.

"I feel like a wreck right now," I said, with more of a pout than I would have liked. My injuries had healed a little by then, but I still didn't feel great. The bags under my eyes felt like they were sagging to the ground.

"Me too," Reid replied. We got up and walked to the other side of the small island, where there was a forest.

"I wish I could go home, but I don't feel like I even have one anymore," I stepped over a large branch.

"You have me and Sirani right now," Reid said, understanding how I felt. "Both she and Kairo are stable." We approached a clearing of tall grass and a fallen tree.

"And barely anything else," I said. "I swear, if any other crazy disaster were to happen, I feel like I'd be next to go. Or maybe Kairo would inhale too much smoke. Or Sirani would get possessed for the last time. Or someone else would die in some crazy way we didn't predict and wish we could prevent," I said bitterly. I didn't want to take my anger at the world out on Reid, but I really didn't have any other words. "I don't even think I fear death anymore."

"This is why your role is as important as it is. You were chosen, Isavna. Mother Everealm knew your potential. How you respond to this makes the difference. Sirani and I, and everyone for that matter, are here with you until the bitter end. I won't lie, this has taken a toll on me, you, everyone. But there's still more we need to do."

"This isn't destiny or fate, though. I was chosen as another disposable Earther for Mother Everealm's convenience," I said incredulously. I could feel my own cynicism and heard Reid's sigh in response. It was hard to retain any positivity. "I hate her. You know, when I first met Mother Everealm, I thought she was some kind of immortal, righteous deity who could never do wrong. A god. She looked like one, at least. But turns out, she was just an old hag too afraid of the world she created, too afraid of losing control, and too afraid of apologizing to do anything meaningful in her old age." I looked over the tall grass we were sitting in. "I don't know what I expected from a world where even the gods are mortal. They just… live longer. Too long."

Reid shifted his position. "I wish I could tell you that you're wrong," Reid said, sounding more weary than anything.

"Sorry, do I sound kind of crazy—"

—"No, you're fine. You can be mad."

I leaned back in the tall grass, letting it cushion my fall. It felt sort of spiky. A thought crossed my mind that maybe there was a rat or fleas in the grass, but I was too tired to care. The gray Dekerei Hovercars Company hoodie felt sort of rough in the way that worn hoodies feel. I considered the prospect of not returning it.

"You seemed surprised when Marathene told you Mother Everealm used to be a spirit like Cavaris," said Reid. "She would've probably been immortal had she kept that form."

"It was news to me," I said, staring at the sky.

"She took humans from Earth, and not just you, all humans on Avukena came from various places on Earth. Along with a lot more stuff, apparently. I've never been to Earth, so I wouldn't know what, exactly."

"Rice, carrots, chickens, cows, horses, birds, certain species of fish, crabs, mollusks, a heck of a lot of fashion styles and inventions, and so on."

"Really? I always thought chickens came from Dekerei. Their snow fowl industry is huge." I heard him shift around.

"So why did Mother Everealm ever want to take a human form?" I asked, still wondering.

"She thought it would give her better control over her people. The same way that Cavaris wants chaos without reason, she wants order without reason. When she took human form, she also took human flaws." The wind picked up and made the grass around me sound like a rattle being shaken.

"I guess what's funny is that she tried to control the entire world, having built it all, but the one thing she couldn't control… was being human. Her ego, her fear, and her body and mind as she aged," I said, rolling over in the grass. "Hey Reid, if Mother Everealm created this world, why did she make it so fragile and hard to control?"

He thought for a second. "Oh, I don't know. Maybe it's because this world was never meant to last forever. Mother Everealm didn't. I wonder if she knew she was going to die."

"She knew." I said, gesturing to my pendant. "That's why I have this. I wish she would've prepared this world more, though. But it probably explains why she was so desperate to kill Jovnelle these past few weeks." We sat in silence for a little while longer. I smelled a bit of the salt from the bay.

I sat up and faced Reid, who was leaning his back on a nursery log, mushrooms coming out of the top. Some weird Avukenan plants were also there.

"Think those reporters are still after you?" he asked while attempting to assess my mood.

"No."

"Do you think they would ask me any questions? A valiant bystander?" He smiled, but the joke didn't land.

"It's too late to be able to tell, unless someone from East Seranoy or something recognized you from holotevision," I said.

I looked more at the log right behind Reid. It had died long ago, but it facilitated new life after its death. So, it was never really gone; it just manifested in a different form.

"What?" Reid asked, thinking I was looking at him.

"Nothing," I said. I looked at the tiny blue mushrooms, fascinated by how something so small and delicate could be so persistent. I traced my finger through the spiky grass. "Gosh, we're so pointless. I know it's obvious… and probably a cheesy thing to say," I said, laughing as I heard my dumb monologue out loud. "But something as permanent as the palace, or even Mother Everealm, we thought could last forever. But it didn't. Even us, as interns or task ops. Yesterday, when we were fighting Cavaris, everyone looked so small. Like flies hovering over fruit or something."

"Well, we're not *that* pointless," Reid said without conviction in his voice. I nodded blankly at Reid. I looked at the clouds, vast and indifferent.

"How late did you stay up?" I asked, tugging on the grass. "I got up to pee around two and the light in your room was still on."

"I stayed awake till four. Slept until ten."

"Gosh, you must be running on fumes right now."

"Yeah," He said wryly, rubbing his bloodshot eyes. I rolled over the spiky grass idly, feeling all the bumps on the ground poke at my bruises. It was almost as uncomfortable as the pullout couch. But not quite.

"So are we going to just sit here forever or what?"

"I dunno, do you have a better idea?" Reid asked.

"Not really." With so much happening in life, the moment I spent with Reid felt like everything was normal again. We sat there a bit longer, sharing small stories and details. The time that passed felt like grains of sand shifting across the windy beach. Fast. Inconsequential. Temporary. Are friends only there to expose these qualities? At the same time, I didn't much care how fast it went. I got a chance to stop moving for a while, and that was enough.

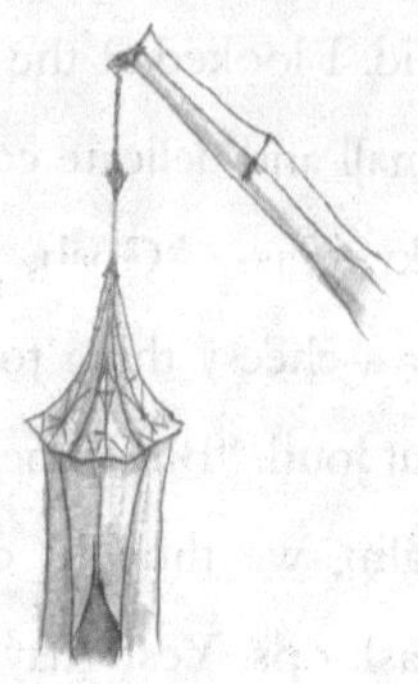

18

Sirani was healing quickly. Avukena's advanced medicine allowed for an accelerated healing time. Reid, Sirani, and I were sitting in front of Avukena Palace, watching the reconstruction.

"How's work been?" Reid asked us. We had been spending a lot of time in the AHL, mainly because we graduated from the Everealm Preparatory Academy, though the ceremony was postponed because of recent events.

"Meetings. Lots of meetings," I replied. "Everyone's talking about internal restructuring to fit the AHL's current goals."

"Yeah. I have a suspicion we might get promotions next evaluation period," Sirani said. "Mostly because they're dissolving our current positions."

"Really?" I said, watching a crane install a spire. "Where'd you hear that?"

"I overheard some execs talking about it in the mess hall. Something about lower-level restructuring." She replied. "Do you know what their game plan for Cavaris is?"

"We might hear about it during the next Div One meeting next week," Reid said. "But I have my own assumptions of what it could be."

"Me too," I said blankly, trying to consolidate my thoughts. "We don't know where Cavaris is, first of all. He has no anchor that we know of, so he can't be as powerful as he was before. But that aside, the first thing we need to know is where he is. Then, we figure out what his patterns look like now that he doesn't have a large source of energy or guaranteed safety like with Jovnelle. Something tells me we might have to keep him around in some capacity; I mean, Mother Everealm emphasized cosmic balance. It was why she died after all." The construction workers on top of the palace were hammering on something, though they were so far away that I could barely hear. "So he wouldn't get any stronger than he is now."

"Right," Reid replied tersely. I felt Sirani shift on the wooden bench. We stood up, silently agreeing to go to work.

The attack a month ago seemed so distant, but its effects lingered as we stepped into AHL from the portals. Saku was walking with a few cadets and a clipboard, telling them about the best ways to kill Mahifers without a blaster. Jovnelle was among us, sitting in the mess hall, sipping tea. She had on a black jumpsuit and gold blouse. She looked fresh, with renewed life in her eyes. Marathene was with her.

"Hello!" Jovnelle said, waving to us. She had her long, white hair, like Mother Everealm's, tied up in a low bun.

"Hi." I replied. "How are you?"

"I am doing fine. I will be returning to my palace soon. The AHL is at work cleaning it out and seeing if Cavaris has remained there," Jovnelle said. I turned to see Zandos, who was bringing sandwiches and shaved ice to Marathene and Jovnelle. He had the same black leather coat he had when I first met him. But it wasn't cracked and broken anymore; he had mended it. He was also wearing Levi's broadsword.

"Hey, Zandos." I asked. "How did you get that?" I saw Jace, who was carrying napkins behind him, too. Sirani came up to him to talk.

"Keya gave it to me." Zandos replied. "She said Levi would've liked it being used in the hands of someone he trusted." Reid approached him, his hands in his pockets, also noticing the broadsword, but he didn't say anything. Jace and Sirani were still talking, walking someplace else. Zandos, Reid, and I sat with the two sisters.

"Hello," Zandos greeted. "How are you?"

"Hey Zandos," Reid said. "I'm fine. So they're rebuilding your palace, right?"

"Yes," Zandos said, a bit surprised to remember that. It appeared as if he had forgotten about that place.

"So, do you think you'll go back to Nojuni? I mean, your mom is saved. Your work here is done," Reid asked.

Zandos looked down, thinking. Jace and Sirani finished talking and sat with us. Reid asked the same to Jace.

"I do not know. I would like to, yes, but I also want to keep working here," Zandos looked guilty. "I feel I should."

"Neither of you guys have to stay. It was an honor for you two to help us," Marathene said.

Zandos smiled softly. "I never really liked living there," Zandos said. "Sorry, mom."

Jovnelle laughed. "No, it's fine. You and I both know that we are a few centuries past due for a remodel. Sadly, we did not have time. Could you imagine a new palace?"

"One with heating," Zandos said. "And without rats."

Jovnelle put her hands over her heart and sighed, fluttering her long white lashes.

"And I can get my room back," Reid said. Kairo had also been released from the hospital this week, making the dorm rooms especially crowded. Zandos, Jace, Kairo, and Reid had been living together for the past week in a two-bedroom dorm, while I was with Sirani.

"You guys are cool and stuff, but I'm sick of fighting over a single bathroom." Reid said. An AHL member approached us.

"We finished cleaning your palace, Jovnelle. Thank you for your cooperation." The man said. Jovnelle nodded curtly and gestured for us to follow her.

"Do you think they remodeled it in a month?" Sirani asked Jovnelle. She smiled knowingly. We walked to the vans and went to the newly founded Nojuni City. We would have taken portals, but to do that, there must already be one there.

We landed after a few hours on the hovercars. The few living liberated citizens were cheering, and construction was everywhere. Gardens with freshly planted flowers lined the streets. Sirani began to sneeze.

We turned a corner to Nojuni Palace. It was still under construction, but from what we could see, it was beautiful. It looked like a more modern take on German Gothic cathedrals. We walked into the palace, and Jovnelle began to squeal. She celebrated and praised the workers in Hakon, though she spoke so fast I could hardly pick up anything. A construction worker approached Jovnelle.

"I see you have found the palace. We weren't able to preserve many of the things before remodeling, except for one ballroom," he said sadly.

"Oh, no, that is fine," She said, waving her hand dismissively. "I am sick of seeing the same walls for a few hundred years, I much prefer new ones," she replied, smiling. Zandos zoomed upstairs to look for his room while Reid, Jace, and I, carrying Sirani and her crutches, ran after. Zandos's new room was elegant and had a new bed, which he immediately dove into.

"It's soft!" he exclaimed, eyes wide. "I may want to stay here after all." I smiled. There was a desk with papers that had been there previously. The bookshelf had all the old books, and the old painting of him was on the wall, too.

Jace didn't speak, but he looked amazed. He put Sirani down on one of the couches. Reid pointed to the balcony. Outside, there were the same potted plants as when I first came. It had a canopy, too, since the snow was frequent in the winter. I saw a herd of felmines fly overhead, casting faint shadows over the gardens.

We decided to explore the rest of the palace and see what else had changed. Jovnelle led us to the throne room, where she gasped in delight. The walls were decorated with paintings of the dark realms and the rest of the Nojuni region, and the stained-glass windows let in plenty of light. Red, gold, and black tapestries hung between the windows.

"This is perfect. I feel like a new empress. I'm so proud of you, Zandos. You've grown so much," Jovnelle said, tearing up. "And you too, Jace. Both of you have done so much to save me." She turned to Marathene and gestured to us. "Thank you for trusting them to help me. You're all welcome to stay here until Avukena Palace gets rebuilt." I looked at the freshly picked millin blossoms in a pot beside the window, colored from the red stained glass. Its fragrance lingered in the hall. The world continued outside, but I felt an earned moment of peace, and suddenly, all the work it took felt worth it.

Later that evening, I sat for dinner with Marathene, Sirani, and Reid in the throne room, as the dining hall was still under construction. We decided to sleep there that night since a direct portal wasn't set up yet, and traveling back would be longer than we'd like.

"When do you think we can return to Avukena Palace?" I asked Marathene.

She finished her forkful of fried vegetables and spoke. "By tomorrow afternoon. They told me it would be livable by then, but a lot of sections would still be closed."

"Wow. Construction on Earth takes months, even years, since they don't use magic," I said.

"Why not? Do they not at least use it to enhance certain things?" Zandos asked.

"No, no magic at all. Magic doesn't exist there, except for the inert potential magic, which only turns usable once you come to Avukena. But we can't use that on Earth," I said.

"It's just a different place, Zandos. They do not use magic, but they're just as strong as us, since they need to find clever solutions for things we use magic for. Really, we are the lazy ones," Jovnelle explained. Zandos nodded with understanding.

I was excited to move back into my home. But thinking about magic reminded me of my own, and how Mother Everealm lied about the pendant to get me to kill Jovnelle. I levitated a plate of roasted potatoes. *No strain. It's easy now.* If nothing else good came from the palace attack, my magic was back in full force. I finished my food and went into an open lounge, near the guest room I was staying in. I spoke with Sirani as Reid was talking with Zandos.

"So how are your knees now?" I asked. They were still visibly bruised and had black braces over them.

"Better. I can kind of walk with crutches. I just need to rebuild strength," she explained. Suddenly, my phone buzzed and rang. It was Toniska.

"Hey, Toniska!" I said. "You're on speaker."

"Are you okay, Isavna?! I called as soon as I heard. Salia told me about the attack," she began.

"Yeah, I'm fine. That, um, happened a month ago. Sirani is with me, and she broke her knees. I'm okay though. By the way, the palace got destroyed, so I'm staying in Nojuni Palace right now." I explained.

"Hi, Sirani. Really? Nojuni Palace? That run-down crack-shack nasty excuse for a palace?" Toniska said with disgust. I saw Sirani smile and shake her head.

"No, it got remodeled. It looked like those mansions we saw when we visited LA that one time." I said. Sirani looked at me, confused, not knowing what LA was, but I continued. "It's really pretty now." Toniska and I spoke more, and I told her about Cavaris, Reid, Jovnelle, and more things that had happened. Then, she asked the question I had been hoping she wouldn't ask.

"When are you coming back?" Toniska asked. "It's been a while. By the way, Adam and Jennifer say hi."

I contemplated. I really didn't want to go back.

"Who are they?" Sirani asked. "Did they go to school with you?"

"My elderly neighbors," I explained. Sirani giggled.

"I'm waiting!" Toniska complained.

"I don't think I really want to go back. I have too much to do here, and I really like it here."

Toniska was silent for a moment, but then sighed. "Okay. Well, I can't say I'm not disappointed. We miss you, you know, when you're not being a nerd. You're my sister, and I wish you were here. But I understand why you want to stay. Avukena's a cool place, I guess. I'm… I'm happy for you. Yeah. You deserve that," Toniska said, sounding sincere but sad. I smiled. I refrained from telling her about Levi's death.

"Thanks for being mature about that, Toniska. I miss you too, but this is where I belong now," I said.

"Glad to hear that. You sound happy. That's cool, I guess," Toniska added. "But promise me, if Cavaris doesn't go away, you're coming back."

"I promise, Toniska. I won't forget. But I know we'll keep him away."

"'Kay. Take care, okay? And call me again soon. I wanna hear more about what happens, with your friends, and I can't wait until I go back to Avukena," Toniska said, chuckling.

"Okay, I will. Take care of yourself too, and say hi to Adam and Jennifer, mom and dad, and everyone else. Bye," I said, smiling.

"Bye, Isavna. Talk soon," Toniska said, hanging up. I felt a mix of emotions, but mostly happiness. I looked outside the giant window to the evening sun and smiled as a sense of peace washed over me, and the last of my tension finally dissipated.

19

Thursday, 7:02 PM, Nojuni Palace, Throne Room

After having watched a movie in the room we were staying in for the night, we entered the throne room for dinner. There was bread, salad, snow fowl, and soup. It smelled delicious. We ate in silence, as the construction noises waned. Finally, Marathene spoke.

"What did you all do?" she asked.

"We watched a movie. *Death and Destruction Six*," I said.

"It was very good." Zandos said. "You should watch it, Aunt. It is great." Sirani nodded excitedly in agreement.

"It was actually good this time, somehow!" Sirani gushed. *I didn't think it was that good.* Marathene looked somewhat interested in the way that parents feign interest with their children's crayon drawings. "Well, maybe I will have to watch it."

I had a feeling she wouldn't get to do that for a while since her duties likely piled on top of each other, now more than ever. She was going to co-rule Nojuni with Jovnelle, at least for a little while, so Jovnelle could learn to run her own kingdom properly. They didn't expect their population to grow rapidly at all. It was as if war had suddenly ended in the Middle East; it wouldn't attract new residents right away.

We ate in silence for a little while, discussing idle topics. I saw construction workers passing by and could still hear drills from somewhere in the palace. Large pieces of drywall were being levitated near the grand staircase, like marching ants.

"Hey mom," Zandos asked Jovnelle.

"Yes?" she replied, wiping her mouth with a napkin.

"You had been possessed by Cavaris all my life. What caused him to possess you in the first place?" he asked. I winced. It didn't sound like a good idea to ask so soon.

She seemed to think the same, grimacing a little bit, but she humored his question. "He gave me an offer of power in exchange for using me as a vessel to possess. Power is a tempting thing. I wanted to grow my kingdom, but I had no knowledge on how, since I did not have any guidance. He promised me that if I allowed him to use my energy, then many citizens would come to Nojuni." Jovnelle said. "But I did not know he would possess them too. I did not care much for riches, or living the life of a queen. I wanted to give people something I never received, which was love, trust, security and hope."

"Things that Mother never gave you," Marathene said quietly.

"That is all I really wanted. Cavaris promised me that with his help, the people would come. It is very easy to take advantage of someone desperate," Jovnelle said, sighing. Everyone in the room looked solemn. "Quite honestly, I'm glad things happened the way they did." Marathene looked confused. "That I am free of Cavaris, but also Mother can live in peace in the stars and her crown." The way she spoke made it seem like she was happy she was dead—or at least, still spiteful about it. I glanced over to Mother Everealm's crown, in the corner. Marathene never told us why. It glinted as if Mother Everealm could somehow hear us. And maybe that's why she brought it, so she could see what Nojuni had become. Jovnelle continued. "I hope that now Mother Everealm understands what she did."

"She can't hurt you anymore, Jovnelle," Marathene said, only partially sympathizing with her disdain. I could always sense that Marathene and Mother Everealm had to be at odds in many decisions, but she still felt some kind of loyalty. After all, she and Mother Everealm had to be extremely close.

"I know. The most complete form of revenge I could have would be to forgive her. She wanted me dead, and if I were to survive she may have never spoken to me," Jovnelle said quietly, putting her fork and knife onto the plate. "I do not know if I can forgive her quite yet. It may take years."

"I agree, Jovnelle." Marathene said.

"Cavaris was the only one who gave me anything. That's why I fell into his trap," Jovnelle said. "It was almost as if he loved me too."

I gasped, and I heard Sirani drop her fork.

"You aren't suggesting that you loved Cavaris?" Marathene ventured tentatively.

"I am. After being betrayed, you learn things the hard way," Jovnelle said.

Zandos looked scared. "Mom, what are you saying? Then… where did I come from? Who are my parents?" Zandos asked.

"Me. And your father is Cavaris… I think. When you're unconscious most of the time you just don't know…" Jovnelle said.

"Then what does that make me?"

"More powerful than me. Eventually," she replied. "You won't get your full power until hundreds of years in the future."

"That explains why the Mahis didn't seem to attack you!" Reid exclaimed. "Back at the palace. When we were fighting Mahis. They were like, trying to run away."

"It also explains your powerful magic," Sirani said. "And the dragon wings. Those are quite rare." Jace's eyes darted between Zandos's twisted face and Jovnelle's apparent indifference.

"This means I will outlive all of you," Zandos said, looking at us. His eyes were bleak, and his face went pale. "Everyone here." None of us said anything or even moved.

We all looked at him, but his eyes looked past us all. Past the palace walls, past the mountain range around the palace, past the sky, past the stars. His fingers curled into his palms, and his lips tightened. He looked like he was trying to comprehend the sudden knowledge of living far past the day the last of us turns to dust. I had never seen someone so afraid, not to die, but to live. Jovnelle broke the silence.

"Yes, you are the newest form of deity," Jovnelle finally replied gently.

"And if Mother Everealm lived a couple billion years…" Sirani said.

"Then I will live almost as long." Zandos blinked, suddenly burying his face in his hands. "I think I am done. I'm going upstairs." My heart broke for him. We continued onto dessert in silence. I tried to empathize and feel what he must be feeling, even though it was kind of impossible.

Would I become numb to losing people if I lived that long? Would I stop finding rosy sunsets beautiful, after having seen several million of them? Would I ever get bored with living? It sounded like some kind of awful curse. I did not envy him in the slightest.

After dessert, we all decided to retire to our rooms. I hugged Jovnelle and Marathene and thanked them for their hospitality and honesty.

I knew it must have been hard for them to share their stories, especially with Cavaris still out there. I hoped they would find peace in the night. Reid, Sirani, and I walked over to the guest rooms. The three of us were sharing a room, with Sirani and I staying in the primary two beds, and Reid on the couch. It wasn't ideal, but construction workers were mainly using the guest complex since Nojuni City didn't have proper hotels yet.

We settled into the room. Sirani was on her wrist projection, scrolling through social media. Reid was going through channels on the holotelevision. I sighed and opened my phone. I saw the news of the New Klethorog anniversary party posted on their social media. Their culture seemed interesting. From what I could tell, they weren't as into tea as we were in Avukena. A lot of old men wore their hair long. Green geometric shapes seemed prevalent in the old people's robes. The young people seemed to be into more conservative, plain, and modest styles there, Saku being an exception. The ends of her hair had been dyed blue for some time now, and she often dressed in a more colorful, fun, and cute style. Kairo, however, was with the majority.

The day got late, Reid gave up on looking for something to watch, and Sirani tucked herself in, so I decided to go to sleep as well.

Friday, 8:48 AM, Nojuni Palace, Throne Room

"I wonder where Zandos is. Or how he's doing now." Sirani said as we ate our breakfast. We had eggs, but they didn't look too appealing since they were cooked poorly and were as tough as a shoe. I didn't even know how they managed to do that. The edges were browned in a very unbecoming way. It reminded me of eggs in an Earth hotel's continental breakfast. Or my pathetic attempts at cooking as a child.

"He came down earlier, I think," Jace replied with his mouth full, eating his food ravenously, even though it wasn't very good. *How could he possibly like it? This is literal dog food.*

"I wonder if he's okay," Sirani said. "After he left." We heard footsteps coming from the stairs, barely audible because of the construction noises.

"Hello!" Marathene said brightly. She had on a wide-brimmed sun hat that matched her pistachio dress.

"Hi," I said. Everyone was poking at their breakfast without eating it, save for Jace.

"Gosh, Jace, will you *please* at least *try* to have *some* semblance of manners? You're nobility, for heaven's sake." Jace wiped his mouth with his sleeve. "It's disrespectful to our host, Jovnelle," Sirani scolded.

"Fine," Jace grumbled. "I lived here for years, though, you know." It was sort of funny to see him be berated by his younger sister.

"Ready to go home, everyone? The palace is ready for us to move in," Marathene said, noticing our disgust at the food. All of us happily agreed, having a reason to leave the table. As we got ready to go, Zandos appeared from upstairs. He had a neutral but tired expression on his face. He had dark circles surrounding his eyes.

"Wanna go to Avukena Palace with us?" Jace asked hesitantly.

"Sure," Zandos replied bleakly. We took a van and left across the smooth black asphalt road.

As the van hovered along the beaten path, the sun blazing through the tinted windows, I couldn't help but feel a sense of anticipation building within me. Sitting next to me, Sirani idly fiddled with her long, blond hair, her honey eyes fixed on the passing scenery. Marathene, dressed in her pistachio sundress, sat in the driver's seat, absently tapping her manicured nails against the window. Reid and Jace chuckled to themselves in the far back, as one of them showed the other some kind of lowbrow meme. Jace was also talking with Sirani about going back to school in the next school year to finish his studies before trying to find a stable job somewhere. Zandos, however, remained silent and lost in thought. At this point in our ride, we were already in the northern part of Sjasa, the city north of Avukena City.

The van beeped. We all looked out the window to see the grand gates of the Avukena Palace down the road. They were adorned with gold and silver and beautiful gemstones of different colors. Marathene put the van into manual mode, and the steering wheel pushed out. She began to drive expertly around the construction materials. The palace was finally coming back together.

We all exited the van and began to make our way towards the palace entrance. The air was warm and humid, and a light breeze rustled through the trees surrounding the courtyard. I could smell the salt from the bay. A feeling of familiarity washed over me as I gazed upon the architecture, the intricate carvings and sculptures that adorned the walls and gardens. It felt good to be back.

"Are you okay, Zandos?" Marathene asked, noticing his unhappiness.

"I am okay. I am just... a bit upset my mother had not told me about my origins sooner," Zandos explained.

"I'm sure Jovnelle would have, she just never got the opportunity," Sirani said.

"I suppose so. I do not know. She was just so... casual about it, like it did not even matter to her, or should matter to me," Zandos said. "I cannot bear that one day I will forget everyone from this short moment in my life." We arrived at the door, and it swung open, leading into the lobby.

It was full of people in high-vis uniforms and hard hats. A butler approached us.

"Welcome back, Madam Everealm." A butler said. It felt strange hearing her being referred to by her last name. It felt like the name was for Mother Everealm, and only her.

We all followed the butler to the elevator. "Most of the floors are closed off, except for floors twenty, nineteen, five, two and one." The butler explained. I itched with curiosity to know what was on floor five, but this was not the time. "Most of the residential units were left untouched except what was necessary for electrical rewiring. We found a major problem with it while we were demolishing and cleaning out the wreckage," the butler said. "Ms. Belanis, your room is also available for you to use once again." I thanked him, smiling.

Reid turned to the group. "Also, we should probably pack our stuff since we need to be in New Kleth *tomorrow*." Reid said. "We're leaving tonight, Kairo told me so."

Zandos's eyes widened, still dazed. "Wow, he only told you so soon before we needed to leave?"

Reid nodded. "Yeah. Kinda bad timing. I mean, I guess we did get the invitation some weeks ago, but these past few days have been busy," Reid said. "Anyway, let's go upstairs."

We got into the elevator and pressed the button for the twentieth floor. Marathene decided to go to her own room and speak with the construction crew. The elevator ascended quickly. We stepped out of the elevator and walked down the hallway into my unit. A butler had handed me my key, which I clutched tightly. The plastic keychain was melted, and the key was tarnished, but I hoped it still worked. I heard rumors from other wards that it would change to biometric security soon.

I opened the door and felt a surge of relief. I was worried my unit was going to burn down or get damaged during the attacks, so I was relieved to see it as I had left it. My bed was messily made, and my desk was somewhat untidy. The middle table on my sunken floor was full of candles that had melted to the bottom, which we had used when the power went out. It still smelled faintly of hairspray and perfume. I walked over to the table and picked up one of the candles. It was lavender-scented, my favorite, although it had run out because of how long we left it running for light during the attack. My bloodied pantyhose were still cast in a pile in the bathroom, and the wrappers of bandages littered the ground. I remembered how Sirani gave the lavender candle to me, along with a book of poetry by a famous poet in Luzuma.

Luzuma. Levi's kingdom. For a moment, I thought about the attack and how he would have responded to everything. Although I was confident he could have defended himself, I felt a little better knowing he didn't have to witness any of that.

Everyone else had situated themselves and relaxed in my unit. Zandos and Jace were sitting in the sunken floor, chatting and laughing. Sirani was on my bed, scrolling through her wrist projection. Reid was in my kitchenette, putting my kettle on the stove to make some tea, after washing out the few-weeks-old water.

"Shouldn't we get going, with packing and stuff for the trip?" Jace finally asked us. I checked the clock. We still had a lot of time.

"Our flight leaves tonight, so we have the whole day, basically," I said. "Plenty of time. I'm excited." I smiled. It would be a red-eye flight; we'd arrive early the following day. Sirani looked up from her wrist projection and looked at me, sitting on the table near the kitchenette. The crutches were on the ground beside her.

"Yeah, I can't wait to go to New Kleth. I don't think I've been there before, but I heard they're showing *Death and Destruction Seven* in theaters over there!" Sirani said, smiling. *So soon, too. Gosh.*

"I've always wanted to visit New Kleth too. It better not disappoint, Saku and Kairo have been hyping it up for like, forever now," I said, laughing.

"How are you going to dance with broken knees?" Jace asked Sirani. She could walk with crutches, but she wouldn't be able to safely dance.

"I suppose I could try and levitate," she said, closing her wrist projection and putting her hands on her lap. "But I'm not that great at it. I get way too tired way too fast."

"Maybe you'll have to skip dancing this time," Reid said, taking cups out of my cabinet.

I sighed, having nothing to do. "I suppose I'd best get to packing." I said, walking into my closet. As I packed, I heard the tea kettle whistle.

Reid quickly dashed over to the kitchenette and poured us all some tea. It was hot and refreshing, compared to the cold state the room was in, having no inhabitants for all this time. We sat down in the sunken floor to relax and talk about our plans and all sorts of things until we decided we'd better get ready for the flight. Sirani, Reid, and Jace left for the portal room to go to the dormitory complex.

Friday, 6:41 PM, Avukena Palace, Lobby

We met with Marathene and Jovnelle in the main lobby as we awaited our plane at the palace garage. We kept cars, vans, carriages, helicopters, and airplanes in there. Keya was with us, catching a ride, though she was on her wrist projection at the moment. I checked my phone for the time. *We're fine.* Zandos came last and noticed we were all already there.

"Are you okay? You look sick," Jovnelle asked in Hakon. Zandos nodded. He looked like a little kid in comparison to Jovnelle's height. She and Marathene dwarfed us all.

"I'm fine, mom. Just a bit tired," he replied in Hakon.

They continued speaking in a different language, maybe their own native one. The one that sounded guttural, like Arabic or Spanish. I was impressed, as that meant English was Zandos's third language. Most people in Avukena City were at least bilingual in English and Hakon, trilingual if they came from someplace else. *Where I'm from, most people are monolingual. That would be incomprehensible here.* She stared ahead as if receiving a telepathic message.

"Our plane is ready," she said. We headed to the garage, our luggage rolling behind us. When we entered, I felt the cool summer air. We saw a sleek and shiny jet waiting for us. It looked to be a private jet, of which we had a few of our own, but it had the emblem of New Klethorog. A group of servants helped us load our luggage, along with gifts from Avukena and the surrounding cities, like Sjasa and the Water Batrans. New Klethorog was a giant and powerful place, the capital of its region, so it made sense for people from everywhere to recognize it.

We boarded the plane and found our seats, where we were greeted by Saku, who was happy to see us. She was dressed differently and did her hair in an updo, something so formal that it didn't fit my image of her. She appeared to have been wearing concealer or something because her usual sleepy eyes looked forced awake. The plane was small but still felt comfortable. It had leather seats, a mini bar, a TV, and snacks. We buckled our seatbelts and awaited takeoff.

"Hello, Avukenan friends, thank you for coming to our banquet." The pilot over the intercom said, in a thick Klethoran accent, similar to Saku and Kairo's. "We are about to depart. Please sit back and enjoy your flight, we are expected to arrive at about three in the morning. We expect an air channel that may cause a bit of turbulence over the Gosbon Islands." The plane moved out of the garage and zoomed over the runway with a loud rumble. We felt a thrill of excitement and anticipation as the plane lifted above the ground. We looked out the window and saw Avukena fading away as we headed northwest. The seats were comfortable. I heard Keya yawn as we reached cruising altitude. I leaned my head back against the cushion as I attempted to drift off to sleep.

When I woke up, it felt like hours later. I checked my phone. *Hm. It's only 9:20*, I thought. Everyone else was awake, too, as Saku was getting us drinks from the minibar.

"Want anything, Isavna?" Saku asked me quietly, trying not to wake up some who were still asleep.

"Whatcha got?" I asked, my voice hoarse.

"Citrus juice, blackberry juice, Lenton berry juice, Jeya, and other stuff," she said, handing me a menu. "And water, of course, if you're *boring*."

"Can you get me some vanilla Jeya, please?" I asked her.

"Coming right up," she said, taking back the menu. She came back soon after, with all of our drinks.

"Thank you for your hospitality and allowing us to stay in your palace, Saku," Marathene said, receiving her tea.

"Of course, Marathene. My parents wanted to make sure you all made it there safely," Saku replied.

"How's he doing?" Keya asked while Saku handed me the fizzy drink.

"He's fine. Just doing dumb-idiot-loser stuff like normal probably," Saku said, snorting a laugh. "Nah. In all seriousness, he's been swamped. He has lots and lots of responsibilities, but he seems to be handling it well," Saku said.

She was wearing more formal clothes than her usual pastels. She had black pants, black ballet flats, and a powder blue blouse. The blue dip dye she had only a week ago had been cut off.

"So when is he going to become king?" Zandos asked. "Or are you going to?" he spoke quietly.

"No, he's going to do it. I'm going to go rule someplace else I think, if I marry some monarch. I don't think I can handle all the duties I already have, so being queen would be worse," Saku explained, chuckling wryly.

"Well, you seem to be holding up fine," Reid said, sipping his tea.

Saku's eyes widened. "No, no way," she said. "It's just easy 'cause you guys are my friends. I suck at interacting with new people. My dad's thinking of stepping down as king too within the next ten or even twenty years. I think Kairo's totally fit for the role."

"Yes, I agree. I have observed him in AHL functions and he always conducts himself professionally," Marathene added.

"He's like, super good at magic manipulation too," Reid added. "He's a natural. He could stand to be a little cleaner at home, though, but I'm sure you know."

Saku nodded slowly, eyes wide. She sat down, and I stared out the window as the sun set over the ocean horizon. I didn't notice myself falling asleep.

20

Late in the evening, after long hours of getting ready, we made our way down to the guest complex's lobby of the New Klethorog Palace. It was a lot colder than Avukena, requiring at least a light shawl.

We found Marathene, Jovnelle, Keya, and Reid. The guest complex was on palace grounds, but separate from the main palace, unlike Avukena. It was on the other side of the courtyard, too far to walk. After waiting a few minutes, punctuated by crickets chirping, Zandos and Jace arrived too.

"Hey guys, the car is waiting for us outside!" Reid said as he stood at the door, holding it open for all of us. I saw a black van, with plenty of seating, parked at the curb, the beautiful palace in view across the court. The car had to be tall; all the vehicles at our palace were custom-built to fit the Everealm council, which were all over seven feet tall. New Klethorog was the territory of the water sister, who was the tallest one. We all went into the car and felt it move forward.

"Hey, Isavna," Reid said as I was sitting between him and Sirani. "You look great. I'll try not to crush your skirts."

"No need, the car's really big," I said. The van really was quite spacious—it must have been custom-built for the water sister. "You look good too, *I guess.*"

"Gosh, thanks," He replied, rolling his eyes with feigned offense. "My suit was ruined from the attack last week. I had to borrow one from Kairo, but it still fits a little too big. It feels like a parachute." It was a dark blue pinstripe suit with a black shirt and white tie. Definitely something Kairo would wear. "At least I can breathe, though. My other one was too small anyway." I looked around the car, and everyone was dressed in their best outfits. Jovnelle had on a red and black dress, much like the kind she used to wear back when she was possessed. Something about the cuts of the dress and the materials made it seem more freeing, like she was embracing who she was and what had happened to her, maybe retaking control of herself.

Marathene wore a white brocade gown and a peach cloak. It had to be Mother Everealm's or a replica made to be a bit shorter. From where I was sitting, I saw the gown details, with delicate, beautiful flowers, making it seem almost like a wedding dress. She held Mother Everealm's crown in her lap; I assumed she was going to wear it later.

"I like your dress," I said in passing. "Is that your mother's cloak?" She nodded solemnly. I could feel Mother Everealm's presence in the room. Maybe that was what it felt like to have a god.

"So what are we going to do there?" Jace asked. "I know it's some kind of party, but what's going to happen exactly?"

"It's an anniversary gala, so the king and other people are going to give speeches about New Klethorog and its achievements. Entecera might give a speech too," Marathene explained. Entecera was the name of the water sister. "And they're likely going to address the attacks on Avukena as well."

We arrived at the palace.

"We're here, thanks for coming. Enjoy the ball," the driver said timidly.

"Of course, thank you for the ride," Marathene said.

We proceeded into the palace, looking at the architecture. We made our way to the banquet hall. There were fewer people there than at the Avukena ball, as this was more of a minor event. The main hall had many round tables with floating digital tents on them to indicate the guests sitting there. We made our way over to the Avukena City table and sat down, waiting for the event to start. Appetizers were being served around the hall with small fluffy biscuits with salty olives, bright orange salmon, and a light vinegar sauce. The hall was decorated with banners and flags of New Klethorog, as well as pictures and portraits of the king and his family. The main table was at the front, with Kairo, Saku, King Gomen, and Queen Luyana. The king was wearing an adorned white suit with gold trimmings and a red sash across his chest. It seemed to borrow patterns we had seen around New Klethorog, like white gold geometric shapes, circles, and leaf patterns. His wife wore a simple, traditional green dress with a matching crown and necklace. The king stepped up to the podium and spoke into a microphone.

"Good evening, everyone," he said as the lively chatter subsided. "Thank you for joining us on this special occasion. Today marks the 200th anniversary of New Klethorog." The crowd clapped. "But first, before we begin, I would like to address the attacks that occurred, interrupting the Flower Festival gala at Avukena City, where we lost our beloved Mother Everealm. We have with us today people who fought that very battle against Cavaris and his army of Mahifers, along with Jovnelle Everealm, who is now free from Cavaris, as is her realm." He motioned for my table to stand up, which drew eyes from all the tables. "And we share our deep condolences for the loss of Avukena's leader. Thank you for coming to our banquet." We thanked him and took a seat. *Saved myself from a speech there.*

He continued. "Entecera Everealm would like to say a few words before we begin." He motioned for a tall, slender woman to take the stand. She had blue hair no longer than her chin that curled elegantly and eyes that drooped at the edges, but still looked pretty. She had a traditional, adorned white, gold, and green dress that had motifs of animals and plants. She thanked King Gomen as she repositioned the floating microphone. Her moves seemed almost choreographed.

"Honored guests," she began, her accent nothing short of endearing. It had a uniquely low and distinguished timbre, just like Jovnelle's, though not quite as delicate. "While it has been some time, I would be remiss to omit a mention of the attack in Avukena City and the associated losses and casualties. As sisters," her gaze swept over Jovnelle and Marathene. "We know the fragility in power and the strength in community." Her gaze dropped for a moment, and her tall and thin frame heaved. Entecera continued with her speech, briefly going over the events and reminding the crowd to stick to the facts and not get speculative. "Treat the situation with kindness, respect, and maturity," she said. "And remember to keep your humanity. People lost their lives or loved ones." Zandos looked enchanted by the way she spoke. I had trouble grasping the fact that he was her nephew, too. I felt a bit of envy for such powerful connections.

She silently exited the stage without any remarks such as "thank you" or "goodbye." The applause that followed was restrained.

"Entecera has always been that way," Marathene remarked to Jovnelle, who nodded.

King Gomen took the stand and spoke about New Klethorog and the purpose of the ceremony, then passed out awards to civilians.

He called up people to come on stage and gave them medals, the audience applauding after each name was spoken. The applause was more and more bare after each person went by.

"This is so boring," Jace complained quietly to Sirani, who was sitting next to me.

"Shh!" Sirani snapped.

"Come on, Sirani, don't you think this is a bit too formal and dull?" Jace whispered. "I just want to get to dinner and the snack table in the dance hall."

"Jace, this isn't a party, this is a banquet. We're honoring Saku and Kairo's city and the people who have done far more than the average person. This is a banquet that we are lucky to be invited to, and lucky to have made it to after what happened. So please, be quiet and pay attention. It'll only be a moment before this'll be done and we get to eat," Sirani said. Her voice hushed. "Gosh, you're such a brute. All you think about is food."

"Fine. I'll be quiet," Jace said, not retorting to Sirani's comment. It wasn't long before the table slowly ran out of medals, and the king returned to his seat. Entrees began to be handed out, with a choice between snow fowl or felmine loins. Kairo came over to our table as we ate and pulled an extra chair.

"Hey Kairo!" Sirani said as he sat down near us.

"Hi," he replied. "So whatcha think?"

"Oh, the food's great!" Marathene said, covering her mouth as she spoke. Jovnelle, now having regained a bit of flesh and color since leaving Nojuni, was holding a fork and knife and cutting the steak into pieces. She appeared to be left-handed. Most people in Avukena were. *Genetics, I suppose.*

"So Kairo," Reid asked. "What are you going to do now that school's over? I've asked everyone but you."

Kairo thought for a moment. "Well, I'm going to university here at the New Kleth Royal Academy, so I can finish the requirement to become king after my dad steps down."

"Wow, you're really dedicated to that," Jace said. "I think you're the only one of us who actually is going to follow through with becoming a monarch."

"That's the plan," Kairo said, tilting his head and sighing.

"What about you, Zandos?" Marathene asked while sipping her light purple wine. I caught a smell of it. It was like any fruity wine with a thick odor of alcohol, but also something peppery.

Zandos opened his mouth to answer, but Jovnelle was too quick.

"He is the direct descendant of us sisters, so he has powerful magic as we do. I will likely live for another several million years longer, so Zandos will have to wait a while for the throne." Jovnelle said. "I do not intend to abdicate it as long as I can help it."

"Let him speak, Jovnelle," Marathene said.

"Well, I do not... I do not know," Zandos said. "After coming to the rest of the world... I realized how much I did not know. And how much more I want to see." We nodded in agreement.

"And you, Isavna?" Kairo asked. "Are you going back to Earth?"

I thought for a little while. "No. Or at least, I don't plan on it. Not unless it's vacation or something." I shrugged. "Cavaris is still out there," I said that as more of a generic answer, but I didn't really know what to expect *if* I went back to Earth. Would they accept my diploma from the Everealm Preparatory Academy? Would anyone besides my family actually remember me? What would I do when an interviewer asks about the gap in my resume?

"Isavna, what sort of responsibilities are you going to get now?" Sirani asked me. "I suppose you've completed the mission already. The 'saving Jovnelle' one, not the 'killing Jovnelle' one."

"Gosh, I hoped you meant the former," Jovnelle said. "I was worried for a moment." I laughed.

"Well, it's up to Marathene to decide. I don't really want to work at Bahana's or Dewdrop for the rest of my life, though."

"You're welcome to continue your work in the AHL or anywhere else you'd like. I think you'll find their new goal more... appropriate." Marathene said. I nodded. During the last Division One meeting, the AHL changed its mission from "killing Cavaris and Jovnelle for good" to "protecting Avukenans, their interests, and their freedoms."

The banquet finished, and we proceeded to the ballroom. We spent our time enjoying ourselves, dancing, eating, and talking. Marathene, with her god-like power, gave Sirani a temporary levitation spell so she could dance.

"Did you see that couple at the Southern New Kleth District table?" Sirani asked as she and I danced around the hall. The musicians played a lively waltz. "They were, like, totally kissing, and it was really gross. They've got to be a new couple."

"Ew," I said. "I'm glad I didn't see that."

"Oh well. Give it a week and whatever they have will probably be over," Sirani said with mock indignation.

I thought for a moment. "Wait, Sirani, do you even like anyone?" I asked. "In the whole time I've known you, you've just been observing other people's relationships and stuff like some weird reality show. You're always on your wrist projection stalking our classmates on social media like it's a reality show. But you never talk about your own relationships. You never told me about how your date with the guy from finance went all that time ago.”

“He was, like, cute, but it wasn’t all there… you know?” she said, fluttering her eyelashes and tilting her head. “He kept bragging about how he cheated on his statistics exam to get the finance position right under Mr. Makorod. And he expected me to be impressed or something.” We passed by a snack table, and I picked up two meringues and passed her one.

“Hey Isavna, Sirani, I think that weird couple is fighting now,” Reid messaged us. We both pretended to get more meringues and watched. The woman crossed her arms and pouted, her movements making her red sequin dress shimmer. The guy rose from the table, responding angrily.

“Jeez, how long are they going to argue?” Reid commented as he approached us. I shrugged, trying not to seem too suspicious, though they appeared to be in a standoff. The three of us sat down to continue watching various couples flirt stiffly or argue. The musicians finished their song, and people entered and exited for the next dance.

Sirani left without telling us, wandering over to the snack table where Jace and Zandos were. I felt happy for her, since she and him seemed to get along well now.

Reid and I spent some time simply taking in the scene. I liked to think that he, like me, was trying to get his mind off the mountain of emotions that had been stirring in all of us for the past few weeks, even as we settled into a more normal rhythm. It was hard to come to terms with all of the sudden changes, both with some familiar servants whose faces I no longer saw in the palace, as well as the change of interior scenery, having grown so used to what was our home.

Suddenly, Reid addressed me. “How about we dance?” *That seemed like it took some courage from him.*

"Okay, sure." I said, slightly stunned at the abrupt but pleasant proposal.

We joined the other people on the ballroom floor who were moving around in a clockwise direction. I almost stepped on another girl's massive skirts a few times. We passed Sirani and Saku a few times. Reid's hands felt somewhat clammy.

"I remember hearing this song on a show my parents watched as a kid." Reid said idly, about the minuet the musicians were playing. A common classical piece here in Avukena. "Some dumb soap opera, I think."

"Oh, really?"

"Yeah. It was always at night when I wasn't supposed to be awake."

"What a troublemaker." I found that I didn't realize how much time had passed, yet we must've been through a couple of songs by now. Even Saku and Sirani were sitting on the chairs by the snack table again.

"I think that you're pretty special to have made it this far, at least mentally, you know?" Reid said. "You're the first Earther to have actually survived as long as you did."

"Thanks. I'm as surprised as you are. But I'm just grateful that things didn't turn out any worse. If Levi taught us anything, it's how quickly bad things can cut into our lives," I said while watching his green eyes widen as we nearly missed an older couple.

As we went around the dance floor, the night seemed like a precious candle slowly melting. But as all things do, it came to an end.

Sunday, 1:12 AM, New Klethorog Palace, Courtyard

Carrying my heels in my hand, I sat on a park bench, watching a fountain with my friends.

"Imagine if I never meet you all," Zandos said. "I am not able to imagine still sitting in my room, not knowing of the world outside. And my mom is now saved."

Keya, who had been silent for most of the event, rested her face upon her hands silently. She seemed at peace with herself, if not a bit pensive. The whole night, I had seen her alone.

"I sort of miss Mother Everealm." Sirani said, picking at her press-on nails. Two had already fallen off over the course of the night. "Even if she turned out evil in the end. I've known her personally ever since I started the junior high boarding program in Avukena. I still struggle to realize that she wanted Jovnelle gone so badly."

"That's tough," Jace said, untying his red tie and unbuttoning the first few buttons of his dress shirt. He loosened his belt, having overeaten. Zandos, seeing that this was acceptable, did so as well. "I never really knew her besides what she wanted to do to Jovnelle, so I guess I can't say I feel the same."

I approached Keya, sitting near a bush of blue flowers. She had on a blue cocktail dress, one I hadn't seen her in before. I sat beside her, but she didn't notice me. She held up her hand to the night sky as she admired her wrist, and the blue bracelet she had on twinkled in the moonlight.

"Did you enjoy the banquet?" I ventured.

Keya lowered her hand and looked at me. "Yes," she said softly. The softest I ever heard her speak. She turned her head to the moon. Among the stars was a great bright one. That was Mother Everealm's. "It… it all happened too fast," Keya said, sounding small. "Mother Everealm's gone. Levi too."

I didn't respond right away. It seemed like an odd thing for her to bring up now, unprompted. Or maybe it had just been on her mind this entire time. I heard her sniffle while the rest of the group discussed tomorrow's plan, on the other side of the blue flower bush.

"I keep expecting to hear him or see him somewhere," she continued. "I'll just turn a corner, and he'll be there to say something dumb or talk with Zandos about weapons." Her fingers tightened around her bracelet, which must have held some significance to her. "Maybe I just gotta let him go. But we were together for all of my teenage years, how can I? If I don't even remember what it was like before?"

I stayed silent. Words would have gotten in the way.

She quickly wiped her cheek and sighed with a shaky breath, trying to straighten herself out, but then she covered her face in her hands and cried. "I thought he'd grow out of his recklessness and energy someday, but he never did. I told him… I said—I told him…that those missions are dangerous and he's risking…But…B—and then he'd grip my hands and tell me, 'Keya, I have to do it,' but then I'd tell him he, that—I, I don't… ugh, Levi, selfish bastard!" she cried out, not loud enough to alert the rest of the group. She sobbed quietly.

"He had a mission of his own," I said. "Did Salia ever tell you about the portrait wall?"

"Damn that stupid portrait wall!" she heaved, breathing for a minute. "And his father for making him feel like he was nothing!"gos Her body shook with a few more silent sobs until she tired out. I rested my hands in my lap, unsure of what to do with myself. Her mouth curved into a tired smile as she gazed at the bracelet. She began to sob again. "I just want him back. I don't even care anymore if it's selfish, I just want him back."

Her breath steadied, and she held the bracelet, like it anchored her to something. *Life goes on.*

She was still, her body leaned over her knees, and for a while, I couldn't tell if she was still breathing. I felt sadness for her, and a bit of guilt for having gotten to dance with people who mean a lot to me. *I wish Keya had at least gotten that with Levi at some point. She deserves that far more than I do.*

"Keya?" I finally asked, as gently as I could. She lifted her body and sat up straight, finger-combing her short red hair.

"We were going to come to this banquet together. We went shopping the day before the mission to find a tie and dress that were the same shade of blue, since every tailor in town was busy. It took all day. Who knew there were so many shades of blue." Her lips quivered. "He promised me a blue corsage for today, and when I saw these flowers I just couldn't hold it together anymore. I wore this blue bracelet I found in my closet hoping it would complete this outfit, but I just feel even emptier now." She looked up and turned her head, her bloodshot, weary eyes meeting mine. Crumbs of mascara littered her cheekbones. "Sorry, Isavna. Didn't mean to dump all of this onto you."

I extended my arms and held her in a silent hug. I heard the fountain, Keya's breathing, the others' idle chatter, and my own heartbeat. I could've sworn I heard Mother Everealm's star, through my pendant, whispering something indistinct. I didn't listen.

EPILOGUE

6 months later
December 8th, Thursday, 6:23 PM, Avukena Palace, Library

I leaned on my knees, sitting on a sofa. Outside, it was raining, the dark sky shrouded by clouds. Construction had been completed by now. The library was old and remained untouched by construction as it survived the attacks.

I watched as the flame of a candle danced around in the air. My phone fell asleep on a text message with Toniska while I waited for her response. I would be returning for the holidays—the first one in a while. I sighed, feeling the stress leave my body. I picked up the book I was reading, *The Cintu People: The Line Between War and Peace*, and tried to focus on the words of the introduction.

The Spevans were a war-mongering people (named after their martyr, Saint Speva), while the Drujans were territorial but more diplomatic. They didn't always get along, but eventually, five hundred years later, a middle culture would evolve, the Cintus. While they were powerful for a short period of time, they eventually lost when the Drujans and Neo-Spevans defeated them. The ancient Spevans would become possessed by Cavaris and move their civilization north.

The insignificant, boring words seemed to float around the page. My mind was elsewhere. I thought about a dress I saw in town that Sirani might've liked.

I decided to go back to my unit and call her. She was studying business and logistics in Elkostet, on the opposite side of the planet. I set down my book and left the library.

I went up to my unit and heard chattering inside. I carefully opened the door and found Reid and Sirani sitting at my table together, sipping tea. A spot was ready for me.

"Isavna!" Sirani exclaimed as I went over to give her a hug. "How are you doing?"

"Pretty good. Sorta lonely since everyone left," I said.

"Hey, I'm still here!" Reid said. I laughed. He was studying locally, like me, at Avukena University.

"So what are you doing here?" I asked Sirani.

"We got a few days off, and the fare for the portals were cheap, so I thought I'd pop over," Sirani said, smiling.

"Oh, good. I was starting to miss everyone," I said. We went outside to the gardens after we finished our tea.

"So when are we going to visit Earth?" Sirani asked.

"Oh, I don't know. It's a hard trip to do, unless you're from Earth. You need to take a space pod from the palace. It's not as cool as it is here, though," I explained, trying to shut down the idea.

"But it still seems interesting, I'd like to see what Earthers do for things we use magic for," Sirani said.

"There's also no unicorns, or alicorns, or any kind of magical creatures."

"Well, at least you have felmines," Reid said.

"Not even felmines," I said.

"Never mind then," Reid said.

Sirani sighed and pouted. "Fine. I guess Earth is boring. But what about all the other planets? There are so many to choose from. What about Mars, Venus, or Jupiter?"

I shook my head. "Can't support humans. They're rocks and gas."

"Oh well. I suppose it's hopeless, then."

As we wandered throughout the courtyard, the moonlight and glowing magic streetlights of the cold winter painted the garden with an ethereal, cool glow. If it weren't for my thick winter coat and the wool hat covering my ears, I would've certainly frozen. The path we were on meandered around the garden until it led us to a stone statue of Mother Everealm in the middle of a fountain.

We all sat down on a bench under a gazebo. Rain pattered on the trees and topiaries. Somewhere in the distance, I heard other people in the gardens, too, laughing and squealing as the rain suddenly came down a little harder.

Reid sighed. He crossed his legs, wearing the same dark wash jeans I had often seen him in, though they looked a little more worn down now. We all were, though that wasn't entirely a bad thing. I could still feel the knotted bump under my jeans from the Jace monster's attack so long ago.

Sirani glanced at the statue of Mother Everealm, which held the kind of peace you see in the faces of bodies in caskets. The statue stood, her eyes closed, holding a scepter where the water spouted from and trickled into the bowl. Bioluminescent birds occasionally flew overhead, in the trees, or by the fountain, but remained silent.

I let my eyes unfocus and look past the statue, thinking about what my mission even meant. Was I supposed to eradicate evil? That wasn't possible. Evil wasn't something you could easily scrub away or even identify easily. Evil was something intangible, a notion created to justify actions and assert that what we did *wasn't* evil. The existence of evil implies the existence of good, which is just as subjective and also difficult to identify at times. To eradicate evil, at least to Mother Everealm, meant weeding out everything she thought was wrong, even when those convictions led to a lot of pain in the end. When she saw herself, she saw a hero, until she set down the mirror and saw what had happened to her world.

But did Mother Everealm's wrongdoing and cowardice really make her a fully, or mostly, bad person? The night air and garden offered no answers, only an embrace of chilly winter air and the smell of rain. *This couldn't possibly be the legacy she wanted.* I thought. *But this is the one she left. And she will forever be remembered for it.* We stood up, Sirani and Reid looking lighter.

Whatever my mission was, I had to do my part to protect this world. I stared at the fountain. *You left me no choice.*

We made our way inside the palace, veering off into the library, feeling a gentle peace settle within us. Mother Everealm's death marked the end of the Everealm age and the beginning of something else. An age as significant as the ones in my books, like Middle Avukena.

I thought about how the Everealm Age would be portrayed in the history books. The Late Everealm Age? A few dozen pages about everything that happened, soon to torture Avukenan History 211 students like me?

Whatever it was, I was one of the many symbols of what was left. Probably the last Earther to be forced into Avukena. A marker of an obsolete practice. A big council meeting four months ago condemning the practice was held, and I was given a small tax exemption for the rest of my life. I thanked them for it, as trivial as the compensation was.

As my life finally slowed down, I traveled more. I visited Levi's grave in Luzuma about once a month. I hadn't yet visited Mother Everealm's at all, even though it was on palace grounds.

And when I was in Luzuma to visit Levi two months ago, something sort of dawned on me. I had always asked myself, *why are they taking all these young, minimally experienced operatives on high-risk missions?* And it was just like Renee had told me—*everything is replaceable.* I had thought for some reason that Mother Everealm's doctrine had only ever applied to Earthers, but it stretched throughout the AHL. When I was organizing files one day, I found one about a meeting that Renee, Brev, Officer Novet, and Mr. Makorod had all had about Zandos, where they treated him as a logistical asset rather than as a person. It disgusted me.

Damn it, Levi. I thought, getting angry that the world had been so cruel to someone with so much potential. He believed that he could prove himself and become someone who mattered. And he mattered to us, his friends, but little to the organization that sent him to Nojuni. Mother Everealm's doctrine had caused this, but there was still time to fix it. There had to be.

"So, Isavna, you going back to Earth for Christmas?" Reid asked quietly, as I snapped back to reality. *Christmas.* It was coming fast, a reminder of the two worlds I called home, a sensation so unique and fractured to me that it warped my perception of belonging for so long.

"Yeah," I finally replied, sitting on the library's soft couches. "It's been a while since I have. Hey, how do you even know about Christmas?"

"I read about it in a book on Earth culture. I think I still have it, actually. I'd like to see how much of it is wrong. It talked about this one holiday where people dress up and beg for candy at night."

"Wait, are you talking about the Hall of Being?" Sirani said.

"What the heck are you guys talking about?" I said. Then it dawned on me. "Oh, you guys are talking about Halloween!" I laughed. "I guess it really is sort of a strange holiday." It started raining outside. It was too warm for snow, so instead we got miserable cold rain.

"Oh my goodness, look at the time. Reid, we ought to go," she said. "It's getting late." I hugged both of them as they departed. Reid, back to his dorm, and Sirani, upstairs to my room. We would have a sleepover, just like before.

Alone, I gazed at the city's nocturnal silhouette, where my mind wandered back to my journey's beginning.

All of it, even what was bad, had already happened, and I couldn't help but think it was necessary, somehow. Or else I wouldn't be who I was. I grew to like the little scars on my leg and the piece of wallpaper the construction workers forgot to patch in my unit. The little mark of soot left from the candles on my ceiling—the scarring on Sirani's knees.

The city's rebuilding had also transformed itself into something new. It bore its own scars, but those were beautiful, too, in their own way. I leaned back in my chair and looked out the window. There might still be problems in the world—there always will be, but for now, I had Avukena. And Avukena was still worth fighting for.

THE END

AFTERWORD

This is the section of the book that nobody reads.

Admittedly, I am part of that problem. I never really gave afterwords or acknowledgments much thought as a reader, since they always started with some form of this sappy preamble:

"Much love to my husband John, for reading and re-reading my manuscript late into the evening, and many thanks to my brother Scott, my sister Amy and my brother-in-law Chuck for always being there...."

And yet, here I am, writing one, three weeks before publication.

My book will be published in April of 2026, right in the middle of my high school's spring break. As someone who is still 17, I haven't experienced much at this point in my life, and I would be ignorant to say that I've acquired all the wisdom necessary to talk about the themes in this book with the depth I would like to. And as I approach the finish line for this multi-year project that has taken up a third of my life, it's left me with unfamiliar and strange feelings buzzing within me.

Maybe those feelings make sense when I think about how much this story has grown up with me. When I first started out writing this as a bright-eyed fifth grader, I would talk about this project to anyone who would listen. Parents, teachers, classmates, and so on. As I became a more self-conscious middle schooler, I kept it more of a secret. Even throughout high school, it still embarrasses me to know that some of my classmates, whom I hardly talk to, have read this project that is rather intimate to me, and perhaps they even made it this far. If so, please tell me in class. I would love to know.

Now onto the obligatory sappy stuff. I'll keep this brief, reader, to respect your time.

Thanks to both of my parents, Juan and Amanda, for their unwavering support (though I will admit, I have heard the phrase "So, when are we going to publish this thing?" an excessive amount of times during the whole process).

Thank you to my sister, Dana, who also grew up with this story back when it was our make-believe world as young children.

Thanks to all the friends, classmates, and teachers who listened when I told them about my book.

And to Jacob, for "reading and re-reading my manuscript, late into the evening." (*Sigh*, I know.)

And lastly, to you, reader, for somehow having the endurance, patience, and curiosity to see what the author blathers on about in the back of a book. Gold star.

One final addendum for you, reader. I just want you to know that you're never too young or too old to start anything. If you have a book, a song, a painting, or a poem in you, I want you to open your journal, laptop, notepad, or phone as soon as you close this book and write it down, because the world deserves to hear your story, too.

Goodbye, until we meet again. I've got big plans for the rest of the trilogy.

-Elena Delgado